Praise for Paris L

"Readers will want to put everything aside, grab a café au lait and delve into Marcia Fine's spellbinding story. On every page her writing shines, especially in the Parisian food scenes, from the conversations over French meals to shopping at French farmer's markets to the art of making goat cheese. Riveting and absolutely splendid."

–Tracey Ceurvels, writer and author of the upcoming cookbook, *The NYC Kitchen*

"A thoughtful portrayal of a woman with a family secret and her son who resents her for it."

–Kathryn Casey, best-selling author of *Deliver Us*

"As always, Fine's rigorous research and fast-clip prose shine in this smart psychological caper. Ancient archaeology, espionage and family secrets unearthed make for a fascinating plot to follow, though the lush descriptions of Paris and its surrounding countryside made me want to linger. A robust, satisfying read!"

–Jessica Leigh Lebos, writer and blogger of *Yo, Yenta!*

"Marcia Fine does it again! Her latest novel, Paris Lamb, *brought me back to my recent summer vacation in Paris. Marcia makes the City of Light come to life with her keen sense of place. I wasn't reading a book about Paris, I was transported to that romantic city–strolling through beautiful Luxembourg gardens, sipping a latte in a corner cafe and window shopping in chic boutiques. . . . Skip the jet lag and pick up her latest novel!"*

–Marsha Toy Engstrom, *The Book Club Cheerleader*

"This fine author has delivered a well-researched novel that delves into archaeology and the art market as well as that ivory tower of academia, a furnace of jealousy, ambition and cutthroat competition."

–Virginia Nosky, author, 2014 Indie Silver medalist, *White River*, 2014 Eric Hoffer finalist, *Blue Turquoise, White Shell*

"Fine's Four A's: archaeology, art auctions, academia and antisemitism intersect in this meticulously observed narrative that opens in a taxi cab in NYC, leaps back in time to Paris with stops in New Haven, Miami and Arles."

–Terrance Gelenter, author of *Paris Par Hasard: from Bagels to Brioches*

"*Marcia Fine is one of my all-time favorite storytellers. Her attention to historic detail, as well as contemporary nuance, makes this story jump off the page with its accuracy and relevance, an absolute page turner! From the last paragraph in the very first chapter, I was hooked, hungry to read what happened next!*"

–Susan Brooks, life and success coach,
Life Solutions for Professional Women

"*Miss Fine's passion for history offers her readers a learning experience as well as fascinating entertainment.*"

–Edith Kunz, author of *Fatale: How French Women Do It*

"*Paris Lamb is a sweeping story of post-Holocaust attitudes spanning two continents. Glimpses of Paris and gardens stir up the chemistry between Michael Saunders and Sandrine Agneau as they seek new answers to old questions and secrets in this engaging novel.*"

–Gail Fisher, freelance writer and author

Paris Lamb

Marcia Fine

Cover and interior design: Kim Appis
Photography: SMF Photography

www.marciafine.com
www.limagepress.com

Cataloging Publication Data:
ISBN - 978-0-9826952-7-2

1. Historical fiction
2. Biblical archaeology
3. Paris
4. Antisemitism
5. 1950s Florida
6. Mother-son relationship
7. Family secrets
8. Romance

Scottsdale, Arizona
www.limagepress.com

Other Novels by Marcia Fine

Historical Fiction:
Paper Children: An Immigrant's Legacy
The Blind Eye: A Sephardic Journey
Also available as ebooks and audiobooks

Satire:
Stressed in Scottsdale
Boomerang: When Life Comes Back to Bite You
Gossip.com

PARIS LAMB won First Prize from the Arizona Author's Association in 2013 for Best Unpublished Manuscript. *The Blind Eye* earned First Prize in the Historical Fiction category of the NABE Pinnacle Book Achievement Award for the Summer of 2014. *Stressed in Scottsdale* won First Prize in Satire/Humor from the Arizona Author's Association and the Living Now Silver Medal for Women's Fiction in 2010. With three historical novels and a satirical series set in Scottsdale, Fine has been a finalist for the Eric Hoffer Award, Foreword Book of the Year, Best Books Award and USA Book News. Her books have also been chosen as a featured selection by Beauty and the Book's Pulpwood Queens, and selected as a Top Ten Book of the Year by bookclubcheerleader.com. *The Blind Eye* has also been chosen as a ONEBOOKAZ winner for 2015, to be read simultaneously by communities across the state of Arizona.

For all my female friends

Chapter One

Newark, New Jersey
September 15, 1993

Maurice Dubois moved into the aisle after hours of being cramped on the L'Avion flight from Paris to Newark, his elongated frame stretched to its full height. He couldn't wait to depart the plane, get through customs and exit the terminal for a smoke.

He patted down his pockets for wallet, cigarettes, lighter and aviator sunglasses, balancing his leather briefcase on the top of the seat. He clicked it open to survey his papers and confirmed his passport was tucked into a pocket. From the overhead bin he grabbed his suit jacket by the collar and shook it, melting away the wrinkles in the lightweight wool. Then he pulled out his trench coat, draping it over his arm. In first class they hang up your garments, he reminded himself. Ah, well. When the auction is over, I will be flying on private jets and pouring a Lafite Rothschild Bordeaux for myself and my friends.

The other passengers took measured steps away from the stale air of a ten-hour flight. A woman in a yellow sweater held up the line trying to snap up the handle of her rolling bag. Another insisted on manipulating her child's arms through a Mickey Mouse backpack. Maurice, impatient with such frivolous delays, shifted from foot to foot.

Finally, freedom. Maurice slicked back his longish, blonde hair with a free hand. He advanced with confidence around groups of people into the large disembarkation room to claim his luggage for customs. His dark-chocolate Louis Vuitton, a worldwide status symbol, was among the first to slide down the shaft. In France, their indestructible practicality was a necessity.

He spoke to no one as he waited in the customs line. Passengers piled their belongings onto the free rolling carts. Maurice placed his brief-case on top of one, his suitcase on the bottom of it. The mother next to him held a drooling baby who threw his bottle on the filthy, tiled floor. Maurice took a step forward to retrieve it and handed it to the young woman, never removing his hand from the cart. She smiled in gratitude. Americans, he thought, a childlike people.

He waited in line. Red light, stop. Green light, go. The glum customs official glanced at his passport.

"Business or pleasure?"

"Business."

"Of what nature?"

"Archaeological research. An auction."

"How long will you be in the U.S.?"

"Two weeks."

The man, a serious bureaucrat with horn-rimmed glasses, stamped his passport. "Welcome to New Jersey. Enjoy your stay."

Maurice knew his route. A men's room stop, *francs* for dollars, a smoke, cab ride into the city.

His mind circled around his meeting tomorrow with Professor Sommerstein. The professor was to examine his research on what was often referred to as God's Gold, three treasures from the time of the destruction of Israel's Temple in AD 70 valued at close to a billion dollars. Maybe more. When he viewed them for the first time ten years ago in an obscure scientific lab in the south of France, chills coursed through his body. Other archaeologists were jealous of his access to the rare artifacts, especially Michael Saunders, a Yale professor who confront-ed him at other symposiums, and Yossi Farber, an arrogant Israeli, who thought the extraordinary discovery was a fraud, despite the carbon dating. They would have to bide their time until the auction preview to see these rarities, ones that had survived centuries of deception and controversy. The beauty of the artifacts in the photographs paled next to the real thing.

Tomorrow was a prelude to delivering his speech at the École Biblique et Archéologique Française symposium the next week. His report would reinforce his reputation worldwide as the expert on these discoveries.

Maurice, preoccupied with the impact these items would have on the open market of museums, governments and individuals clamoring for them, stood behind the painted line on the floor at the airport money exchange. *Merde.* Such an advantage in the U.S. with the *franc*-to-dollar ratio. How did the rate go down while he was crossing the ocean? Best to change money at a bank, but no time now.

He opened his briefcase at the window, handing a credit card to the woman dressed in a navy jacket.

"Ten thousand in American dollars, please."

She raised her eyebrows and checked his credit limit on the computer. "Large bills, okay?"

"*Oui.* Yes."

A nervous tremor coursed through him. He glanced to his right. No one. He observed the woman, obviously a smoker too, from her yellowed fingers and lines around her mouth. Not like the Parisian women he knew who smoked after dinner for effect. He watched a kid to his left in a black nylon jacket and sneakers, hunched over, a walkie-talkie to his ear. When he saw Maurice gaze at him, he turned, his jeans baggy.

The teller counted the bills out below the counter. Maurice watched her lips move as she thumbed through the bills. She placed the cash into an envelope and slipped it under the bulletproof glass. Maurice took the envelope, pulled out a few bills and stuffed them into his pants pocket. The rest of the money he stored in his briefcase under his report and laptop.

On the curb he stood in the taxi line smoking, his lungs filling with relief. He thought about ridding himself of the cash in the safe at the hotel, a hot shower, a glass of Bordeaux. He dropped the cigarette, stepping on it when his yellow cab pulled up to the curb. The Vuitton suitcase was loaded into the trunk as a drizzle began.

The cabdriver seated on wooden beads wore a crocheted Muslim cap.

He peered into the rearview mirror. Maurice shifted his trench coat onto his lap, his briefcase close to his thigh.

"The Pierre at Fifth Avenue and Central Park."

With a wordless nod, the cabdriver melted his vehicle into the traffic heading away from Newark. Maurice noted the cabdriver's photograph and name, his credentials displayed in a plastic sleeve on the back of the window. Absolem Halim. The windshield wipers thumped a steady rhythm as the drops grew fatter.

The skyline of industrial parks, factories and the haze of pollution brushed a grey wash over Maurice's view. The ride from Orly or de Gaulle in Paris was not attractive either, but a historic skyline made up for a lot. Americans created architectural buildings like the Twin Towers, not monuments for eternity, like Monsieur Eiffel.

The cabdriver spoke, turning his head over his shoulder, "Bad traffic this time of day. I take another route."

Maurice shrugged his shoulders. "No matter. Just get me there."

He leaned his head back and closed his eyes for the hour ride, anxious to go over his paper again before meeting with Sommerstein.

As the taxi picked up speed, Maurice swayed in the back. After a toll on the New Jersey Turnpike, the driver manipulated his cab, running a route parallel to the expressway. A known shortcut, other vehicles ignoring the speed limit zipped by his cab. A car slid dangerously close. The driver jerked the steering wheel. Maurice, now alert, watched signs glide by: Corbin Street, Port Eatery Truck Stop, even a billboard for Rutgers University.

The symposium, subsequent celebratory party and auction of the actual items had already drawn worldwide attention. I will be one of the most sought-after *académiques* in the world, Maurice thought.

The cab sped up, keeping up with the fast-moving traffic.

Merde. These are the best taxi drivers in the world? Why the rush?

A large truck spun past them on the right. The cabdriver jerked toward the guard rail.

"Hey, slow down. I want to arrive alive." Bile crept up his throat.

"Not my fault. Rush hour. Shortcut. Relax."

His attitude annoyed Maurice. Rude. I will not tip him, he thought as he leaned back, his eyes watching out the right window.

A semitruck lumbered by, veering into the taxi's path. The truck driver over corrected, squealing his brakes as he cut off the cab and slammed into the guard rail. The taxi spun out of control, the cabbie gripping the wheel, his foot pumping the brakes.

Maurice's head lurched forward. As the cab slammed into the truck driver's side of the front wheel, the impact started an engine fire, flames licking around the truck's tires.

Commuters leaned out of their car windows shouting, "Get those guys out of there!" A few Samaritans exited their vehicles with warnings. "Watch the gas tank." "Call 9-1-1." "I'm a medic. Let me through." Foreign tongues added to the pandemonium of ambulance and fire-truck sirens, a stuck horn, a radio blasting rap music. Wails to Allah rose in the din. The jackknifed truck blocked the street.

The Mack truck driver was slumped over his steering wheel. Two men in rain gear climbed up to reach him, pulling on the door. A few others headed for the cabbie and Maurice. More shouts enveloped the air.

"Hurry up. Before it explodes. Get 'em out!"

Maurice's twisted body was crumpled into the well of the back seat, his briefcase underneath him.

Traffic piled up as the accident became the horror show of the frontage road, the steady rain washing the scene. Sirens wailed closer, bathing the street in pink and red, until the rescue vehicles advanced through the crowd, lights spinning, noise amplified. The teams, anxious to do their jobs with efficiency, nudged onlookers out of the way. Firemen lunged with hoses toward the wreck as the fire turned into steam. A crowd hunched under umbrellas gathered to one side. In moments three bodies were stretched out on the asphalt. An officer covered the three men's faces with cloths.

Chapter Two

Paris, France
August 4, 1993

When I first arrived in Paris after my mother's death and the beginning of my sabbatical, I thought about contacting Maurice Dubois, the star of the upcoming conference in New York. We had attended a number of archaeological symposiums, acknowledging one another with intellectual confrontations, but he was such an egocentric prick, I dismissed the idea. With his supercilious attitude, he let us know he thought American professors inferior. He might have provided some intellectual stimulation in a city where I knew only a few people, but why bother? Sadness made me vulnerable and I wasn't in the mood for sparring.

We both agreed the artifacts in question were genuine; although Maurice had the advantage of actually being present for the carbon dating, I knew he wouldn't be gracious. He did not have many fans. With the upcoming École Biblique et Archéologique Française and Scholars Conference, an amalgam of the French keynoter's research and a nod to the rest of us, we would cross paths a few times.

Instead, I saw all the typical tourist sites that most Americans do—the Batobus tour down the Seine to the Eiffel Tower and the galleries of the Grande Palais, the Paris City Tour for the Champs Elysees, the train ride to Versailles.

I fell into the Parisian lifestyle, sitting in a café on Saint Germain watching people, or taking the Métro to explore new neighborhoods. I was practicing my French, especially the word *arrondissement* until it rolled off my tongue so I could ask for directions as I wandered for hours searching for a landmark, the weather a bit sticky but not a deterrent to discovering the City of Light.

It was on one of those relaxed afternoons that I met her.

I ventured to the Place des Vosges, the oldest planned square in the city, an elegant refuge among the most beautiful in Paris, and surrounded by red brick homes with stone strip quoins above a vaulted arcade that stretched its way around the perimeter of the park.

On the way I stopped at a small shop where the proprietor leaned out the window to serve me. I purchased a ham sandwich and a cold bottle of beer. Ah, the simplicity of the French lifestyle. No whole wheat, rye, sourdough choices. Just fresh-baked French bread with a hard crust and unmatched flavor.

I took a seat facing the statue of King Louis XIII riding his horse, watching children on school break play near the fountain among the clipped lindens set in gravel and grass. A young couple kissed, sitting on a worn blanket, her hair shielding their faces for privacy, while an Orthodox couple strolled the pathways hand in hand, he with a skull cap and long sideburns wearing a white shirt and black pants, and she, younger, pale-pretty in a long dress, her pregnant belly leading the way. They probably lived in the Marais nearby, which flowed across the third and fourth arrondissements, a hub of upscale boutiques, bagel shops and yeshiva schools, the marble plaques on the outside walls a reminder of past horrors. For a moment it triggered thoughts of my mother and her recent revelation.

I crumpled up the sandwich paper and threw it in a receptacle along with my beer bottle. I wandered around the interior of the covered arcade that rims the park, past No. 11, the former home of Marion Delorme, a famous courtesan, to No. 6, Victor Hugo's house on the corner. I consulted my guidebook.

"A successful author who wrote *Les Misérables* while living here from 1832 to1848, his most acknowledged work appears on stages in theaters throughout America."

I meandered afterward into a tea shop with elegant containers and enticing aromas. I purchased black tea and a tin of biscuits for later in the evening. I strolled into art galleries, some with oils and sculptures too abstract for my taste, until I passed a custom shirt shop.

Lining the window on covered hangers was a display of attractive shirts with elegant collars and French cuffs crisp with starch.

I went in.

Dark wood fixtures lined the walls, displaying shelves of shirts next to a distressed leather love seat placed near the door. A rack filled with fashion magazines sat nearby. As most of the buildings in this city, it had been standing for hundreds of years.

"*Bonjour, Monsieur.*"

"Do you speak English?"

"*Oui.* A little." Then she smiled. "American, no?"

I nodded. She wore little makeup except for well-drawn lips and arched brows. "*Bienvenue* to Paris, City of Light. I am Sandrine. You would like assistance?"

Her throaty voice captivated me with its seductive accent. I liked the way she made eye contact. I had to think of an excuse to stay in the store. Beautiful, but not in a perfect way, she was petite with large coffee eyes, a straight, elongated nose and a red, sensuous mouth.

I stammered, "I would like some shirts." What an astute beginning.

She gave me a tour of the store. "On this wall we have prototypes of the shirts our tailor sews for you. You pick your size to try on. Then we discuss collars, size, cuff types." She eyed me up and down. I noticed the length of her lashes. "You will be a 42/16." Her small hands pushed aside a few shirts on the rack as she reached for one. "Here. Try this. The dressing room is behind the curtain. Please come when you are ready."

"What are the ties for?" I asked, fingering a few thrown over the end of the brass rack.

"Only to see how a collar will lie on you."

Lie on me? My boyish humor. I'd better go into the dressing room.

When I reappeared in the light of the store, she frowned. She reached up to grab my shoulders and faced me toward a standing antique mirror.

"You have the good physique but we will taper on the sides. You go to a gymnasium, no?"

She fussed around me like a mosquito deciding where to land, touching and flecking, smoothing my back. She pulled at a few places and clutched them. "You like?" She slid a measuring tape from around her neck and placed it against me, wrote down a few numbers on a pad of paper with a pencil that had been hidden in her hair.

I scrutinized my reflection. I was taught it wasn't good for a man to be vain, especially in scholarly circles, so I used the necessary toiletries, got haircuts at a barber shop and wore serviceable clothes from the local department store. But now with her peeking out behind me, I could see my father's six-foot frame, blue eyes and thick, dark, sandy hair. It's a wonder how you can look so much like someone and be nothing like them inside.

"*Parfait*. The shirt you wear was not fitted properly. This makes your shoulders more broad. How many will you order? We have a summer special. You take three, the fourth is free."

It wouldn't hurt for me to look more professional for the upcoming conference, an opportunity for me to present my knowledge in a well-researched paper. This could cost me. Not that I have to worry, but with the bad economy I'd reined in my spending.

"Monsieur, what is your name?"

The French are exceedingly polite. "Michael. Michael Saunders."

"It is nice to meet you, Monsieur Saunders." Her lips parted to reveal her perfect teeth in a smile. "What about something for the casual?"

"Sure." I found her English charming and acknowledged it was much better than my French. I didn't need anything casual, but it was an excuse to stay longer and engage her. Of course every man who wandered in must approach her.

She led me to the other end of the store with an inventory of shirts already made up in pinstripes and florals. I observed what she was wearing—a man's shirt with tiny red polka dots and white starched cuffs, a few buttons opened to reveal a bit of a lacy bra and cleavage. It reinforced that unselfconscious way French women are comfortable with themselves. She had tied it at the waist in a knot so her belly peeked out above very tight, well-worn jeans. On her feet she wore red high heels.

"Your size is up there," she said as she rolled a ladder across a brass bar and climbed the first few rungs with ease. Her ass was eye level to me.

"Wait. Let me help you. I can reach up there."

"No. This is my job." She descended with a half-dozen shirts, a panoply of designs and colors. She displayed them on the front showcase next to the computer. "I see you in this. It will match your eyes."

I felt a pang. My mother said the same words to me when she dressed me in blue as a child. She stroked a grey and blue faded stripe with contrasting cuffs of navy. In moments she pulled the pins and collar cardboard out, shook it and held it against me.

"Ah, yes. This one. Fantastic with jeans."

I fingered the fabric. Soft. "Egyptian cotton?"

She stood close to me with her neck bent forward, a few tendrils of hair curling into the white collar. Her dark hair, fastened to the crown of her head, smelled like spring. Or was it perfume?

French women know how to wear a fragrance so that it permeates without being overwhelming. Her perfume was seductive enough for me to want to ask about it. Too intimate a question, I thought. I read an article that French women applied a fragrance by dabbing it behind their ears and wrists, then touching it to pulse points between their breasts, the indentation of their throat, the navel and pudendum. Their body heat released the aroma.

"Monsieur, no. Our fabrics are made in France of Boussac cotton. *Tout naturel.* The finest quality. So. Two for work and two for pleasure?"

"Yes. Of course. And please call me Michael. I slipped back into the dressing room and changed. She assisted me with the choices, packed up the two ready-made shirts and let me know the others would be ready next week.

She handed me a white shopping bag embossed with a gold fleur-de-lis, tissue paper at the top and her card with *Sandrine Agneau* scrawled across the bottom.

I stared at her mellifluous name, the *Agneau* lost in my scrambled vocabulary.

"What does it mean?"

Eyebrows raised, her expression registered puzzlement.

"Ah, *Agneau* is lamb in French and *Sandrine* means protector of men."

"Are you both?"

She gave me a wry smile.

"Sometimes. *Merci beaucoup*, Monsieur Michael." She lowered her eyes for a moment and then stared at me directly.

I felt a connection, the kind a man knows well.

Chapter Three

Paris, France
August 14, 1993

I spent time at the American Library looking for more sources to back up my research, refining my paper and being nonproductive when images of my mother distracted me. Her passing was definitive and also confusing. She would have loved Paris. I stewed until the end of the following week when I couldn't wait anymore to see Sandrine. I headed for the Latin Quarter to sit on stone bleachers at the ancient Roman amphitheater in the Square des Arènes de Lutèce wearing one of the shirts I purchased.

My imagination was good enough to picture the seventeen thousand screaming inhabitants who viewed the entertainment of battling gladiators and wild circus animals in the first century. A brutal spot that took the Parisians more than sixteen hundred years to excavate, it was sacked by barbarians in the second century AD. The destroyers carted off most of the stone work to reinforce defenses near the Île de la Cité–just to drive archaeologists crazy two thousand years later as they dug through rubble.

Five years ago when I visited the Arch of Titus in Rome for research, I saw in clear bas relief the arch that depicted fifteen triumphant Roman soldiers celebrating the emperor Vespasian and his son Titus's victory over Israel in the First Jewish Revolt. They erected the arch with sacred treasures on the southern wall to immortalize the destruction of Herod's Temple in AD 70 after the murder of six-hundred thousand Jews.

The Romans paraded the broken dreams of a nation on their shoulders–a pair of silver trumpets, a gilded candelabra and a gold table studded with gems, often referred to as God's Gold. The ransacked booty not only had material value. For the religious it represented the sacred intimate symbolic communication between God and man, a triumph for the Israelis.

Situated on the summit of the Sacred Way in the Forum, the popular monument had limited access as ordered by the Italian prime minister after a special request by the Israeli government. As though the Israelis could right all the wrongs. Passage through Arco di Tito was now blocked from public access out of respect for the conquered people. Yet, Mussolini and Hitler passed underneath it in anticipation of another triumph decades ago, thinking they would rule the world. Only Jewish tour groups traversed it now, many spitting on the ancient rock.

The biblical treasures in question were released into the marketplace in the late seventies without fanfare through an antique dealer in Rome, not unlike the Dead Sea Scrolls that leaked out in Bethlehem. So many frauds had come to the marketplace, including the Shapira texts of Deuteronomy in the 1880s displayed in the British Museum, that healthy skepticism reined in academic circles.

It didn't take long to trace back rumors to the Catholic Church. After all, no one could verify what the Vatican had hidden in their vaults after so many centuries. The presentation of my paper was to be at the École Biblique et Archéologique Française and Scholars Conference in New York in a few weeks, an opportunity for me to curry accolades from my peers. In academia we have to rise above the pack with knowledge, exotic digs or a great discovery. Seymour Sommerstein, the department chair at Roscom College, must have pulled some academic favors to sponsor the prestigious event.

I wasn't the keynoter. That was Maurice Dubois, the academically adept Frenchman who worked directly with the scientists who verified the exceptional pieces with carbon dating. Tight security moved them to various underground labs in Europe while archaeologists speculated on their validity and value. I didn't like Dubois, but I believed his evaluation that they were authentic. This symposium, celebratory party and auction of the actual items would draw worldwide attention.

When I examined photographs of the extraordinary discovery, they inspired regret that I hadn't the opportunity to examine them in person. Dubois bragged about the beauty of his first viewing ten years ago. We all had the credentials to authenticate them, but he knew the right people. Jealousy flourished everywhere.

The rest of us would have to bide our time until the auction preview to see the treasures, ones that had survived millenniums of deception and controversy, stirring current responses from all over the globe.

I glanced at my watch every few minutes. Too early to show up at the shirt shop. I read over my conference paper, "The Journey of Sacred Biblical Treasures from the Essenes to Their Hiding Place at the Vatican," a treatise that would spark some refutations from my academic counterparts.

Our job was to dispute theories. I often thought Brooks White, my nemesis at Yale, stayed up at night thinking of ways to hassle me. I'd had disagreements with Yossi Farber too, an Israeli archaeologist, who had confronted me in person and in print. If you could prove someone wrong, you didn't necessarily have to be right. You had to cast doubt. Maybe I should have gone to law school to hone my skills of argumentation. Even though our field was in the scientific realm, so many areas existed that could not be proven from antiquity. Archaeologists are supposed to be objective, utilizing scientific theory; however, someone who followed Catholicism might take offense at my theory of the church hiding treasures.

I strolled into the shop a few minutes before five when she was closing down the computer and register. I felt nervous. A man takes risks when he approaches a woman, although I admit I hadn't been turned down very often.

"Monsieur?" The same red lips, but I had forgotten the aroma of her intoxicating fragrance. It floated in the shop.

"I was in last week and ordered some shirts," disappointed she didn't remember me. Maybe I misread the signal of interest.

"Ah, yes, Monsieur Michael. I was going to call you today, but the shop was busy. One moment." She walked from behind the counter to the curtain in the back, pulling it aside. She emerged with two dress shirts on hangers.

"Please try on," she said with a nod toward the dressing room. I took my briefcase with me. I trust no one when it comes to my paper after twelve years of exhaustive research, even though there are versions on my laptop and at my office in New Haven. I glanced at it whenever I had a spare moment to memorize key phrases so I could look out during the presentation. Most academics never meet the eyes of their audience, who view only the tops of their heads as they read every word. Fortunately, I don't have a bald spot or a bad comb-over. And I don't have to peer at them over reading glasses. Yet.

I stripped off my shirt and tried on the white batiste one. I didn't bother tucking it into my jeans. I pulled aside the curtain and stood in front of the mirror.

"*Ah, ça tombe parfaitement bien.*" She touched me at the shoulders, inserting inexpensive links into the cuffs. "Now you see how a shirt should fit onto you." She focused on me in the mirror, her lashes lowering. "*C'est très bien.*"

"*Merci beaucoup,*" an immediate response with one of the few French phrases I knew. It took a moment to realize she complimented me. I didn't know if it was another sign or I was misinterpreting interest.

"I will get the bill ready. It is almost time to close," she said, meeting my eyes again in the mirror. I followed her with my gaze as she turned away. Jeans with an awesome fit.

At the register I paid with a credit card. She was very efficient, handing me the receipt to sign and then the shopping bag. "*Bonsoir,* Monsieur Michael. Come again."

A flush rose on my cheeks. I headed for the door and stopped. "*Mademoiselle* Sandrine, would you like to meet me for a glass of wine at the café a few doors down since you're closing?" In the past I might have made a larger offer of dinner, but something made me keep it simple. I expected a no, an excuse, a story of a previous engagement or a boyfriend.

She opened her eyes wide. "*Oui.* I am almost ready. You go to Ma Bourgogne. I will meet you there."

And so, that is how it began. Wine, conversation, later a salad. Then *coq au vin* with roasted vegetables and more bread and wine. Talkative outside the store, she lived with her mother in the third arrondissement; her brother-in-law owned the shop; she was thirty-one and never married. And there was a boyfriend. Damn. We sat for hours. I spoke about myself and my work as an instructor at Yale University, being on sabbatical, my research into the hidden biblical treasures held by the Vatican for centuries and why Paris was an aphrodisiac for my soul.

She asked more questions and I played into her lovely eyes. She ate everything we ordered. "I did not have a lunch today. Sometimes I close shop and go home for the afternoon meal. But today I stay in and leave early with you." She gave me a slight smile. Whatever she said sounded enticing with her accent.

"You don't have set hours you keep the store open?"

She shrugged. "The French will come back if there is no one. Only the Americans keep rules."

During dinner she asked questions about my research. She wanted to know what proof there was that the Vatican had been holding the spoils of war for so many centuries. Did the pope know about the artifacts? Did Israel's rabbis have a right to demand the return of silver trumpets and gold treasures two thousand years later? What was their significance? I found her bright and engaging.

At first I responded in general terms, but she pressed me. I became more specific, sharing recent research about an unpublished inscription on a mosaic in the basilica of St. John Lateran of Rome dating to 1291. I memorized it because it was so crucial to my premise that the artifacts had been hidden by the Catholic Church after passing through the hands of barbarians, Vandals, Byzantines, Persians and thieves.

I quoted the lines for her. "Titus and Vespasian had this ark and candelabrum and . . . the four columns here present taken from the Jews in Jerusalem and brought to Rome." I admit I was showing off a bit, but she was someone worth impressing.

With the artifacts part of the public domain and the world watching, would the church admit to hiding them? Rumors circulated that the lawsuits against the church for the priestly scandals with children worldwide had grown to such astronomical amounts; it was a simple solution to raid the Vatican Secret Archives to raise money. The

Tower of Winds that held the papal collection of books from the 1500s meandered for more than seven miles down white marble steps, through two basements of musty parchment and paper, only opened to archivists.

As valued and priceless objects appeared on world markets with little explanation for their discovery, they created havoc in the antiquities arena. Some of the archaeological discoveries were breakthroughs that gave credence to the Israelis and the validity of their right to the disputed land, as stated in the Bible. Others reinforced the early power of the church to plunder in God's name. Still others were elaborate fakes.

I explained I had spent years ruminating about the skullduggery that must have ensued to smuggle these particular artifacts out of their clandestine tombs and into reputable hands to report a discovery of world-wide significance. At last, these priceless treasures would be auctioned in front of a world market next month in New York.

After the owner came out a second time to see if we wanted anything else, I paid the check, sorry our meal was over.

I avoided touching Sandrine as we strolled along, her impudent stride keeping up with mine, the crowded streets lit by a late sun, weaving by cafés, people leaning with their arms draped over chairs, gesturing with cigarettes in hand, the smoke circling around them. I was cautious. It was bold of her to dine with me. I didn't want to make her skittish. Men and women acknowledged us as we passed—the pointy red shoes leading the way, her sunglasses on her head, a black leather jacket slung over her shoulders. A quintessential French woman.

In France the air is intoxicating everywhere. Scents of lavender, musk or the fragrance of women amplify fresh croissants in the morning and red wine in the evening. I walked her past the Saint Paul stop to the Métro at the Hotel de Ville.

"*Bonsoir,* Michael," she said, lifting herself up to kiss me lightly on both cheeks. The perfume again. I took a subtle deep breath.

"And Thursday?" I regretted it the moment I said it. A bad move. Too soon to ask for another date.

"Roland meets me. We motorcycle to the cemetery." I looked away, knowing I'd blown it. She brightened. "*Père Lachaise* where all the famous are buried. Have you been?"

I nodded. "I spent last Friday in the rain looking for the graves of Jim Morrison, Gertrude Stein, Modigliani and Proust."

"Ah, the flower shop across the street from the entrance sells maps."

"Now you tell me."

She laughed, biting her lip for a moment. "Roland leaves to holiday in Biarritz Friday."

"And you don't go with him?" I had picked up her pattern of speech.

"No." She pursed her lips. "I stay with the store. It is a family business. The shirts they make in the eighteenth arrondissement by the Muslim women. We own a small factory. There are many orders now."

Okay. The door was open. I was infatuated with her. I watched her disappear down the steps of the Métro, her diminutive ass fading away.

Chapter Four

New York City
September 16, 1993

Seymour Sommerstein, the head of the Antiquities and biblical Studies Department of New York's finest liberal college, was shocked. Maurice Dubois dead? Why? A scholar doing something as innocuous as riding in a taxi? What the hell? He put the phone down, fell back into his leather chair and sighed. His chin sank to his chest. He didn't know the French professor well. They had been cordial at a few conferences over the years, but the competition between academics was fierce. Intellectual discourse, acceptable. Friendship? Well, that was something else, especially with a pretty-boy "Frog" who had attitude. Ach, and his aroma of Gauloises, those French cigarettes he smoked, hair hanging onto his forehead and over his collar, a look for students trying to be nonchalant—but not credible for a professor. There were always a few who stayed in the university system because they harbored an image of youth.

He leaned forward to place his elbows on the cluttered desk in his home office, an unused bedroom with metal file cabinets and stackable bookshelves. The ancient, wooden desk with one pencil drawer and a shabby, circular rug were hand-me-downs from his mother-in-law before she passed away years ago. A folded academic journal kept one of the legs level.

Unlike his office at the college with a view of the Hudson River, paneled walls, framed diplomas, club furniture, this barren room reminded him how empty his life was without his wife.

His head settled into his palms. It was enough to spend the last two years putting the conference together, a coup for his department to be the host. NYU wanted it. Brandeis wanted it. Even Harvard made a bid. But he got it with a promise of academic excellence and top-notch organization.

And now? Should it even go forward? Was it appropriate in light of a death? And not an old-age retiring professor either—a youngish academic with credentials. He would need a replacement for the keynote speaker and a liaison for potential donors. What about the printed programs, press releases, journals to be distributed?

He groaned, then slammed his hands on the desk. He said aloud, "The poor *schmuck* comes to deliver a research paper and gets killed on his way out of the airport. That's great for tourism."

Sommerstein dragged himself down the short hallway to his living room and clicked on the television. He brushed away the *New York Times*, settling into his worn, brown, leather sofa, easing his shirt out of his pants. His knees creaked as he set his feet onto the coffee table.

Of course it was all over the eleven o'clock news. A black-and-white photograph of Maurice flashed on the screen. The bloodthirsty public loved accidents like this: an Arab cabbie, a long-distance trucker fifty miles from home, a handsome Frenchman and an esoteric conference coupled with priceless artifacts. It was a plot from a bad novel. How did they get this stuff so fast?

"The renowned professor was in the city to present a paper about biblical relics that will be on display next week at the Judaica Cultural Museum prior to an antiquities auction at Shropshire, the international auction house." The broadcaster turned over a piece of paper to start her next news story. "If you or anyone you know has information regarding this accident, please call the New Jersey authorities or your nearest NYPD."

He felt a concrete weight land on his chest. Instinctively, he rubbed his heart, knowing it wouldn't make a difference.

Oy, I forgot my cholesterol meds this morning. I've got to eat better. My Sondra of blessed memory would be nagging me if she were here.

He clicked off the news and struggled to get up, knowing he had to salvage the conference. He reached for the phone on the end table next to him.

"Heather? Sommerstein. Am I calling too late?"

"No. It's okay." She stifled a yawn. "Marianna and I were just getting ready for bed."

"You saw the news?"

"Yeah, I was going to talk to you in the morning. What are we going to do about the conference? Maybe we should cancel. People would understand."

"What? No, we've been planning this for ages. The prestige of the college depends on it. People—even government representatives—are flying in from all over the world."

He heard her say a muffled, "It's the boss." She placed the phone against her ear again. "Maybe not if people are getting creamed who arrive in Newark."

"Never mind. That's Jersey. They'll come into Kennedy or La Guardia. Call Dr. Levy and see who we can get to replace Dubois. If I can get my hands on his research paper, I'll get someone else to read it. At the very least, get hold of his secretary in Paris."

"I don't speak French."

Ach. A pain in the *tuchas*.

He wanted to hang up. He had no patience for excuses, but Heather was invaluable to him. An efficient Ph.D. candidate in archaeology was what everyone needed. Thank God she was on the six-to-eight-year plan.

He hated it when she took off an entire semester to go on digs in Caesarea or Herod's tomb in Israel or traveled to Tikal in Guatemala. Kid thought she could dig up the world overnight. He just didn't want to hear about her weekends spent in a Melissa Etheridge haze.

"Sir, do you want me to set up a short memorial service at the conference after I find a possible list of replacements?"

"Excellent idea. You're always thinking." And then he visualized her in a man's shirt and khakis with her boy's haircut, arm around the girlfriend's shoulder and an earring in her eyebrow. Damn, she was smart.

Chapter Five

Paris, France
August 16, 1993

I couldn't stay cooped up all day so my exercise and fresh air therapy sent me on excursions around Paris. As I wandered through the Musée Carnavalet, a mansion devoted to French history with symmetrical small gardens, I learned about Madame de Sévigné who had lived there for twenty years and wrote prodigious letters. She reminded me of my mother with her obsessive love for her daughter who resided in Provence. My mother's adoration and sacrifice for me still echoed in my head.

"I did it for you, Michael." I couldn't digest the lies and secrecy, but she felt compelled to tell me "how things were in her day."

"I'm only telling you this, Michael, because I don't want you to judge me so harshly. Times were different after the war. I didn't want you to suffer too." She paused, sitting in an upholstered chair in a silk robe I had given her for a birthday or Mother's Day, a terrycloth turban on her head, loose from hair she'd lost during the last round of chemotherapy.

When I was growing up in the 1950s, *stunning* was the word people used to describe her statuesque figure and lovely face with clear azure eyes. She'd come to school for a conference or pick me up early, and the other boys, even some of the girls, would tell me she was "a looker." She had always been blonde too, her wavy locks cut into a short, chic style reminiscent of Lana Turner or Kim Novak.

As an only child I spent a lot of time observing others or reading books. I took swimming and piano lessons, played tennis, stayed within my social milieu. But, even then I knew there was something I couldn't put my finger on about her. I asked about my grandparents when I saw other generational families attending church. My mother's answer was, "They've passed."

But with my eight-year-old persistence I wanted to know where, how, why. She would rebuff me until I pestered her for so long she would relent and say, "New York."

"Where did they live in New York?"

"In the city."

"Where in the city? What street? Why don't we go there? Where are they buried?"

After a sigh she repeated what I already knew.

"I was an only child too, and my father was killed overseas in the war. I don't know where's he's buried. My mother and I had to struggle to survive afterward with so many servicemen coming home, taking all the jobs, going back to school. I worked as a secretary in a munitions factory in Jersey but that went away—"

"And then you met Dad. Tell me that part again."

Her sigh let me know she was bored with the story but she continued anyway.

"I got a job at Gimbel's in the millinery department. I came to work every day, put on a hat that enhanced my outfit and modeled it as encouragement for women to make a purchase. They were so glad to be back in fashion after the dreary days of grey, khaki and a shortage of silk stockings.

I'd get a customer to sit down on an upholstered stool and gaze at herself in a three-way mirror while I picked out a few hats for her to try. Most didn't know how to wear one so they'd place it at the crown of their head. I'd gently move it forward and tilt it. Some needed hat pins to hold them in place. I got to know my clients, asked questions about their families, encouraged them to be a bit bold. We all needed to lift our spirits. We had lost so much fighting the Nazis."

She reached for a few tissues knocking over a glass of water. The chemotherapy had made her clumsy. I jumped up to mop up the mess with a towel. She apologized and then with encouragement, continued.

"I did very well and the assistant manager came down to tell me I had exceeded the quota of all the other departments the previous month. Even dresses. A strapping guy with hair parted on the side, darkened from its blond hue with oil men used then, he always had a few hairs that stood up at his crown. I knew who he was because he strolled through the aisles on a regular basis to make sure we were all doing our job, not sitting down or chatting without paying attention to customers. His boss stayed upstairs in the executive offices and barked orders."

"And that was Byron, the assistant manager?"

"Yes. He took a liking to me and always stopped to ask questions. The other girls said he was sweet on me. But management didn't mix with sales help. Plus, I knew he was from the Upper East Side."

She paused a moment. "Also, he wore a wedding ring." She fiddled with a loose sapphire ring on her hand.

"When I asked about it, he slipped it off his hand into his pocket and said, 'I just do that so the ladies don't think I'm available. But I am. For you.'

"Oh, I was suspicious, cautious, terrified. I didn't want to lose my job. I was damned either way. I couldn't fraternize with him or refuse his overtures.

"But then my mother had to quit working. She couldn't stand on her feet anymore. At first I thought it was the varicose veins, but later I sensed it was something more. We still had my dad's army benefits, but the landlord raised the rent and we were squashed into two rooms. I gave momma the bedroom and I slept on a cot in the kitchen. The bathroom was down the hall. We were poor. I handed her my paycheck every week when I came in the door.

"In the meantime, Byron would stop in my department every day. It embarrassed me because the other girls teased me. Then some turned ugly because they felt I had advantages, although I hadn't accepted a thing from him."

"Then what happened? What happened to my grandmother? What

was she sick from? When did he ask you to marry him?"

My mother clammed up. Details became hazy. She claimed she couldn't remember much about that time period because it all happened so fast. I couldn't even get her to tell me her maiden name. She'd brush me off with a wave of her hand, lips set in a thin line.

"We just got married in a small ceremony at city hall. It was crowded because all the soldiers had honeys waiting for them after the war. And then you came along, the joy of my life."

I bought the story until I was about twelve when we were living on Greenway Drive in Coral Gables down the street from the country club. My father had accepted the position of general manager at the new Sears Roebuck, the gateway to Miracle Mile with a few blocks of fancy stores and a Food Fair. It was a big promotion. My mother was the perfect corporate wife cultivating friendships with the wives of other important spouses in town—bankers, airline pilots, physicians.

She entertained often with Estelle in the kitchen—dinner parties with cocktails, a table that took all day to set, fancy desserts. She spent hours creating floral arrangements, a low one for the table, another for the piano and a spray of baby breath for the powder room. After picking up a pressed tablecloth at the dry cleaners, she'd get her hair done at J. Baldi's, a salon on Miracle Mile where the owner's portly Italian shape and dyed black pompadour could be seen as he worked on clients through a plate glass window.

I don't think women pictured themselves in any other role. It was before Betty Friedan wrote her tome about housewives' ennui. She played bridge twice a week, swam at the country club for exercise, flew to Cuba with my dad on gambling junkets. She seemed content waiting for me to come home from school to drink milk and munch cookies.

When Estelle arrived with a shopping bag wearing a dark felt hat on Mondays, Wednesdays and Fridays at 9 a.m., she'd change out of her clothes into a uniform. Her closet off the kitchen had three mint green ones hanging in it. They had grown tighter on her corpulent backside over the last few years, the buttons in the front straining a bit. With her back to me as she washed the breakfast dishes, she'd start a new pot of coffee for my mom. I loved her. She answered endless questions, baked cookies and left me alone to read comic books.

My dad left in a starched white shirt and tie about the time Estelle arrived, greeting him as "Mistah Byron." He'd make his exit, jacket over his arm, briefcase in hand, an imposing figure at six-foot-one, to drive the Lincoln ten minutes to work. If my mom needed to do errands, she drove him or took the bus at the corner.

On one of those weekends while they were gone, I decided to look through their nightstands. Just a kid's curiosity I guess. There were activities at the club, movies, swimming tournaments, and a friend's mom picking me up to spend the day with them on Sunday. Estelle was sleeping over, but she busied herself in the kitchen and slept in the maid's room, which my mother had decorated in English chintz roses.

With my parents out of town Estelle tuned the radio to her gospel station at a higher decibel so it ricocheted through the house. She sang along dusting, mopping, vacuuming even though she couldn't hear it with the loud Hoover sucking up debris. Builders were clearing lots of pine trees to the south and east of us. My mother and Estelle commiserated about the mess on the terrazzo floors and wall-to-wall carpeting from the soil, bark, needles and sap.

On this particular Saturday she sat across from me at the kitchen table while I thumbed a well-worn comic book. I had a collection of superhero comics in my room, but my favorite was the one where Lex Luthor lost all his hair in a lab accident accidentally caused by Superman.

"Mistah Michael, whatcha goin' to do today with your momma and poppa gone?"

"I dunno." I rested my head in my hand. "I'm bored." A fresh squeezed glass of orange juice sat in front of me, the beige linoleum shiny from a recent scrub.

"Your momma says for you to go swimming and meet your friends at the club. I'll be right cheer when you come home with a peanut butter and jelly sandwich. Come on. You get your trunks on and get goin'."

I didn't move. A fly spun by my head. I took a sip of juice. I turned another page. We sat like that in silence for a while longer.

"Well, I don't have time for staring. I promised your momma to get all the silver polished and that's one back-breakin' job so I'd better start. You let Estelle know if she can do anything for you. You want to hang out here for awhile, that's okay too." She pushed herself up with both hands, started singing "Swing Low, Sweet Chariot" and busied herself in the kitchen.

After a bit I closed up the comic book and wandered into my mom's room. I lay down on her side of the bed knowing I'd have to fluff the pillows and smooth the taffeta spread when I got up. I was closer to her than my dad because he was gone so much.

My father intimidated me so our interactions were stilted. He didn't know how to talk to me, asking a few awkward questions about school. Evenings he'd come home, collar loosened, and walk straight to the bar, his briefcase left near the door, jacket thrown over the back of a chair.

He'd mix a scotch on the rocks or a gin and tonic. Sometimes he'd make martinis for himself and my mom but mostly he drank alone, sitting in a chair with an ottoman in the Florida room, the jalousies tilted for a breeze, reading the afternoon paper. *The Miami Daily News* was delivered by my classmate's older brother on his Schwinn. After a bit he'd pull off his tie, open another button and call for my mom to mix him another drink.

She'd come in wearing heels and an apron smelling of the roast that was cooking or spaghetti and meatballs, my favorite, the garlic bread doused in butter. I always helped mix the iced tea or tear up the lettuce for a salad but she wouldn't let me handle a knife to slice the tomatoes even though I had learned to use one in Boy Scouts.

"You'll cut your finger."

"Sara, you baby the boy too much."

"Hello, honey," she'd say, bending down for a quick kiss. "Easy day at the store?"

Usually he'd grunt, preoccupied with the paper, but sometimes we'd hear a story about another assistant manager whose name I don't remember who was gunning for his job, undermining him in the men's or sporting goods or appliance departments. He'd have at least three drinks before dinner, only getting out of the chair when my mom said it was time to wash up.

Most Saturdays he worked because that was the busiest day in the store, people coming from faraway places like Hallandale and Homestead to see the newest modern convenience, an escalator planted in the middle of the shopping emporium. So Saturday wasn't a baseball or bowling day with me like some of the other dads I knew.

Chapter Six

Paris, France
August 17, 1993

After a stroll through Luxembourg Gardens with its chestnut trees planted in rows, I searched for the Medici Fountain, an Italian Renaissance gem with a reflecting pool. The anguished mythological sculptures, a contrast to the tranquil beauty of the spot, seemed out of place. I sat for a while on a mossy stone bench enjoying a respite from the shrieks of children watching a puppet show or pushing small sailboats into the lake.

I lounged around Les Deux Magots, a café on the Left Bank, to read a copy of the *International Herald Tribune*. The paper was installed on a long wooden dowel so people couldn't walk off with it. It was Bill Clinton's first year as president and I was curious as to how our leader, a mere four years older than me, was faring. I skimmed through articles about pope John Paul II visiting Mexico and the United States, an inspiration to Catholics around the world, the upcoming marriage of Kim Basinger and Alec Baldwin and a collapsed hotel in Thailand that killed 114 people until I was satiated.

I sipped espresso, taking small bites of my croissant so I wouldn't have to leave too soon. I watched some of the eccentrics wander by with pampered pups in jeweled collars, others wearing feather boas left over from the night before and a large man wearing a small derby. A couple in their sixties wandered by, she, petite with a silver 1920s haircut, clutching at her partner's arm. She stood on tiptoes to whisper something in his ear and they laughed. I couldn't recall my parents having many intimate moments. Maybe they had secrets from each other.

—

On a particular afternoon as I lazed in my parents' bed reading comic books, the roar of Estelle's vacuum cleaner brought me out of my reverie. It meant she was occupied. I rolled to the other side of the bed to rifle through my dad's nightstand drawer, the metal pull easy in my hand. It matched the bedroom suite my mother had insisted upon made from blonde wood.

I never stole anything like some of my friends who shoplifted candy or gum, but I was a curious kid. I liked exploring nightstand drawers after Eddie showed me his Dad's hidden gun. In fact, we looked at it almost every time I went over, stroking the cold steel barrel with our forefingers. We never took it out of the drawer. My mother's cautionary words always reverberated around my head. She was protective, more so than most of my friends' parents.

Her final coup when I was desperate to participate in something she felt risky was, "Eddie's parents have four children and I only have one." That was a killer. Guilt personified.

The drawer slid open with ease on rollers, unlike some that fell out when you pulled them. My mother insisted on top of the line from Modernage. I remember my parent's argument because my dad wanted to get the best Sears had. She won.

The first layer was cigarettes, matches, a cigar in cellophane, two white hankies with his initials, folded papers that I glanced at—an old telephone bill, a parking ticket, a birthday card from my grandparents, some numbers scribbled on a pad, a racing form from Hialeah Track, and a Mickey Spillane pulp novel. Underneath that was another layer. *Argosy*, a men's adventure magazine with a marine, gun in hand, dashing across the cover—and underneath that, girlie ones, the top one *Beauty Parade* with a woman posed in a red bikini, her chest spilling over the top. Under that, *Titter, America's Merriest Magazine.*

He had a collection of them with provocative women on the front in stockings and garters, open sheer robes and my favorite, a fallen ice skater with her panties showing. I was dismayed my father looked at such things while he was married to my very proper mother. Intrigued, I pulled them out, a flurry of tobacco falling to the bottom of the lined drawer. I picked up a tin box.

On the back was written "Ultrex Platinum prophylactics are tested on new, modern equipment for your protection."

Condoms. I was shocked. I knew what they were for and heard some older boys talking about carrying them in their wallets. It was foreign to me but the reality hit. I fell backward into the neatly bolstered pillows. They did it. How often did they do it? Why did they do it? I wished I had an older brother to ask questions. Why didn't they want more children? I was a good kid. Wouldn't they want more of me?

I put everything back in the drawer mostly the way I found it. I couldn't remember anymore.

"Mistah Michael, you okay?" Estelle said, knocking at the door. "You been in there a long time. I'm going outside to sweep the patio. Let me know if you're leaving for the club or you want that peanut butter sandwich, okay?"

Chapter Seven

Paris, France
August 18, 1993

I leaned my head back on the park bench in the Student's Garden at the École normale supérieure, where Simone Weil, a Jewish woman who became a Christian mystic, graduated with a degree in philosophy. According to my trusty guidebook, the quadrangle off rue d'Ulm had a pond known as Cour aux Ernests, the "Ernests" being the goldfish that glimmered in the sunlight.

My neck wasn't comfortable, but it didn't matter when I reflected. I kept revisiting my childhood seeking answers. I closed my eyes, drifting back to Miami, a city on the verge in the mid-1950s with Yankee refugees escaping winter, blacks sustaining in poverty, mob bosses establishing themselves in the hotel industry and lots of sunshine, clean beaches and inexpensive real estate.

Months passed with me stealing into my father's nightstand several more times. I smuggled one of the magazines into my room for an afternoon knowing he wouldn't be home for hours.

It also raised more questions for me about my mother. I knew where my dad came from, who his people were—good, honest farm folks. I also saw how hard he had worked to separate himself from them by moving to a big city, attending some college, becoming sophisticated, modern. He wasn't a war hero, but he had served and that gave him credibility in conversations, when I could listen in after a dinner party while the men sat in the living room and the women gathered in the kitchen. Everyone smoked.

My dad didn't reveal much of himself. It was all about ball scores and the track and business. He could rattle off percentages of improvements in various departments at Sears. "Women's hosiery is up twenty percent now that there's nylon. All the little ladies want a washing machine so appliances are doing well. Whole country's having a sigh of relief now that everyone's back where they're supposed to be, men at work, women at home."

I never heard my mother complain of boredom. She lunched with her friends, a group that sometimes gathered to shop at Daniel's, a specialty store off Miracle Mile or on a rare occasion, visited Bonwit Teller on Lincoln Road in Miami Beach. Once, as the light faded outside, I heard her ask her best friend Linda McNair, while they smoked and sipped Bloody Marys at our kitchen table, if she wanted to make a day of it on the beach–lunch, shopping, a movie.

I busied myself with the cookie jar, a large Aunt Jemima, round ceramic piece whose head came off to reveal the chocolate chip cookies Estelle had baked the day before.

"Come on, Linda. I'll get the car from Byron and have Estelle stay late for Michael. There's a big gala happening at the club in October and I'd love a new dress. I heard Bonwit's and Lillie Rubin have Dior and Balmain. We might even find some things in that polyester fabric. I can't stand the way white nylon yellows. Besides, there's that great Wolfie's deli down there where we can get a pastrami sandwich. Or a bagel."

"I don't know." Linda hesitated, sipping her drink, pulling at her collar, the cigarette perched at the edge of the ashtray.

"What's the matter?" my mother asked.

"I can stay by myself or go to Carl's," I piped up. "I don't need someone to watch me anymore."

Of course I was thinking about how to get back to those magazines in my dad's drawer.

"Well, I just don't want to go over there for a hot hour's ride to be spoken to rudely," said Linda, punching out her cigarette.

"What are you talking about?" My mother tapped her ash on the tray. I saw her foot gyrating under the table, getting agitated. When she wanted to do something she pushed to get her way.

Linda sighed. "Earl says there's too many Yids there, that I shouldn't shop in their stores. Next you know they'll start moving to Coral Gables. Bad enough the new music teacher at the junior high is one."

I saw my mother freeze, then recover, pressuring her cigarette out in the overflowing ashtray. "Well, okay. Maybe another time." She got up to carry a plate of Ritz crackers and cheese slices to the sink. I could see her face because I had my hand in the jar again. She paused to look out the kitchen window to our expansive backyard, the St. Augustine grass green like a Disney cartoon, her eyes damp.

What did that mean? Why was she sad her friend didn't want to go with her? Enough to cry?

She walked Linda to the door, past our living room reserved for special occasions, the long white sofa, matching end tables and coral chairs placed exactly in a layout my mother had seen in *Better Homes and Gardens*, its formality a testament to a successful family and as inviting as a closed door.

It was months until I was alone long enough to explore my mother's nightstand drawer. By then my parents had window air conditioners installed in our bedrooms courtesy of Sears. The one in my parents' room whirred and dripped, a never-ending source of promises to send a repairman to fix it. My parents argued about the stained wood floor, a permanent bowl and towel underneath the unit to collect condensation, and the chipped paint on the rose wall that the installers had ruined.

Chapter Eight

Paris, France
August 19, 1993

My studio apartment, compact and clean, didn't offer many amenities so I spent a lot of time in Parisian parks. Besides being a good way to explore the city, it offered solace from the finality of my mother's death. I lived such a cerebral life that examining emotions was awkward for me. No question I loved her. That was clear. Where I ran aground was why she kept a secret for so long that impacted my childhood, one that made me vacant without faith, traditions, an extended family. Yes, I was grateful for her substantial departing gift that allowed me to indulge in a foray to Paris, a dream we shared, but I had missed so much. Would it have made me a better, well-rounded person? Or would I have gravitated to a solitary life anyway, discarding the distractions of family and religion to bury myself in academia?

I had explored Parc Citroën, named after the famed French automaker, which had opened a little over a year ago; the Tuileries Garden with its promenade and ponds near the Louvre earlier in my stay, and the Student's Garden at the École normale supérieure in the fifth arrondissement yesterday.

Today I took a bus to the east side of Paris to wander through Bois de Vincennes, a tree-filled refuge and former royal hunting ground of almost twenty-five hundred acres, three times larger than Central Park. I discovered Parc Floral behind the Château de Vincennes. Although it was late in summer and most of the roses had dissipated, the dahlias bloomed among noisy peacocks, an errant butterfly–it was the epitome of nature. It was easy to find a spot to think.

I was seeing Sandrine on a regular basis but proceeded with caution. I kept it casual, meeting her after she closed up the store for dinner on weeknight evenings. She spent time with her family or her boyfriend and I had to leave in September for the conference. Commitments were damning.

A young man nearby broke my reverie. With his legs folded under him, he picked at a guitar, humming a tune under his breath. A group of children in front of me kicked a ball back and forth, shouting when it flew out of their imposed circle. I observed to see if I could spot the leader. A lanky boy with stringy hair and dirty knees kicked it hard. It landed at my feet. He appeared before me, an expectant look in his eyes. I bent down and tossed it to him, with a thought as to how some children can be in the moment.

As a child I only met my grandparents on my dad's side when we traveled to their goat farm in Wisconsin one holiday. We stayed in a hotel in downtown Racine. I didn't meet my cousins until dinner on Christmas Eve. I was the outsider from the East Coast, a rare Southerner residing in Florida.

In the bitter cold my grandfather marched me to the barn to show off his goats. He explained how to care for them, the process of making cheese and showed me the extra hay they needed in winter. Although I liked a kid that nuzzled me with its white-starred forehead, I was bored.

When we came in, my grandmother, who was preparing kringles, chided him for keeping me out in the cold for so long. In the large farm kitchen, pots and utensils displaying dents and scratches hung on the wall, a testimonial to how long they had been in use. She retrieved bowls and ingredients from open shelves. I noticed her faded apron was shredded near the bottom.

She told me with a tinge of resentment in her gravelly voice that my father had surprised them by leaving for the University of Michigan to study business. "Course your dad got called up to do his duty in the war. He's hardly looked back since. Shocked us by never coming back home 'cept for a few weeks after his discharge. Your grandpa thought the boys would take over the farm. Then we could move to town, but looks like I'm going to spend my last day's right here."

She sat down with me at the all-purpose table. Her hands, rough and red, were unlike my mother's with her manicured nails. She hand-rolled pastry as we chatted.

"First, Michael, we're going to make remonce, the filling. The butter, sugar, cinnamon and raisins need some strident stirring to get creamy." I must have looked puzzled because she explained kringles were a butter pastry made by Danish bakers who settled the area. I took my task seriously, wishing there was a way to add chocolate chips like Estelle did with cookies.

"So why'd he leave?"

"He'd always had big ambitions, a real hard worker. He wanted to make a lot of money, drive a fancy car. I think sometimes he's ashamed of us, but I try to be tolerant. His Daddy's hurt though. Don't repeat that. I shouldn't have said it."

She stopped her rolling pin for a minute in the awkward silence. I loved her in that moment of regret.

I glanced out the framed window, the panes frosted and the sill covered with knickknacks, salt-and-pepper shakers and a few stained recipe cards. "So what was my dad like growing up?"

"A good kid. He's the oldest of my three boys so he'd get them into a lot of mischief. But a farm is getting up early, doing chores before school, helping afterward, Sunday at the Danish Lutheran Church. Smartest of the bunch his teachers told me. Read with a flashlight in bed."

She took my bowl giving it a few more swipes with the wooden spoon before she started laying out the pastries on a cookie sheet. I missed the red and green sprinkles we used on cookies at home. "Once he got to the high school in Racine he was all grown up, good-looking, the star of the football team. He had a job part time at Coopers Underwear in Ludington. Strictly commission. Later it became Jockey and he could've stayed right here, close to home, the way that business has growed."

Her voice got soft and she stopped mixing. "That's when I lost him. It was too far to come back and forth so he'd sleep at a friend's house and work after school and on the weekends. His brothers had to take his chores, which made his daddy real mad. Once he got a scholarship and left for school we didn't see him much. Like now. You're going to have to leave by Christmas afternoon so he can get back for the sales on the twenty-sixth." She paused. "You like living with all that sunshine?"

I shrugged my shoulders. "Guess so." I liked listening to her country talk. The oven door closed with finality and we sat down to wait for the first warm kringles, twisted like pretzels, the aroma permeating the kitchen.

"Let's start another batch with nuts this time." She handed me a cloth bag bulging with walnuts. "Crack them open, pick out the meat and chop them up fine with a knife." I didn't mention my mother wouldn't let me cut a tomato.

She stood up, pressing her belly to the counter, adding ingredients, stirring the mixture of flour, vanilla, sugar and butter near the sink, her shoulder moving in rotation. Wisps of grey hair crowned her head in the window light.

"So when did you meet my mom?"

She stopped, turning to look at me. "I met your mom in '55, a good ten years after the war ended. Your Dad was working in New York at Macy's or Gimbel's or one of those fancy places—trying get ahead. We didn't hear from him much. Boys aren't so good at writing. I got a letter one day that he had married. Later, he sent one that they had a child with a picture of you. They wanted to visit before they moved down to Florida. Oh, the kringles!"

She grabbed a well-worn dishtowel and set the kringles on the counter. My mother insisted I always pull out a trivet for her. My grandmother fanned them a bit before grabbing a spatula and lifting a few to check the bottoms. "Goodness. Caught 'em just in time. Wait a minute before you try one. Very hot."

I got up to hover over the treats, the smell almost tempting me to burn my tongue. She handed me two on a plate, blowing on them.

"Now finish those nuts. I'm almost ready to add them to the mixture."

"So then what happened?"

"Well, you were little. I don't know if you remember. . . ."

I did have a few memories of playing on the floor under this table, feeding the goats, but I couldn't remember the people.

"No, not much."

"Well, it was short. Just an introduction but your grandaddy wanted to know why they were high-tailing it out of New York and your daddy said it was a better opportunity. Your mom told him to tell the truth. 'It's your family, Byron. We can trust them.' But your daddy hushed her up and said they were starting over without snow and ice. Everything was real new in Florida after the war."

As a child I got prickly all over knowing something was a secret. More than the usual "I must have been adopted" fare kids think about. I looked just like my parents, sea-blue eyes like my mom and my dad's square jaw and build.

"So what do you think she wanted to tell you?" The warm pastry melted in my mouth. I'd never tasted anything so delicious.

"I'm not supposed to say but your momma's background . . . was different."

Hints had been dropped over the years. At one point I was convinced my mother had been a harlot with her red lips and blond hair. Arguments rattled behind closed doors, epithets screamed. Certain subjects brought a hush. Maybe they weren't really married. Maybe it was a fake and I was illegitimate, like the story about a girl in our class who didn't have a father. Or at least one anyone knew about.

"In what way?"

"I'm not one to judge, and the good Lord our Savior started—"

"Mom! Please don't fill Michael's head with tall tales." My father burst into the room and herded us into the living room for a holiday toast.

I pulled her arm as my grandmother slipped the apron over her head. "Will you finish?"

"Your Daddy doesn't want me to say."

"But I want to know," I whispered.

She grabbed my hand as we entered the living room where my mother sat, relaxed by the fire with a drink in her hand, wearing a soft blue sweater that I loved to put my head against when I hugged her.

Chapter Nine

Paris, France
August 20, 1993

I didn't want to think about Sandrine, but I kept going back to our dinners and how charming she was ordering for us in French, sipping wine, sharing tidbits about customers. Was it the romance of the city? Was I being as selective as usual? Or was I lonely in an unfamiliar environment? It had only been a few weeks and I didn't want to rush the relationship.

I'd been so wrapped up in the details of my mother's denouement, I hadn't spent much time on my social life. Was now the time to pursue someone? How much should I share? My mother at the end of her life remained an enigma. How could I have been so close to her all those years and not have known who she really was? Was it a flaw in my character that I hadn't been a better observer? I plagued myself with questions and found few answers.

When I woke this morning I had a flash of dizziness, a sign a migraine might have tracked me down across the ocean. It could be the red wine I was consuming or the aged cheese we ordered with fruit instead of sweets after a meal. Both were known to contain tyramine that could trigger a headache. I took a precautionary pill and left for the Monceau *quartier*, a neighborhood with a park near Montmarte. I was impressed with the colonnade, lily ponds and rock gardens with statues of Frédéric Chopin and Guy de Maupassant, whose short stories I read in high school many years ago.

—

I came to a new level of awareness when I scoured the drawer on my mother's side of the bed. On this particular day I sat at the kitchen table, my hand propping up the side of my head with *Tales from the Crypt*, my favorite comic book, when she came in wearing a scarf, a few of her blond curls popping out the front, sunglasses and her pocketbook over her arm, keys in hand.

"Michael, I'm going to Food Fair. Want anything?"

"No thanks, Ma."

"I'll be back soon. Answer the phone if it rings. It might be Martha giving me details about the school fundraiser. Write down her name and number. And don't forget to answer 'Saunders residence. Who's calling please?'" I attended Ponce de Leon Junior High and since we were in an affluent area, an active PTA urged moms to donate their time and resources.

I was laconic until she walked out the door and I heard the new Cadillac rev its engine. I waited until she got out of the car and closed the garage door. I turned a few more pages of my horror comic in case she forgot something and came back.

Then I slipped into her room with the air conditioner humming and sprawled out on the bed, even though I knew I'd have to pat down the chenille bedspread, a recent replacement for the taffeta one, to make it look like I hadn't been there. They kept the door closed all the time to keep it cooler. I rolled onto my stomach and slid open the drawer of the ash nightstand. It smelled of her perfume, Chanel No. 5, when I opened it. My father's drawer was sexy. My mother's held nothing of interest.

I rifled around trying not to move anything too far out of its place: stacked crisp white hankies with her initials were in one corner, a few packs of Chesterfields in the other, matches, a cigarette holder I had never seen her use, two *Reader's Digests*, a *Good Housekeeping* magazine, a group of pencils with a rubber band around them, a small sewing kit with a tin Sucrets box of straight pins, tissues in a blue and white box. Boring. Pond's Cold Cream, a hairnet, clippies that she used to hold the curls in front of her ears, a copy of *Marjorie Morningstar* by Herman Wouk—even the cover looked dull with a young woman looking worried—and an old red lipstick worn flat down. Underneath the floral lining paper a corner of an envelope peeked out. I lifted the paper to pull it out. Blank on the outside.

When I slipped it out the other items shifted. I hurried to move them back into their spots. My mother was organized. She'd know if something was moved. My father read those girly magazines and tossed them back on top of the drawer's contents. Not my mother. She had a place for everything. I pulled out the envelope shoved in the back.

My hands shook a bit because I knew it had to be private the way it was hidden. Inside I found a piece of paper folded in thirds.

March 15, 1950

Dear Sarah,
I miss you every day. I understand your decision and your reasons for it. I want you to have a better life, an easier life. Byron seemed kind the one time I met him. Can I see the baby before you move? We could meet at the luncheonette on the corner of Lexington and 52nd.

Mommy

I couldn't understand what I was reading so I read it again. My mother's mother, my grandmother, met my father only once and wanted to see me? I had bought the story that my grandfather died in the war and that my grandmother became ill and passed away too. My mother seemed uncomfortable when I asked about her family. She never gave me any new information so I had stopped inquiring. Why couldn't her mother just come over to where they were living? I panicked trying to fit it back into the envelope.

She'd return soon. A trip to Food Fair, even with parking on Miracle Mile and a few friendly exchanges with neighbors and the manager—we get the best cuts of beef she told me—meant she'd be back within the hour.

Estelle knocked on the door. "You in there, Mistah Michael?"

I scrambled to put the envelope back and smash the drawer closed. I leaned back against the pillows.

"Sure, Estelle. The air conditioning works better in here than my room."

She opened the door, waving her arm. "Look how you scrunched up your momma's pillows. Come on outta here so I can re-fluff the bed."

I rolled off, heart pounding, and slipped by her.

"Michael?" I heard my name from rooms away, an echo that stung me.

At first I couldn't speak when my mother called. My throat closed up. She was lying to me. Why? What was she hiding?

"Michael, come and help with the groceries."

"Coming, Ma," I yelled, opening my bedroom door.

Chapter Ten

Paris, France
August 22, 1993

My mother came up for me every day in some way. She would have loved us being in Paris together–the museums, cuisine, fashionable women. We had talked about it for years. It was always a someday. Work, schedules, meetings, money–we kept putting it off. We spoke on the phone weekly, but maybe if we had traveled together, outside our meeting in New York City for a few long weekends, the opportunity would have come up to share more. Maybe I could have figured out my mother's story years ago. It was only since she made her final exit that I had time to go back and reflect on what I missed. It seemed incredible, but as shocking as it was finding a letter from someone who claimed to be my mother's mother, I forgot about it for awhile. Mostly, I was oblivious.

Little League season rolled into summer and the end of the school year. My mother signed me up for advanced swimming lessons at Venetian Pool, a structure built in the 1920s by George Merrick in an elaborate Italian style with vine-covered loggias, shady porticos and a cascading waterfall that spilled into a free-form lagoon. Fed by an artesian well, the water was freezing but I loved it. My friends and I hid in the coral caves and climbed the three-story observation tower for hours. It was a brief respite from the sticky, sweaty air that hung in clouds of humidity, mosquitoes and gnats. She drove me, waiting with the other moms in pastel shirtwaist dresses along the covered deck, smoking, chatting, eyes and hair hidden behind glasses, scarves and hats.

The country club down the street also had a roster of activities so we often walked down there for dinner. My parents sipped highballs or martinis with their friends on the patio, a breeze cooling down the heat of the day, while my friends and I ran around the grounds searching for mischief. Eddie had been shipped off to a relative for the summer. Arthur Brady, my best friend, was a pilot's kid whose Dad flew for Pan American Airlines. Russell Smart, who was anything but smart, always made us laugh and Andrew Van Shimmel made a point of reminding us his name was Dutch and not German. I didn't understand the distinction but he was a little older and a troublemaker so I never challenged him.

It wasn't until the fall, late October actually, that my suspicions about my mother renewed. I wanted to look for the letter again. Or maybe a marriage certificate. I knew it took nine months to make a baby and somehow the dates she told me seemed off.

I had a weekly after-school piano lesson with Mr. Rosenbaum, the music teacher from Ponce de Leon Junior High. I was a seventh grader, small for my size, and petrified one of the ninth graders with their nascent muscles and sprouting hair might pick on me. I never saw Mr. Rosenbaum during the school day because I wasn't in the band or orchestra, but I looked forward to my Friday lesson.

A stocky man with wavy dark hair and glasses he pushed up with his forefinger, Mr. Rosenbaum wore blue or white cotton short-sleeved shirts, a pencil and pen sticking out of a plastic protector in his front pocket. With a wry sense of humor and infinite patience at my lack of skill, he remained encouraging at my ineffectual sounds.

Although I did follow the practice regime of thirty minutes a day with my mother's urging, my favorite part was when he assigned a new piece and played it through for me. I'd scoot off the bench so he could move over from the dining room chair that we had dragged into the living room, his fingers flying across the keys.

My mother took this as a signal that the lesson was almost over and would come in and settle herself on the sofa. I admired the wonderful sound he got out of our baby grand, a Steinway my parents had purchased from someone at the club who had been transferred to Chicago.

She usually got him to play a Gershwin song while she listened, her eyes dreamy. She loved *I've Got Rhythm* or *Rhapsody in Blue*. When he was finished he'd push back the bench to stand as she handed him three dollars for the lesson. I sat down trying to pick the right hand through the new assignment. I had no talent, but I liked music and enjoyed his jokes.

After the first few lessons Mr. Rosenbaum brought his wife, a dark-haired, loquacious lady who sat in the kitchen with my mother while they shared cigarettes. Their daughter Ivy, a ten-year-old who never took her head out of a book, wore blue cat-eye glasses. One time I pulled the book she was reading out of her hands and snorted because it was Nancy Drew. Girl stuff. Anyway, she didn't bother me. She sat curled up in a corner of the rattan furniture in the Florida room, the light from the jalousies over her shoulder, and only got up when it was time to leave, hiding behind her parents.

Ruth and my mother became friends sitting at the canary Formica kitchen table. I'd hear an occasional laugh or the warm buzz of their voices during my lesson. Later, the ashtray would be full and Ruth would emerge with an armload of magazines. My mother liked Ivy and gave her a few small gifts—barrettes, a new book, a package of Chiclets. It occurred to me she might miss having a daughter.

Sometimes I thought about the letter I had read in the drawer and got angry at my mother. I was taught not to lie and she was doing that to me. But I never confronted her. I just simmered and then forgot about it. My world was school, my friends, the club. What adults did was often mysterious and usually uninteresting.

The last weekend of October came as a surprise. It was after my Friday piano lesson and I was itching to go outside and look for the boys.

"Michael, Ivy's staying with us for the weekend while Mr. and Mrs. Rosenbaum fly over to Cuba," my mother told me, her arm draped around Ivy's shoulder. I shrugged because I didn't see how it affected me other than that she'd be sleeping in the spare bedroom. I remembered there had been discussion about it, but I didn't know when it was going to happen. "It'll be great for me to have a little girl for the weekend." She took a long drag on her cigarette.

Ivy ate dinner with us in the kitchen that night. My dad was working late again. We chatted a little because basically I was a nice kid and none of my friends were around to tease me. Russell hated girls except for Betty West, a popular ninth grader with big boobs. He drooled over her every time we were hanging out together. Unfortunately I made the mistake of showing him my dad's magazines so he pestered me constantly about when we could sneak back into his room and look at them again.

After dinner I wanted to see my favorite show, *Gillette Cavalcade of Sports* but we watched *Life of Riley* and *The Thin Man* instead. Ivy laughed during the first show but remained shy. My mother took her to the other end of the house to get her ready for bed. "Night, Michael," she said with a small wave of her hand.

Saturday the club was having a Halloween party with a costume contest. I spent the afternoon making myself look like a bum, tearing and cutting up some old clothes, putting dirt on a cap that already had a stain and ruining a pair of Keds. My mother fussed over Ivy making a headband with a feather to match a slip she created into a flapper dress with a few rows of fringe hand stitched onto the bottom. She even took out her costume jewelry long pearls.

Before the boys arrived to walk down the block to the club with us, my mother sketched a black eye and beard on my face with her eye shadows and eyebrow pencil. Ivy was the recipient of blue eyelids and red lips.

Arthur, Russell and Andrew rang the door bell shouting "Trick or treat!" I swung the door open and we howled, pushing each other's shoulders, exclaiming over our costumes: another tramp, a store-bought Superman with attached cape and a Mexican with drawn mustache and large sequined sombrero, obviously a souvenir from a vacation.

My mother handed Ivy and me bags we slid onto our wrists. Russell, the troublemaker, spoke first, "Who's she? She's not coming with us, is she?"

My mother placed her hands on Russell's back and mine. "Ivy is our houseguest this weekend and I trust you will make her feel welcome." Ivy looked awkward but hopeful. "There will be lots of candy and games. Don't get spooked. The committee put together a ghost house. And, Michael, you're responsible for Ivy. You understand?"

"Yes, ma'am." I wasn't happy about dragging along a strange little girl, but once we got inside I knew she'd see some kids she knew from the elementary school and I could dump her. For a while anyway.

The boys walked in front, munching on candy, throwing the wrappers on our neighbors' front lawns, bags swinging with Hershey's Kisses, Bazooka bubble gum and Reese's Peanut Butter Cups. I trailed behind with Ivy who had given up wearing my mother's heels down the block because she kept falling out of them. She carried them in her other hand.

Decorated with Jack-o'-lanterns, ghosts fashioned from starched sheets, and lots of twinkling orange lights, the double doors of the Coral Gables Country Club stood open. I could hear the music playing and see the party happening in a semidarkened room, the bar on the back patio for the adults.

The club maitre'd greeted us from behind a podium stationed outside. He was wearing his standard tuxedo with a nod to the holiday by sporting a crazy brown wig that stuck out all over his head. It was hardly a disguise. "Good evening, gentlemen," he said, waving to all of us.

Our costumes weren't that clever so he recognized us from our parents' memberships. Most of us had Sunday brunch in nice clothes, a buffet, which entitled me to multiple desserts. Arthur's family met us there after church. I had asked my mother why we didn't go more regularly. She didn't answer, looking away with an uncomfortable stare. I didn't pursue it. I didn't really want to go anyway. Other than seeing some friends the few times we attended, it wasn't fun.

"And who might this be?" the maitre'd asked, stretching a hand out toward Ivy who was hidden behind us. He pulled her forward. I have to say she looked cute the way my mom had fixed her up, her eyeglasses left behind. She squinted a bit and stumbled forward, the shoes back on her feet.

The maitre'd repeated his question. She looked petrified. I gave her a nudge with my elbow. "Tell him your name."

"Ivy."

There was a silence so I spoke up. "She's with me. A houseguest. My mom called ahead and they said it was okay to bring her."

I smelled his wig as he leaned down to address Ivy closer to her face.

"And Ivy, are your parents members here?"

"I don't think so."

"What's your last name?"

She stood there frozen, the lights flashing orange across her face. The other boys were getting restless with the delay and wanted to abandon me.

"Guys, wait a sec. We'll go in together."

"Ivy what?" This guy was persistent. I could see kids lining up in two teams at either end of the room behind him.

"Rosenbaum."

The Colter girls, identical twins who had matching costumes, rolled by us with a wave as ballerinas in pink tights, short tutus and tiaras.

He stood back up and moved behind the wood podium looking through the list. "I'm sorry, but I don't see your name here, Ivy Rosenbaum. I'm afraid you'll have to go home."

I was stunned and stuttered, "But-but my mom called ahead and they said it was alright."

"Well, I'm sorry, but we can't allow any more guests in tonight."

"Michael, come on, let's go in," nagged Russell. "Leave her here. Let him call your mom. They're starting the games and giving out prizes." Arthur and Andrew were standing in the doorway motioning me inside.

A few older kids from the club tennis team rushed by us, the air from their hurrying creating a slight breeze on my soiled face.

"No, I can't leave her. I promised my mom."

"Crap, Michael," said Russell. "Well, we're going in. Walk her home and come back. We'll be waiting for you. Betty's here in her mother's dress and she looks stacked." Andrew cupped his hands on his chest.

So I took Ivy by the hand and walked her back down the street. I knew she had to feel terrible that she was turned away, but I had no clue why. I opened our front door and called for my mom. She came out of the kitchen wiping her hands on a dish towel, wearing an apron. "I'm just getting your father some dinner. Why are you home?"

I shrugged my shoulders. "I don't know. They wouldn't let Ivy in. I want to go back. They're starting the games."

"What do you mean they wouldn't let her in?" My mother's voice went up a pitch.

"We got there and they asked her name and then Gordon looked at the list and he said she couldn't come in."

"Did you tell him I called ahead?"

I nodded, glancing at Ivy, lipstick smeared, her glasses back on her face, pathetic in my mom's slip. She looked expectant.

My mother's face turned harsh and she picked up the black phone from the small table outside the kitchen dialing with her forefinger. The spin-around dial clicked as it hit all the numbers.

"Hello, Gordon, this is Mrs. Saunders. I sent Michael down there for the Halloween party with our little houseguest and they've just returned. I don't understand why they were sent home."

There was a silence while some sort of explanation was given. My mother's expression evolved from confusion to anger.

"Wait a minute. You mean to tell me this child can't come to the party?" I saw Ivy's shoulders slump, forlorn, as she sat down on the edge of the flamingo-print hassock in the Florida room. I could see my mom was getting steamed up because her face turned red, her foot tapping out a furious rhythm. Suddenly she took the phone and receiver to disappear into the kitchen, the swinging door reverberating behind her. I couldn't make out what she was saying, but I knew she was mad.

She came out and slammed the phone down. "Michael, you can go back and join your friends. Ivy, you'll stay here with me. We can play Parcheesi and bake a chocolate cake. I have everything to make icing. Why don't you go and wash up."

I couldn't know what was going through Ivy's head, but on some level I knew she understood she had caused a problem. Her excitement for the evening deflated, she nodded at my mom, pulling off the headband, the high heels with tissue paper stuffed in the toes, fallen on their sides.

"Uh, it's almost nine o'clock and the games are over. I think I'll stay here and help with the cake," I said.

Chapter Eleven

Paris, France
September 15, 1993

It's not that French women don't wash often. They do. They just allow their own pheromones to mix with the musk of their perfume by waiting a day or two, unlike American women who foster squeaky-clean bodies twice a day with too many perfumed soaps.

Sandrine always bathed after we made love in my apartment. Some evenings she lolled in the tub but most nights she showered, removing the shower head from where it was attached to the wall. She wet herself first, then soaped under her arms, her chest, her breasts, lifting her leg onto the side and cleaning between her legs. Her hands and soft soap explored every area of her body. She threw her head back and let the water run down, closing her eyes when the warm water trickled into her dark curly hairs.

I watched from the bed through a mirrored reflection on the door many times. Did Sandrine know? Maybe. Even when she vacated the bed after sex, I savored her through the lingering aroma of *Heure Exquise*, the perfume she wore. Once when we exited the historic wooden doors of Saint-Suplice after a Sunday organ concert, she pointed out the Annick Goutal perfume store next to Yves St. Laurent. She was in a hurry to get a good table at her favorite café. I made a note of the location for a future gift. Might as well get women what they want. I didn't feel it was a manipulative hint. She pointed to a few balconies and told me who they belonged to as we strolled toward our destination.

"The balconies up there? The shutters are closed, but it is the apartment of Catherine Deneuve so she is out of town," she told me in her guide voice. Parisians take pride in their city and its denizens. Except when they're on strike. But that's another story.

"Have you ever seen her?" I asked, reminiscing about Deneuve's tango scene in *Indochine.*

"*Oui, oui.* In a scarf without makeup. She is *magnifique.*"

We had fallen into a wonderful habit of meeting after work a few times a week and spending some Saturday afternoons together. Sundays she accompanied her mother to Mass and visited with her family—except for last week. She spent Sunday with me because everyone was traveling. I had the impression Roland was still hanging around. Perhaps that's why she didn't proffer any invitations. No questions from me and no answers from her.

I couldn't have been a secret because she returned home late a few times a week, but then again, her mother had a boyfriend. The French style was not to be curious about one's personal life, unlike Americans who interrogated any deviance from a routine. Not ready for any commitments, I was copasetic with the situation. And I used condoms. No point complicating my situation.

The unofficial schedule gave me time to work on my paper for New York. My delivery of a similar topic at the Sorbonne the week before had been well received in a small auditorium filled with French students. They looked the same as American ones but a little scruffier. No perfect wedge haircuts for the women, just an air of ennui. The guys looked as though they had slept in their jeans for a week and of course no one was clean shaven except for me.

Arm in arm, Sandrine and I strolled in a light drizzle to St. Germaine, the popular and busy shopping district, she in a classic beret and me in my Burberry trench coat, a gift from my mother. I felt as though I had known her all my life instead of a month. Les Deux Magots, the hangout of Jean-Paul Sartre and Simone de Beauvoir, was crowded so we went next door to Café Flores, filled with stylish Parisians reading the paper, a few men arguing politics and a young couple feeding their dog scraps from the table. We were guided to a spot out of the sprinkle.

I hesitated before I approached her. No question I was infatuated, yet I was a gentleman and gave her options to back out. The French are so natural about their bodies and fulfillment. She wore wonderful lingerie that accentuated her flat stomach, a sheer bra and lacy bikini underwear in melon colors.

The first time I removed her clothes she remained quiet, although my hands shook a little. I made a comment about my nerves and being with such a beautiful woman. I turned her toward the full-length mirror on the bathroom door, a few steps from where we stood. I stood behind her and cupped her breasts in my hands and tantalized her until she turned to me.

Our kisses began tentatively. Soon I was holding the back of her head and pressing my lips onto her mouth, the ever-present red lipstick smearing across our faces. I walked her over to the mirror and we laughed like clowns. I kissed her again. She backed away and began to unbuckle my belt. I slipped out of my pants and dropped them to the floor, unbuttoning my shirt with haste. Her hands roamed my chest.

She gave me a flirty smile and her eyes fluttered at me. "*Oh là là.*"

I assumed she liked what she saw. I led her to the bed.

In our subsequent encounters she unclothed herself in the most unselfconscious manner. After our lovemaking, she would turn on her stomach, chin cupped in her hands, and ask me questions about my work. She created an intimacy I had not felt with my former wife or previous girlfriends. And, although it usually took a while until a couple developed a rhythm to their lovemaking, we were sensitive to each other from the beginning. It became a dance of passion, some laughter, intimate whispers of shared delights and a long post-coital exchange.

We shared cigarettes on the balcony after we dressed. It wasn't a habit for either of us but another shared private pleasure. After a few times—we were meeting almost daily at this point—I asked what she told her mother and if Roland was wondering why she missed his beeps, her pager sometimes vibrating in her bag while we made love. Sandrine responded with a shrug. "It is my business."

"Don't you feel some obligation to explain your whereabouts?" I asked, sitting on a metal stool while she stretched her legs out on a canvas chair. I passed her the Gitanes we were sharing, the blue package of a gypsy and her tambourine on the floor between us.

"I am my own woman. My *mère* does not wait for me. She has a boyfriend too. And Roland is at the ocean for holiday. He will meet a nineteen-year-old and come back to me when the fun is over. We live independent lives."

After that I didn't question her about relationships. We were enjoying each other's company. I spent my days reading, researching, working on my paper about the treasures, the complicity to hide them for centuries and who would be the ones to own them. The Israelis, the Chinese, the Arabs—all had a vested interest. The focus was on the auction, the splashy publicity of the released artifacts and subsequent carbon data testing long over.

Once in a while I would wander toward memories of my mother, my absent father and my strange childhood. The anger and confusion roiled up like heartburn. I forced myself to push it aside. I had plenty of time to deal with it after the conference. Better to anticipate my evening recreation. Sometimes it was hard to focus because the expectation of being with Sandrine distracted me.

I pushed myself to the task at hand. I still needed more proof about the eyewitness account of Isaac Herzog, the chief rabbi of Israel who met with Pope Pius XII, the pope from 1939 to 1958.

The meeting took place in March of 1946 to discuss Jewish children who had been hidden in monasteries or by Christian families during World War II. The rabbi wanted them returned to their families or the Jewish people. Upon visiting a few monasteries Rabbi Herzog recited the sacred prayer called the *shema* in front of children in classrooms. When some instinctively used their small hands to cover their eyes, he knew they were of the faith.

During that visit there was documentation that the pope showed his esteemed guest, who was also the first chief rabbi of Ireland, the menorah from the destruction of the Second Temple. There is no record of the rabbi's reaction, but it was noted the pope refused the rabbi's request to return the candelabra when asked. That eyewitness report by the chief rabbi stirred great speculation about whether the church held the rest of the artifacts. No one knew what the vast city called The Vatican held. Secretive to a fault, they refused to answer any questions about the speculation of what was held in the bowels of their structures. They didn't have to. The pope, a religious leader, was also a head of state. Now the whole world was going to see the treasures that had been inspired by what believers said was the word of God.

As an atheist, it didn't move me. My religious views from childhood were pedestrian, a rejection of some forced church attendance and a vacant spot in my soul. I admired others who felt a deep commitment, a link with the past and future. My mother's rejection of faith, only later to embrace it, left me confused. But as an archaeologist and historian it was phenomenal, a seminal event for the twentieth century along with the Dead Sea Scrolls.

With the artifacts and their authentication proven true, it gave credence to the Israelis' assertion that the land and Jerusalem belonged to them from the beginning of time. It meant that others who wanted that same sandy strip would have to accept their reality. An apocalypse could be avoided with compromise, an unlikely scenario in that region, but always a possibility. The eternal territorial issues that kept the region in turmoil might trigger more unrest, but with reasonableness it could be a holy site for Jews, Christians and Muslims.

I supported the Israelis for a number of reasons. Anyone who visited the region could feel their passion about the history of the land. I also thought they'd be more equitable than the other forces. They respected knowledge without so many restrictions, except for their Orthodox, of course, who decided who could marry whom and who was a Jew. After the symposium and auction on the world stage, the findings could no longer be disputed. Once I started down the antiquity and religious path, the hours flew by.

On this particular evening my gaze shifted back to Sandrine's reflection as she toweled herself dry. It had been a most satisfying encounter with the rare occurrence of simultaneous climaxes. She rolled off and we both laughed in delight. I made a silly joke about wanting to preserve the ecstasy forever, that she was my Paris lamb—soft, delicious, a treat with big brown eyes, a moniker I used when I found out her last name, Agneau, meant "lamb." She kissed me and then dozed for a bit before she got up for her toilette. I watched with fascination every time. Her sensuality was so French.

She didn't rub herself dry, but patted herself all over with one of the plush towels I purchased at *Printemps*, the high-end department store on Haussmann. First she dabbed her face, flushed from the hot water and lovemaking, then her neck and her breasts, carefully moving each one to the center of her chest to dry, creating the cleavage that drove me wild. Her rose-pink areolae appeared dark in the dim light of early evening. I hadn't bothered to light any lamps. As she started between her legs, the black phone rang next to the bed. It took three times before I reached for it never shifting my eyes from the mirror.

"Professor Saunders? This is Heather Salvador from Professor Sommerstein's office in the Antiquities Department at Roscom Liberal Arts College."

"I'm sorry. Would you repeat that more slowly?"

She repeated her introduction. I calculated what time it was in the States. I grabbed a pillow and pushed it behind my head. "Sorry to bother you but we've had a tragedy here and Professor Dubois will not be delivering his paper at our conference. Even though you're scheduled for the afternoon on day two, would you be able to stand in for him as the keynoter?"

I hesitated while I digested the information. "How early would I have to be there?" Sandrine stood before me, dry and nude. She teased me by stroking her bushy triangle. I hadn't seen anything this glorious in ages. She dropped to the bed and snuggled in my arm, squirming her body closer to my torso, her chaste smell making me consider whether I could go again.

"Sir, right away. The conference, the presentation of the display of antiquities to the press and the auction need a visible figurehead. Professor Sommerstein thought you'd be an excellent fill-in."

"But why me? I'm on sabbatical. I planned on coming in late next week. What happened to Dubois?"

"He's had a tragic accident. I'm sure it's on the news in France. Professor Sommerstein said he needs you now. Can I tell him you'll take a red-eye and be here within twenty-four hours?"

"What kind of accident?"

"Sir, did you know him?"

I chastised myself for not buying an international paper without access to a television in the studio apartment. The use of the past tense clobbered me.

"We are acquainted." I inhaled a measured breath as a vision of Maurice sailed by me. Sharp features, tall and thin. Smart, supercilious prick. He challenged something I said at every conference we attended. Felt he knew more than everyone because he had connections to the radiocarbon-dating people. "What happened to him?"

"I don't have all the information, but he was killed in a taxi near the airport. Mack truck. Three dead. Looks like they found meth in the truck cab."

"What?" I sat up without regard for Sandrine. She rolled over, grabbed the sheet and stared at me.

"When?" I may not have liked the bastard but he was a colleague.

"I really don't have any more information." An awkward silence engulfed the space. "Uh–I have a lot of calls to make and the decision has been made that the conference is going to proceed. I'm sorry for the loss. Can I count on you to assist us and be here ASAP?"

"Twenty-four hours? I have to change my airline, check out. I'm not even completely finished with the final draft of my paper. Why does Sommerstein need me so much earlier than I planned to come in?"

"Sir, he wants you to be a liaison for the press, which is all over this story. And he needs you to handle some of the distinguished guests who need extra attention."

It's not like me to get cranky but I felt put upon. "Can't he get someone else from your department to lead around the insipid press, the wealthy patrons? For Chrissakes, why can't he do it?" Sandrine pushed my hand between her legs. She's ready again. Nothing like a *réchauffé* woman to use the warmth of her body as a distraction.

"Sir, my job is to get you here. The boss says it's urgent. I'd hate to keep calling you back in the middle of the night every hour."

"Damn, when did you assistants get so pushy?" I have a habit of frowning, especially if I feel a headache coming on. Sandrine reached up and tried to smooth the well-worn lines stitched between my brows. I was having trouble digesting that Maurice was dead.

"With all due respect, sir, since they upped the doctoral program to an interdisciplinary one with archaeology, anthropology and historical architecture, plus a double dissertation and four hundred hours of digs."

"Hold on a minute." I cupped my hand over the phone, touching my chin to the top of Sandrine's head. "Will you come with me to New York City? There's an emergency."

"*Moi*?" She twisted to look up at me, wide-eyed. "Yes, I sleep with you, but travel? That's another something else. How you say? A commitment."

"Will you come with me? They're waiting. You'll see the artifacts I told you about, we'll go to a fancy cocktail party, I'll find time to take you to a few museums. There are beautiful shops. And there's the auction, bound to be a spectacular celebrity event." I pressed the phone to my chest.

She hesitated. "If I find a replacement for the shop, yes. Maybe my mother or sister."

I removed the phone. "Tell Sommerstein I'll be there, and he owes me."

"Thank you, professor. I'll let him know."

"Hey, one more thing. Why'd he decide to pressure me when he has Abe Golden, Ed Morey and Sam Austin on the program with excellent credentials?" Sandrine stroked my chest, throwing her leg over mine. I could feel damp hair pressing into my leg.

"Sir, I don't really know, but I overheard him say you came from a classy country club background and he needed someone with panache."

Her mispronunciation of the last word bugged me. I dropped the phone and leaned back against the headboard as my hands circled down Sandrine's body with distracted intention.

Chapter Twelve

New Haven, Connecticut
September 16, 1993

I settled into my airline seat with Sandrine next to me. Soon, she nodded off. The conference paid the difference to change my ticket, but I bought hers, not an inconsequential sum at the last minute. I couldn't leave her.

I was preoccupied on the flight because of my hasty Parisian exit and the hornet's nest waiting for me to replace Maurice. I also had nagging regrets about inviting Sandrine. Maybe I should have thought it through instead of succumbing to an impulse. What was she going to do while waiting around for me? I needed to gather up my professorial papers and wardrobe from my New Haven condo and travel back to New York on the train. The fancy French shirts wouldn't cut it in the academic crowd. Besides, maybe an affair only worked in the place it originated, especially Paris.

Yale University, an enclave of Ivy League sanity amid a drug-infested, crime-ridden neighborhood, had mansions of yesterday that were now crack houses. I imagined her reaction to the homeless sleeping on once-manicured front lawns from another century. What a contrast to the respect for ancient architecture in France.

Sandrine couldn't be by herself other than the few blocks around the university where upscale preppy shops, bookstores and a few home décor emporiums enticed students. I felt guilty in advance that I wouldn't be able to spend enough time with her to show off some of the historical sites.

Sommerstein's assistant Heather was driving me crazy with directives. The preview event at the Judaica Cultural Museum was being held in three days and I didn't even have a pressed suit. Plus, I needed to be a gentleman and offer to buy a cocktail dress for Sandrine, a remembrance of her rash decision to visit New York. I had no idea who was "in" for women's fashions. I missed my mother who taught me to look for quality. I caught a flash of her buying me a tuxedo when I graduated from college, her forefinger and thumb testing the lightweight wool and examining the construction.

"Michael, if you have a tuxedo in your closet, it'll open doors for you. Renting is for the prom."

I proved her right many times. I got invited to some fancy places with classy ladies. With her fashion expertise she would have loved this assignment.

I glanced at Sandrine curled up next to the window, sleeping peacefully. We'd been booked into first class because of our last-minute arrangements. After accepting every glass of champagne offered, she slept, a child at rest with delicate features, mink-like lashes, her slim body huddled under a blanket. The sensual mouth that had given me evenings of pleasure was now soft and relaxed and devoid of lipstick.

Something made me not want to leave her behind. Was I getting emotionally attached? I did my best to stay away from involvements, but this seemed different. My emotions ricocheted, a rubber band stretching beyond my comfort zone.

I wanted to focus on the conference with its myriad of details and my new role, but I felt unsettled. I got pulled back to my mother and her revelation. It happened so quickly—the diagnosis, the treatment, her confession and then her passing. I hadn't distilled, digested or incorporated it into my psyche yet. Why did she wait so long to tell me? I thought I knew everything about her. It's hard to imagine a parent's secrets. Ah, well, she would have liked Sandrine, with her entrepreneurial spirit and easy glamour.

Or, maybe it was the badgering thought of Maurice dead. The newspaper report Sandrine translated for me said he was carrying ten thousand dollars in cash in his briefcase. It sounded suspicious to me. I never quite trusted the guy, maybe because I didn't like his competitive brilliance. It wouldn't be unusual for academics to be involved in skullduggery.

Academics may be eccentric with their tunnel vision, but they usually develop some moldy disease from sitting around too long, become senile and go away. Accidents happened, but I couldn't wrap my head around an international academic leaving the earth so ignominiously, especially with the artifacts drawing worldwide attention.

We arrived at JFK and made our train connection to New Haven. When I opened the door to my apartment it smelled musty and looked worse. I left not dreaming someone would be coming back with me. Not exactly a place for a tryst. I called my cleaning lady to come by and freshen things up.

After showering we walked down to Chapel and York Streets for a brief tour of the campus. In my best professorial voice I treated her to the trivia of New Haven and Yale's more than three hundred years of history. I was acutely aware of what a spit that was compared to France's chronicle of almost eight hundred years.

"Besides the twelve million books in the library, we also invented the hamburger, the lollipop and the corkscrew."

She smiled and took my hand. It embarrassed me. What if I ran into someone? I've been a solitary and private character who kept my life just that. I didn't want to have to explain a French-accented darling to any of my colleagues in the international scholars program or a post-doctoral fellow that happened by. Not that they would ask outright.

Most everyone here was too self-absorbed for that. But there could be looks and the potential of rumors. Gossip was rampant in all departments on campus. I still had my upbringing of not wanting to call attention to myself or make a scene. My mother's favorite word was "class." She studied old money—who had it, who didn't, where it came from. She couldn't stand *nouveau riche* types. Her line was, "If people have it, they don't talk about it."

Late in the afternoon the lunch crowd fled to the library or their dorms. I slipped into the back of my favorite restaurant off Whalley

Avenue to avoid anyone I knew, sitting away from the door. I didn't want to answer any questions about the research, the events, the girl. We ordered fresh arugula salads. Sandrine was quiet. Maybe she was having second thoughts too. Or maybe I wasn't as appealing in my own environment.

"Everything all right? You're not sorry you came, are you?" I asked.

"No, of course not. I am happy." She gave me a cheesy smile, playing with me.

"Look, maybe this wasn't a good idea." I reached across the table to touch her hand. "I can send you back tomorrow. . . ." My voice trailed off. The thought of being without her clutched me.

"No, Michael. I want to see your world. I am interested in your subject and seeing the city of New York."

A hand slapped my back. "Michael, I didn't know you were back in town. I thought you were out on the cushy sabbatical."

Brooks White appeared in my line of vision, his bad-boy blond hair combed into a perfect sweep across his forehead. He took in Sandrine. "I see you're working hard."

"Hey, Brooks." I introduced Sandrine.

"Agneau? My high school French tells me that means lamb."

"Yes, I am from Paris."

Brooks assessed the situation. "So, you're the Paris lamb?"

Leave it to Brooks to take a term of endearment and turn it into sarcasm.

"Ever heard of the Paschal lamb?"

Sandrine looked confused.

I wanted to dismiss his tasteless reference without having to explain about the sacrificial lamb killed the night before Passover, when blood was smeared on doorposts so the first born weren't killed. But I didn't. As usual, Brooks pursued it.

"In politics or literature the sacrificial lamb is either a candidate with little chance for victory or a supporting character that dies. Which do you think you'll be?"

"Aren't you being inappropriate?"

I could see he was unnerving Sandrine.

"Ever thought you might be overstepping boundaries?"

My comment made him pause.

Brooks, an anthropology professor in the undergraduate school, was an Oxford scholar who made it clear his subject matter was a hobby. He reminded us in not-so-subtle ways he was a trust-funder, the recipient of a flour-and-mill fortune. He often returned from holidays tan and fit from sailing in Newport or hitting the links. He'd show up in a worn sport coat that screamed old money.

He didn't flaunt his affluence, but he didn't hide his blueblood background either. In the rarified air of an Ivy League school, especially one known for being egalitarian, he stood out. We teased him about his Mayflower patronage and his great-great-great-great grandmother's membership in Daughters of the American Revolution.

Oddly enough, my "country club background," as Sommerstein had labeled me, was closer to his, but I never bonded with him. After my mother's confession, I understood why.

He made me slide over so he could sit down. "So Dubois was killed. Think it was an accident?"

I raised my eyebrows toward Sandrine. I just got to town. How did I know what was going on?

"You replacing him?"

"I'm supposed to."

He addressed Sandrine. "And you're along for the ride?"

She nodded.

"If Michael's too busy, here's my card. I do a great tour of the anthropology department and the medical school exhibits. Did you know in *The Great Gatsby* Fitzgerald's narrator was from Yale?"

She smiled. I liked that she got his come-on, pompous ass that he was.

"So the preview event is still happening?" he asked.

"Yes, I'm stepping in. They have the exhibit displayed at the Judaica Cultural Museum, then the conference and the auction, which is really what everyone's waiting for."

"So you know that Yossi Farber has been in New York stirring up trouble?"

"No." I glanced at Sandrine, weary from travel. "What's he doing there?"

"He's refuting the entire conference and planning a public forum. Really will throw a snare into your theory."

"What?" I pushed my plate away from me. Brooks was always trying to one-up me.

"Will probably kill the pricing on the artifacts you've been touting if they turn out to be fakes."

"Not going to happen. These are bona fide world-class treasures the Vatican has been hiding for eons. Hey, they even have pieces of the Dead Sea Scrolls no one has laid eyes on since their discovery in 1946 through '56. Maurice's paper backed that theory too. Besides, it's not in Yossi's or the Israelis' best interest to dispute this find."

"Yes, but you can count on the Israelis to stir things up. That's the culture. They question everything."

Brooks's comment caused me to pause, but I didn't want to get off topic. Yossi was irascible and difficult. I knew he was the child of Holocaust survivors. I gave him a pass when he became argumentative over small points. The waitress came over with a menu for Brooks and he sent her away. He continued as though we had asked for his company.

"Yossi's the leading authority on the early history of Israel. He absolutely opposes the scholars who say their excavations confirm biblical narratives. One of the biggest areas of discrepancy is tenth-century Jerusalem, the time of Kings David and Solomon." He nodded to Sandrine. "He disputes the idea that it was a thriving city and says the archaeology shows it to be a village or mere tribal center. That theory drives the other Israelis crazy. Or people like your boyfriend here." His thumb pointed in my direction, an affront.

I stiffened a little. Why was he assuming the relationship? Sandrine caught it. We hadn't discussed the boyfriend/girlfriend part of our relationship. It seemed more than that to me, but she already had a boyfriend. In Paris. I steeled myself for an intelligent response. In academia, one always had to be ready to defend his hypothesis.

I responded with confidence. "Look, Yossi's always been a nut. He believes in 'low chronology,' a method that rearranges the dates of biblical events. He dismisses everything literal. These auction artifacts could support believers' points of view that the Bible is factual. Many of us think it's a book of stories set in a real place, but for those who do not question the existence of God it reinforces his word. Or hers." I gave Sandrine a quick look. "The impact is going to be felt worldwide."

"Aren't you exaggerating a bit?" Brooks was such an arrogant prick.

I'm getting hot. I take the bait.

"Besides evangelicals who think we're all going to be raptured into heaven with the imminent apocalypse, and the Orthodox rabbis trapped in the eighteenth century, there are believers across the globe who accept the Bible as truth. These artifacts confirm the history and land belong to Israel. It's their case in the world court that the Palestinians don't belong there."

Brooks stared at Sandrine who was marginally interested. Jet lag made her lackadaisical. He addressed me.

"You may think Yossi's advocating the hypothetical, but in order to dispute this find, he's garnering a lot of attention for the improbable and the absurd." I decided to let it end. I wanted to take Sandrine back to my apartment and head for the library to do some research.

Brooks slid over to stand up. His smile let us know he preferred the superior position. "Well, hey, I've got to go. Nice to meet you. I'll see you in the city. Keep your eyes open for Yossi. He's gunnin' for you."

He patted me on the shoulder.

Chapter Thirteen

Miami, Florida
June 15, 1993

My mother took my hand, her paper-thin skin reflecting blue veins. "Michael, I always did what I thought was best for you. You know that, don't you?"

"Sure, Ma." I guess every mother wants validation she did the best job she could under the circumstances. She had always been there for me, even when I was in that long stretch for my doctorate, working and trying to raise money for digs. She supported me longer than most parents.

She loved the pursuit of knowledge and she had been generous with what she had. When I landed the extremely competitive job at Yale a few years later, she flew up to take me to dinner and see the campus. She was so impressed.

"My Michael, an Ivy Leaguer," she repeated in disbelief, until I finally said, "Mom, you act like you and Dad didn't pass on any brains to me, that I wasn't a diligent student."

"No, you were. It's just that I never imagined the academic life for you."

"What did you think I'd become?"

"I don't know. A corporate lawyer, a CPA, something like that."

"You're not disappointed, are you?" I asked, hoping she wasn't going to dash my dream.

"Oh no. I am bursting with pride. My parents would have–"

"What?"

"Nothing. Show me the building where you'll be teaching. I can't get over how the campus looks with all the brick and ivy. Like a scene from a movie."

The doctor told me on the phone in May it might be our last visit. "Your mom has responded very well to the treatments, but I can't guarantee you she'll make it through the summer. She has a very aggressive type of breast cancer related to the BRCA gene. It's metastasized in two other places, even after the chemo."

"So what are you telling me?"

"I'm telling you to make sure her papers are in order. She doesn't have long."

I remember hanging up the phone and feeling angry and cheated, a throb launching in my temple. A migraine invaded, annoying zigzag lines dancing across my brain. It holed me up for two days. I needed to go to Miami for more than the weekends I flew down for support. Nothing was holding me in Connecticut. Maybe I would be a comfort to her. Maybe she would share her secrets.

My sabbatical came at an opportune time. As soon as I finished the semester and turned in grades, I flew to South Florida. At least she wasn't alone anymore.

I stayed in her apartment with her for a few weeks. We both knew it was grim after the doctor's prognosis, but she remained hopeful. I did my best to be matter-of-fact, keeping her busy when she wasn't sleeping–disposing of the furniture, clothes and bric-a-brac she had accumulated. Any valuables, mostly jewelry, were already in my possession.

I made a search for the letter I saw so long ago, but she had thrown out a lot of files.

Then she became too weak and had to be hospitalized. It didn't seem fair to go through all that and know it was coming to a close. Once she went into the hospital I knew she wouldn't be coming back.

The situation was the worst I'd ever been through, a combination of every tragic word I could muster. I functioned in a vacuum, making my mother comfortable, closing up her affairs, spending time with her. I couldn't allow myself to tumble over a sea wall of desperation and dissipate into the ocean. My goal was to remain strong for her. I hadn't even begun to deal with the grief of losing her. I'd have plenty of time to cry later.

At this point in life my mother and I didn't have much to dispute. We agreed my father had been a poor choice, Miami was a good place to live and we loved Italian food. Now, however, we were reaching a denouement. Young, only in her sixties, she remained trapped in the proprieties of a woman's role. She fussed about how she looked, who would look after her *objets d'art* she had collected, what neighbors would say when they learned she was moving out for good.

I leaned forward in the chair I had pulled alongside the hospital bed. Light filtered into the room. I glanced outside at a sun shower. It would be over by the time I left to walk back to my motel, but I thought about how heavy the air would feel outside. The strange phenomenon of when the sun persisted and the sky poured made Miami unique. In the Northeast, the sky greyed over and left gloom for days.

"Mom, you've got secrets. You and I know there's not years left for us to talk. It's right here, right now. Why don't you shed some light on your relationship with Byron, why you married him? I know you don't like to talk about it, but soon we won't have the chance."

"I'm too tired to talk about him now." Her eyes fluttered closed and she slept while I daydreamed the afternoon away.

I was staying near Jackson Memorial Hospital since I had closed up her apartment. I walked so I could get some exercise every day even though I had rented a car. The humidity drenched my shirt with perspiration in the stagnant Miami heat. Summer break, when most professors explored their real passions like fly fishing and gardening or furthered their research on digs like in my department, I was on a death watch. I felt incredibly sad, bereft. We had both been alone people, ones with an ability to socialize but often choosing not to go in that direction.

Without any close friends to call, I just broke down one afternoon. It wasn't so much feeling sorry for myself as feeling miserable for her.

The indignity of her life closing up, caving in, the embarrassment she felt about her hair. I just sobbed to let it all out. No point letting her see me like this.

A year-long sabbatical meant I was free. I planned on working on the paper I was delivering in New York in September. After that, maybe I'd get back to the rudimentary starts of a book based on new discoveries of the Pool of Siloam and the Tower of Siloam at the southern end of the city of David in Israel.

It had become a hot topic in academic circles as well as evangelical churches. With the rise of the latter's fervor in politics, the columbarium tower and a dovecote seemed to match descriptions in Luke and John in the Bible.

As a wary skeptic with ideas based in scientific proof, I had visited the site that was drawing worldwide attention. It made strange bedfellows of conservative Christians and Orthodox Jews. I tried to stay out of politics. The academic life is a rarified one, especially for professors who wanted to explore and discover, perpetual students without a graduation date.

I was a solitary soul. That was what my mother and I had in common. As self-contained individuals, we were satisfied with our own company. It's not that we weren't social; we just didn't need anyone. Even after our divorces, neither of us remarried. Sure, I had a few long-term relationships, but I wasn't willing to blend my life into someone else's on a daily basis, be accountable for my whereabouts and feel obligated to talk about my day. I wrapped myself in information, current events and the next scientific dispute.

I'm not saying a smart, pretty woman couldn't distract me. But I loathed getting involved. I found most women, wrapped up in the drama of their families and friends, more than willing to drag a host of characters into the relationship. Obviously I stayed away from students and university personnel. The students were sometimes quite bold, approaching me during office hours as though a wide-eyed, intellectually honest coed was a unique experience. As for others, anyone who worked on campus could spread stories.

I had girlfriends in New York, a train ride away on the weekends. Dinner at an ethnic restaurant, a show, a rendezvous—that worked for me. I imagined my mother felt the same way. Commitment without attachment.

She dated some nice gentlemen who were introduced to her by friends. One in particular caught her attention, a connoisseur of the arts and a well-respected member of a chamber music group whose father had been a renowned artist with pieces displayed in major museums. They were an attractive couple and attended many of the symphony debuts and gallery openings in Coconut Grove and Ft. Lauderdale. Once, in my twenties while I was in graduate school, I asked her if they would marry. She laughed, throwing her head back.

"What's so funny?" I asked. "The two of you seem to get along well. He's cultured, intelligent. Different from Dad in that he's not a drinker."

"Oh, Michael. I'm his beard."

"Huh? What's that?" I admit I felt a bit humiliated that she thought what I said was funny.

She took her pinky, wet the end with the tongue and stroked it across her eyebrow. Then I got it. He was gay. People weren't open about their preferences in those days. You never came out, even to close friends or family. People just whispered behind your back or used euphemisms like AC/DC to imply someone went both ways.

The realization jolted me. I hadn't ever considered that. '"But why do you go out with him?"

She took my hand. "Because he's wonderful company, kind, generous. And he doesn't intrude in my life. He's a 'walker.' I must have looked puzzled again. "A man who accompanies wealthy widows to society events, owns a great tuxedo, remembers flowers. He likes the company of women."

"But you're not a wealthy widow."

"No, his relationship with me has taken him out of that realm. People assume he finally made a choice. I'm a wonderful girlfriend. But in name only."

I was floored. "But don't you want to marry again someday?"

"Why? What for? I'm not having anymore children. You're as good as it gets. I have enough money to sustain myself and my job at Sandra

Post gets me out of the house and keeps me glamour-dressed." She smiled, pleased with herself.

"But what about security? Lots of men like a woman who's a gourmet cook, knows how to entertain, can meet the boss."

She gave me a grim look. "I did that already." Then she gave me a little push on my shoulder. "Since when are you advocating for traditional roles for women. Your ma is liberated. I can take care of myself. Keeps it simple."

"Don't you get lonely?"

"No. Do you?"

I shrugged. "Not really. Maybe that was the problem in my marriage with Francine. I didn't need her enough."

Fran had been smart, funny and attractive in a bohemian way, plus she got along with my mother. But she wanted children, noise, a house filled with people all the time. And I wanted quiet, time to think, travel. After seven years it turned out we weren't meant for each other. No rancorous drama. Just a parting of ways. She married a guy with kids and had one of her own a few years after she left me. I couldn't give her enough of what she wanted.

My mother steadied her gaze at me. "We're a selfish sort, only allowing others in when they insert themselves. There's always the pursuer and the pursued."

I thought about that conversation for a long time afterward. I wanted to be the pursuer. I liked being able to choose.

My mother let out a small moan of pain and I floated back into the hospital room. I took her hand so she'd know I was still nearby. I had some academic obligations and no classes until the fall semester of next year. With only a few things lined up, I needed to be here right now.

She stole her hand away from mine and took a hankie from under the blanket to dab at her eyes, her gaze settling on my face. Grey hair was growing out in patches, not in the blonde waves I knew. The sterile white room was so clinical, so unfriendly. The red roses I brought on the previous day were the only splash of color, their wilted necks beginning to hang in shame.

"Ma, why don't I ask questions and you answer honestly." She looked down. "Can you do that? Tell me the truth this time?"

Her eyes filled with tears. I knew she was a weeper, but it didn't stop me from wanting to break through what she was guarding inside for so long. I pulled a bunch of tissues from the box next to her and passed them over.

"This is hard for me," she said, sighing with reluctance.

A pang of guilt shot across my chest. Was I going to interrogate this sick woman because of my need to know? Maybe it wasn't the right thing to do. How many times had family secrets been buried with people?

"Me too. I want to know what you're hiding." I paused. I had been brought up to be reserved, nonconfrontational. "I'm uncomfortable too. I'm going to make a confession. I looked in your drawer years ago and saw a letter from your mother."

"You looked in my drawer?" Shocked, her voice was stronger than I had heard it in months.

"Yes. I read a letter from your mother. That's who died, wasn't it, when you flew to New York that time?"

"Michael!" Her voice took on the tone I knew so well from my youth, as if she could browbeat me into being a child again.

"It doesn't matter now. With only a short time left I want us to be complete. Byron's dead of the drink. What can't you tell me? I'm an adult. I can handle it." I didn't want to sound impatient, but it seemed ridiculous not to say what needed to be said.

"You were in my things?" She turned her face away from me, as if my presence would dissipate into the sanctified antiseptic smells of the room.

"Michael, I wanted to share more with you, but you were a kid, a naïve one at that. I was more protective than some of the other mothers. I've had some insight over the years. We do pass on our family history whether it's acknowledged or not. When my mother died, I grieved for longer than I let on, especially because I felt guilt about abandoning her. When you're in your thirties, you think you've got years ahead of you to make things right. Sometimes I fantasized about taking you up to New York to meet her. She would have been thrilled to know you. Then I was in my forties and she was gone. What was the point? Ach. So many regrets and guilt. Before I knew what transpired, I was meeting with lawyers about the divorce. It didn't seem right to drag you through one more upset."

"Ma, tell me now or I'm leaving. There can't be secrets between us anymore." I wasn't sure I had the heart to walk out on her, but I was so frustrated with her repression of facts, memories, family history.

"Okay." She gulped in a big breath, turning her head toward me. "But I have to start at the beginning."

Chapter Fourteen

New York City
September 20, 1993

Sandrine squeezed my hand in the cab from Grand Central Station to the Pierre, known for quiet elegance and Turkish marbled bathrooms. I wasn't the type to try and impress someone, but this place had cachet. Weary from travel and the stop in New Haven, I remained silent.

"Sometime you tell me about your mother, yes?"

"Of course. We haven't had the time. And there's a lot to tell."

Her eyes appeared glossy in the darkness of the cab. "Did you love her?"

"Very much. But some things happened at the end of her life that I found upsetting." I squeezed her hand back. "It's for another time. It'll be better after this week is over."

"But I am curious. I want to know everything about you."

"Oh, you will. We're going to be together a long time."

She smiled a self-satisfied grin. "I feel this too."

I relaxed my neck against the worn seat for a few minutes. The emotional exhaustion of the last three days drained me. Brooks. Yossi. Maurice's death. I drifted off as Sandrine absorbed New York life flashing by the window.

I came home from school one afternoon and my mother was sitting at the linoleum table in the kitchen with balls of tissues around her.

I dropped my school books on the floor. "Ma, what's wrong?"

She looked up with red-rimmed eyes, her nose larger than usual. "Michael honey, come here." She reached out her arms to hug me.

"Why are you crying? What happened?"

"It's nothing. I'm fine."

"But you're crying. Something must've happened."

"No. Well, yes. A distant relative died." She snuffled into another tissue smearing her makeup.

"Who? One of yours? You said everyone was already dead."

"Yes, well, most of them." She reached for a glass with amber liquid in front of her. I'd never seen her drinking during the day before. My dad, yes, but not her.

"Who was it?"

"Nobody. No one you'd know."

"What was their name?" I thought about her nightstand drawer with its hidden contents. Maybe in this vulnerable state I could get some more information.

"Ma, who was it?"

"I don't want to talk about it." She put her head down on her arms and looked at me from the side. "Go get washed up. Your piano teacher will be here soon. I'll be fine."

After my lesson I went into the kitchen to let my mother and Mrs. Rosenbaum know the lesson was over. I thought it strange they didn't come out for the usual concert. They were saying something I didn't understand when I came in, leaning forward, heads together, whispering. They stopped and sat back, surprised.

I didn't know what happened but I was on alert. I heard my dad come in from work, mix a drink and swing through the kitchen doors. Their voices were muffled. I crept out of my room to see if I could eavesdrop by squatting between the television and the wall.

"Sara, you need to go. I'll call the airlines about a ticket. Go up there and straighten things out. You'll be back by the weekend."

I heard a chair scrape and froze. "Oh, Byron, thank you. I can be back by Friday before the holiday dance at the club."

"Go ahead. Do what you have to do. Estelle will be here."

"What should I tell Michael? He came home and saw me crying."

"Probably best not to say anything."

My mother left for New York for almost a week, telling me she was going Christmas shopping in the city and might be making a visit to FAO Schwarz, the most famous toy store in the world. I had been asking for Boom or Bust, a two-sided board game some of my friends had.

She left while I was at school. Honestly, I hardly noticed she was gone. Russell, the most adventurous of our gang, had found a place for a tree house and we were spending hours looting a nearby construction site for bits of lumber and nails.

Five days later, after my mother returned from her New York trip, Mr. Rosenbaum, his wife and Ivy showed up for my Friday piano lesson. While I pounded through a few scales, my mother took Mrs. Rosenbaum's hand and led her into the kitchen. Ivy curled up with a book on the Florida room lounge chair, knees tucked beneath her, her dress pulled modestly over them.

At the end of the lesson both women came out and I could see they had been blowing their noses and their eyes were rimmed red. I couldn't figure out what was going on, but I bet Ivy had the scoop. I didn't know how to get to her. Ever since the Halloween party incident she could barely look at me. I was at the junior high and she was still at the elementary school. Besides, it would have been weird for me to talk to her.

The two women hugged as the Rosenbaums left. Outside the door, Ivy's mom turned to my mother.

"Sara, it'll be okay."

What had my mother shared that I didn't know? I tried to pry something out of her, but she mixed herself a drink, crumpled up a few more tissues and disappeared into her room with the door closed.

She moped for a few weeks and drank some more. I caught her standing at the sink, her back to me when I came home, pouring a drink down the drain, the ashtray on the kitchen table overflowing with cigarette butts. She'd turn around to greet me and I could tell she had been crying.

"Ma, everything okay?"

"Of course, sweetheart. How was school? Isn't there a field trip to Vizcaya next week?"

I didn't want to upset her by asking more questions. Even I knew she didn't go to New York just to buy me Christmas presents. I snooped in her closet and found wrapped packages stuffed onto the top shelf. I contemplated picking the scotch tape open on one end to see what was in there, but my friends came over and I was out the door.

During the beginning of Christmas vacation, I checked my parents' nightstand drawers when they were at a club dance.

November, 1956

Dearest Sarah,
I am devastated that you don't write a note with the money. How is Florida? You? Michael? I wish I could see how he's grown. Is Byron's job still secure? Aunt Lottie spoke to me about taking the train down in the winter when we get a few days off but I don't think it's possible. Plus, I don't know what you'd do with us there. I don't want to harm our agreement.
Know that in this lifetime I will always love you,
Mommy

This was a new letter added to the envelope slipped underneath the drawer liner.

Did that mean I had another grandmother? How could that be? It took a few moments until I realized my mother's tears must have been because she died. She wasn't Christmas shopping. My mother went to New York for her funeral. Why had she been sending her money? Why couldn't I have known her?

Chapter Fifteen

New York City
September 21, 1993
9 a.m.

We waited after placing our orders in Katz's Deli. The men behind the counter, dirty aprons emblazoned with lettering, yelled out to each other and the customers. "It is just like the American movies," Sandrine said, clutching my arm.

I admired the excitement that registered on her face. In this new environment dressed as a sophisticated woman, she appeared as a *naïf.* The din of stacking plates and shouting orders with retorts from staff as well as customers became deafening. We stared at each other, our eyes communicating amusement. She tilted her head. I wished we were back in bed.

"These are the best bagels in the world. Hard with a crunch on the outside and soft and chewy on the inside. It's the New York water that makes them better than anyplace else. I ordered us two 'everythings.' Try your coffee." I felt obliged to be a tour guide just as she was for me in Paris.

The platters arrived. I spread cream cheese on both halves of the bagels, stacking pink-orange lox with a piece of tomato on top. I ignored the thick slice of onion out of selfishness, a nod to our frequent kisses. She followed my lead. I pressed my bagel with the flat of my hand so it became bite-sized.

She leaned back in her chair. "I cannot eat this."

"Why not?"

"It is *trop grand*." She opened her mouth wide for emphasis.

"It was never a problem before."

We laughed.

I pulled her plate toward me, pressed the bagel together with the flat of my hand and turned it toward her so she could take a bite.

Her eyes sidled up and down in a flirtatious way. She loved to tease me. I was susceptible. Opening her lips, she took a medium-sized bite, widening her eyes as the sweet cream cheese and salty smoked salmon melted in her mouth.

"It's wonderful," she said, chewing daintily as I chomped down on my bagel.

In a moment her expression shifted and a frown appeared. "Ow."

"What's the matter?" I stretched my arm across the table to touch her elbow.

"My tooth. Something is broken."

"Oh no."

Her lips parted to let her tongue explore. She winced. "It is sharp. I think I break a tooth. I need a dentist." She poked her finger in her mouth and pulled out a small piece of silver filling.

I motioned to the waiter to bring the check. He arrived with a look of disdain, his posture a question of, "Whaddayawant?"

"The check."

"Suppose ya wanna to-go box too, huh?" The waiter tapped his finger on the check placed under the salt shaker when the food was served. Sandrine placed her hand over the spot that hurt, the rest of her expression in a worried frown.

I took two more big bites before reaching for my wallet, throwing down thirty dollars on the table. I guided Sandrine through the chaotic restaurant with the slight pressure of my hand on her back.

"Hey!" the waiter yelled. "Ya supposed to pay at the register."

Before I hailed a cab, I called Sommerstein's assistant Heather from a phone booth, worried about being late for my meeting. I explained that my friend broke a tooth.

"I'll make some calls and have a dentist lined up by the time you get here."

When I hung up Sandrine said, "Michael, I do not want to make trouble for you."

I put my arm around her. "You're no trouble."

In the taxi Sandrine closed her eyes, her hand covering her jaw. I could see she was uncomfortable. I should have stopped at a drugstore to buy some aspirin.

"We'll get it taken care of," I said, patting her hand. She frowned at me. "What's the matter?" She shrugged. "Tell me." She turned away to look out the window. "Is it the cost?" She shook her head no. "What? You don't think an American dentist can be as good as a French one?" I teased her.

She skewed her head to look at me, removing her hand. "For me, going to a new dentist is like seeing another gynecologist. It is personal." I squeezed her hand. I can't say I understood the female point of view, but any dental visit could be intimidating.

A half an hour later we were standing in Sommerstein's office. After brief introductions, Heather tore off a piece of paper and handed it to me.

"Best in Manhattan. Only took me twenty calls. Can fit her in as an emergency. But it'll cost ya."

"I'll get her over there and be back for the meeting."

"No way. The boss is waiting for you at the Y. He's frantic with details. I'll call a car to pick her up. You've got to start walking now. We're on deadline."

I glanced at Sandrine who had taken a seat. I walked over, sat down and explained why I couldn't accompany her to the dentist. A part of me wanted to escape being responsible for another human being.

"A car will be here shortly to pick you up."

She shook her head no. "Michael, I am a Parisian. I take the Métro all the time. I insist. A car is an extravagance."

"How do you know?"

"Because I hear you. One hundred fifty francs for a ride? Ridiculous!"

"One hundred dollars. It's cheaper." Of course in my mind I added up what my little foray was costing me with airfare, a special car and the dentist. And we hadn't even gotten a dress yet. Damn the way my crotch leads me around sometimes.

"No. You walk me to the underground and I do it."

"You cannot navigate the subway. I'm afraid you'll get lost." Who knew she was going to be so stubborn? Shit. I'm really attached to her.

She stood up and placed her hands on her hips. In a pencil skirt and a white filmy blouse she looked like a model, a red belt cinching her tiny waist. I couldn't stop myself from looking her up and down.

"I do not get lost. And I ask the questions. Look how good my English is."

"You don't understand. It's not like Paris. There's no artwork from the Louvre and nice tiled signs in the subway. There's graffiti and bad people. I think it's too dangerous." I shook my head no. My beeper buzzed in my jacket pocket. Sommerstein again. I ignored it. Heather gave me a hurry-up glare.

"Excuse me. I'm sorry to interrupt, but the boss expects you to be at the Ninety-Second Street Y in ten minutes. And the car is waiting." Heather sounded annoyed and adamant, turning her back away from me in her swivel chair, her face illuminated by a computer screen.

I rubbed the back of my neck in frustration. Fuck. I don't have time to deal with this either.

I rose to face Sandrine. "Here's the address. It's on Lexington in the sixties. Too far to walk but an easy ride. It's all paid for. You probably need a temporary crown. I'm not a worry wart but this is New York City. Take the car." I pulled a bunch of twenties and a fifty out of my wallet.

Her eyes hardened. "I do not want to do this."

Disheartened at her stubbornness, I said, "Please. This is walking-around money in New York City. Tip the driver. The car is booked for both ways. Meet me at the Y. You can prove yourself another time. Later we'll pick out a dress for tomorrow night. If you still want to go on a subway, I'll take you tomorrow." My voice edged toward impatience.

I had to get the tooth problem solved. I needed a little cooperation here with Sommerstein waiting, an irritable guy from previous encounters. With all this tension about Maurice's death and how the symposium will be run, everyone's cranky. Why did I allow myself to get distracted?

"*Oh là là*," she said, making me laugh. Her mood shifted. She lifted herself up to kiss me on both cheeks. I gave her my best professorial expression, the one I saved for students who came in to beg and cajole for extra credit when they were dissatisfied with an evaluation.

"Don't smile. Don't talk to anyone. Watch your purse. Here. Take my beeper for an emergency. You can dial 9-1-1. Heather will call the dentist with my credit card number. Don't even think about protesting. It's my fault you chipped your tooth. Do you have any walking shoes with you?"

Sandrine ignored the question, giving me a cocky grin with a tilt of her head. "I know what I do."

We walked out of the office together. A black Lincoln town car idled in front of the college. Unlike the Yale campus, Roscom appeared as another high rise in a city overflowing with buildings.

"I know how to take a métro," she murmured. "I do not like men who try to make control of me." But she got into the waiting car anyway and sat back.

I leaned in toward the driver, a man wearing a skullcap sitting on wooden beads, and handed him the piece of paper with the dentist's information.

"Pretend you're a spy on an important mission," I whispered to her in the back seat.

In the late morning, light crowds thinned as office workers reached their destinations and other determined souls propelled themselves forward through the extra sidewalk space. Sandrine gawked out the window in wonderment at the sprawling city and people. So much to see, do, try. Sounds of horns, sirens, snippets of music enveloped her. She'd almost forgotten about her toothache. The car pulled in front of a skyscraper.

"The dentist is in there on the fortieth floor," said the driver, passing back his card. "Dispatcher's number's on it. Call when you're ready to return. I'll pick you up on that corner." Sandrine checked her purse to make sure Michael's beeper was nestled there, drawing a breath of security.

Sandrine walked into a barren lobby and took the elevator to her destination. The hallway stretched in front of her. The doors, painted the green of old hospital walls, displayed black lettering on marbled glass. She glanced at the name on the piece of paper and then opened the door with the matching name, cautious.

"I am Sandrine Agneau," she said to the nurse behind a glass cage.

"Follow me. It's a good thing Dr. Beaufort had an opening this morning."

The dentist, an attractive woman in her forties, greeted her as she entered the room. After inquiring about Sandrine's accent, she added, "My people were from France originally. I'd love to see it someday."

The dentist invaded Sandrine's mouth with a tiny round mirror, tapping on a tooth. Sandrine winced.

"You need a temporary crown. It'll last about four weeks. Will you be back home by then?"

Sandrine nodded, mumbling, "But I don't know if I want to be."

Efficiently, the dentist administered two shots of novocain, shaking her cheek to ease the pain of the needle. After a minimum of drilling she completed the procedure. Sandrine poked her tongue over the spot.

"It feels better."

Sandrine leaned in to pay her bill at the small window. The nurse informed her that it had been paid. She expelled a sigh of relief.

"Should I call a car for you?"

"No, thank you. I want to see a little of New York. It's a city of dreams, no?"

Outside, Sandrine paused, stroking her numb jaw, observing the rush of activity. The pleasant weather, unlike the sticky moist heat of Paris, attracted the city's denizens to stay above ground. In a lifetime of mythologizing New York—the colors, the people, the streets appeared surreal. Her tongue traced her lips. She reached for her lipstick and felt Michael's beeper. She pulled it out halfway. In an instant she shoved it back into her bag.

Chapter Sixteen

New York City
September 21, 1993
Noon

A series of store windows with chaise lounges and iridescent throw pillows caught Sandrine's eye as she sauntered, purse clutched under her arm. She thought about calling for the car while admiring the abundance of goods on display.

She decided to bring something back for her *maman* and maybe Roland, her understanding Roland, although it was *fait accompli* after her unexpected trip. As childhood friends she knew the romance couldn't sustain itself. Michael was on her mind. All the time.

Sandrine meandered a few more blocks, stopping to buy some chocolates and a scarf for her mother. Michael warned her about high heels. She stopped for a moment, leaning into a doorway to pull her foot out of the pointy shoe, squeezing her toes. A blister rose red on her heel. A teenager with a small radio against his ear bumped her and kept walking, his shoulders dismissing her with a shrug. Stumbling, she didn't lose her balance. "*Excusez-moi*," she uttered.

Sandrine walked another block, the blister rubbing, looking for a pay phone. She passed some with people bent inside, others waiting impatiently outside. She glanced at a clock overhead.

Sandrine stepped off the curb, her arm thrust upward to flag a taxi. In Paris taxis lined up, organized at certain corners. With a few frustrated attempts at waving, she watched occupied cabs whiz by her. She gave up and continued walking, unsure of her direction, looking for a pharmacy. Instead, she saw a sign for the subway. With her blister throbbing, she made her way toward it, hesitating. Michael warned her it might be dangerous, but it was daylight with lots of people around. She dismissed him as a nervous American, her independent spirit ready for a new undertaking. She inhaled a deep breath and followed the steps down, ignoring the chipped, rusted railing.

A few people stood at the bottom of the stairs in front of a large map trying to figure out their stop, gesticulating and speaking another language. Sandrine, limping a bit with her foot not completely in her shoe, approached the window to buy a ticket. She asked the dour young woman with purple nails so long they curled about the stop she needed. The woman mumbled something, not meeting her eyes.

"Can you please repeat?" Sandrine asked.

The woman, blocked behind heavy plate glass with only a small opening at the bottom for a change tray, repeated the instructions, adding hand signals to go downstairs. "Catch the first train going uptown," she told Sandrine with exasperation. "The Lexington Avenue subway."

Sandrine teetered toward the turnstile, a not unfamiliar habit, and dropped in her token, pushing through the metal bar. A kid with dreadlocks and a baseball cap hopped over her and jumped the turnstile without a ticket, brushing past her.

She acknowledged that some people in Paris cheated like this too, but they weren't so flagrant. No police in sight.

Sandrine found her way down another set of stairs just as a train pulled to the platform. People pressed through the subway entrance while the doors remained open. She followed them, picking a spot next to a mother holding a child's hand and two shopping bags. All the seats filled. Sandrine hugged the pole as the train lurched forward, holding her purse under her arm, the bags on her wrist.

With sweat gathering on her forehead in the claustrophobic heat, Sandrine peeked over the woman's shoulder at the map, searching for a sign of recognition. She couldn't remember what the woman in the glass enclosure told her about the Ninety-Second Street Y.

Her foot pulsed. She glanced down at her heel, pulling her foot half out of the shoe. Red, raw, oozing, the blister had broken. She knew she didn't have a Band-Aid with her. She inhaled a breath. A young man with a belligerent frown scrutinized her up and down, chains hanging from his pocket. She shifted her body away, observing she was the whitest face on the train. Suddenly she felt lost, confused, her environment unwelcoming.

"Excuse me," she said to the mother. "Where is Ninety-Second Street Y?"

The woman, her face shiny with sweat, responded. "What? You're way far away . . . that's on the Upper East Side of Manhattan. You'd better get off at this stop and go back the way you came. You're heading toward Brooklyn." The child pulled on her arm. "Just wait a minute, Jeremy."

Sandrine panicked, a rising heat coursing through her chest and neck. The subway screeched to its next stop. Impulsively, she decided to get off, limping with purpose to the platform, following the crowd, passing signs. The young man who had stared at her exited the stop too, taking the stairs two at time. Everyone seemed to have a destination.

Precarious because her foot was not fully shoved into her shoe, Sandrine placed one hand on the tiled wall, the other holding her two purchases, the purse tucked under her arm.

She knew she needed to steady herself. Her mind repeated the word *sparadrap*, searching for the English word for Band-Aid.

In her ascent, crowds of commuters rushed by her—kids in neon shirts, older women shuffling with bags, a few confident businesspeople. She took a few steps and stopped, the heat from below billowing around her. A wave of dizziness swept over her.

Three teenage boys in sweatshirts touched Sandrine's skirt on their run up the stairs. She didn't see their faces, only a flash of silver chains. Disoriented, her upper arm muscles tightened as she gripped her purse under her arm. She guided herself up a few more steps, muttering, her hand touching the wall for support. Halfway between the fading sounds of the subterranean train and echoing street noise, lightheadedness swept upward, teasing, wrapping itself around her forehead, a turban of fear. Her fingers bent to clutch the wall but the tile didn't give. Without warning Sandrine fell forward onto her knees, her foot pulsating.

A man, hunched over, raced by Sandrine, his jacket flying, a hard briefcase with brass fittings swinging from his hand. He stumbled over her, the case making contact with her face. With a pause he righted himself and never broke his pace. "Sorry," he yelled over his shoulder.

Sandrine's grip on her packages and purse loosened, dropping, sliding down a few steps behind her. She screamed, "*Aide, aide*!" the English word for help lost on her tongue.

A few drops of blood spotted the step. She touched her face, her fingers staining pink, the area near her eye throbbing. She regained her balance, but she felt disoriented. No one stopped to assist. In an effort to calm her panic, she repeated to herself, "An accident. Someone in a hurry. I am okay. But I am invisible." Colors swirled by her. She sank to the steps.

An older woman with short grey hair cleared the space near Sandrine by swinging her cane. "Someone call 9-1-1," she yelled to a small crowd gathering.

"No, please." Sandrine pushed her way back onto her feet, breathless. "I am fine. No harm." She palpated her face again. Blood.

She inspected the stairs for her belongings. Without words she pointed to them, scattered a few steps behind her among the subway debris of cups, food wrappers and sticky spilled liquids. A few buttons on the front of her blouse popped open, one lying on the ground at her feet. She grabbed the two pieces of fabric to cover herself.

"I am fine," she repeated.

"Ya sure, honey?" said the woman handing her a tissue.

Sandrine reached for it and held it near her eye with pressure. When she took it away she saw blood was still oozing.

"Yes. Please. I will call a car." Her fingers scrambled through her unzipped purse for Michael's beeper. Gone. Wallet. Missing. Oh no. My money. Her hand rose to cover her thumping heart. Thank God not my passport. She searched around on the steps, but with the volume of people moving, it could have been pushed in any direction. Or picked up. She sank down on the filthy steps, her back against the wall, hair touching the tile. She pressed the tissue to blot the cut near her cheekbone.

"Where do you have to go?" the woman asked, bending forward, her wrinkled face registering concern.

"Ninety-Second Street Y," said Sandrine, her eyes welling with tears. "My wallet, my money."

The woman, weight shifting onto her cane took charge. "Come. I'll help you get a cab. You really should report this to the police. That bastard should have stopped. I saw the whole thing. People in such a hurry nowadays."

Sandrine straightened herself and stood up. "Thank you. I get the taxi myself." She scouted around the steps again. The bag with the scarf wrapped in tissue paper was a few steps behind her. She reached for it and tied it around her neck to cover her torn blouse, abandoning the trampled chocolates. Still unsure of herself, she climbed the stairs with caution, heading for the street.

"Young lady, how will you pay for the cab?" called the woman. "Call the police. They need to know."

Michael. I must get back to Michael. My face hurts. He will be angry his beeper is gone.

Chapter Seventeen

New York City
September 21, 1993
3:30 p.m.

Sandrine returned to Sommerstein's office at the college. As she stumbled in, Heather hung up the phone.

"That was the car company wanting to know why you didn't call after the dentist. He even went up to look for you." She paused for a moment to take in Sandrine. "What the hell happened?"

Sandrine did her best to explain while Heather grabbed her purse, leaving to go downstairs and pay the driver. Buttons were missing from the front of Sandrine's blouse. She had tied the scarf to hide herself. With a small cracked mirror she took out of her purse, she examined her face. Besides the cut on her cheekbone a bruise near her eye exploded in purple. She covered her face with her hands and cried.

Heather came back, placing her purse in its hiding spot. She moved around the desk to comfort Sandrine, surveying her face.

"Hey, hey, hey. Come on. You're in one piece. Let me get your boyfriend." She guided Sandrine to the desk chair and pulled it out. She loosened her taut body into the worn leather as Heather pulled a bottle of water out of an insulated lunch bag, handing it to her. "Take a drink and rest your head on my desk for a minute while I call."

I rushed in, worry crisscrossing my face. I placed my briefcase on a chair, lifting Sandrine to her feet and holding her. She whimpered in relief.

"I am so sorry," I repeated. I pushed her away from me gently to examine her face.

"Maybe you need a doctor. Does it hurt?"

"No. I do not go anywhere else now. I will be fine."

After some prodding she told me about the boys that touched her rushing by, the man swinging his briefcase like a weapon and the older woman who rescued her.

I didn't want to interrogate her, but I had to ask, "Why didn't you take the car I ordered?"

"I am a fool. I want to see New York."

Exasperated, I tried not to show it. I thought to myself, poor kid has been through a lot today between the dentist and a mugging.

"You're a real New Yorker now. Do me a favor. Stay out of trouble 'til I get back."

"An accident. People hurry here. But that is not the bad part. Your beeper is missing. I searched my bag and my wallet is disappeared too. All my money for New York. And your beeper, *non*."

Heather hung in the doorway, eavesdropping.

"No, Jesus. You don't think someone targeted you?" I loosened my hold on Sandrine and leaned against a wall, rubbing my eyes.

"What about your passport?"

"I leave at the hotel in the safe."

I stood frozen for a few minutes and then lifted myself to my full height. "There's something weird here. Anyone follow you?"

Sandrine shrugged her shoulders, shaking her head no, thinking.

"What do you mean?"

"One young man with chains looked at me on the train and I see a flash of chains. Maybe. Maybe not."

"Oh Jesus. This is a nightmare. Has to have something to do with the auction. Do you think you were targeted in the subway? Like someone knew who you were?"

Sandrine frowned with worry. "Unless someone was watching from this morning."

That creeped me out. The idea that someone was watching us made the hairs stand up on my neck.

"Because you're replacing Maurice," offered Heather, her intrusion accepted.

"It still doesn't make sense. What do I have that someone would want? My paper? Do they want to scare me away from presenting Maurice's? Someone else will read it. It has to mean someone doesn't want the artifacts authenticated. Or they're targeting Sandrine to get to me. I can see where my beeper with all my contacts might be useful to someone trying to cause me grief, but why?"

I puzzled over what I couldn't figure out. "Thank God you weren't hurt more seriously. If you ended up in a hospital—" I hesitated, "or worse, I'd definitely be off my game."

"What? You think someone wants to hurt me to get to you?" Sandrine's face registered an alert. "But I don't know anything. Ay, and all my money, ID, pictures of my nephews . . ."

"Sometimes that doesn't matter. They just want to get someone off-kilter to distract them."

"Heather, can you move us out of the Pierre to another hotel closer to the symposium?"

"Of course," she responded with cheer. "Will save us two hundred bucks a day."

"I'm going to switch hotels. I'll need another pager. Lost over forty contacts—department heads for interdisciplinary studies, graduate students I advise, friends at other universities, my mother's doctors." I paused with the remembrance.

"I won't need those anymore," my voice dropping.

I glanced at Sandrine who didn't hear me. "Then my Paris lamb and I—"

I paused. It sounded like a term of endearment even though Brooks had bastardized it. Was she a sacrificial lamb? Who was trying to get to me? I felt a pang of guilt. Have I exposed Sandrine to danger?

"—are going shopping for a new dress. Sandrine, you stay here with Heather. I'll be back in a couple of hours. Watch my briefcase. Don't let it out of your sight."

Sandrine gazed up at me. "No. I want to go with you. I have to change."

"I want to make sure no one follows me. I'll bring you another blouse. And sensible shoes."

Heather interrupted. "I've got the key to the restroom so you can clean up. And I need to get you some ice for that mouse."

Sandrine's eyes opened wide. "A mouse?"

Heather tapped near her eye area.

"Oh." Sandrine touched the spot with the pads of her fingers and winced.

I turned my shoulder to the wall and bowed my head.

"What are you doing?" Sandrine asked.

"I'm trying to remember when I updated all my names and numbers in the beeper."

"I'll walk you down to the restroom and wait, but I'll tell you, I'm the most dangerous person you'll meet in this building," said Heather to Sandrine, tucking Michael's briefcase behind her desk and taking the restroom key.

Sandrine's mouth pouted in confusion.

"Just a lesbos joke. You're really beautiful. Let's look in the lost-and-found box for a T-shirt or sweater."

Reluctantly, Sandrine followed her.

I returned to the Pierre, worried about the subway incident. Someone must have followed us when we left the hotel this morning. They probably thought we'd be together all day, but when Sandrine went to the dentist, maybe it was an opportunity. Did her spontaneity to avoid the car afterward shift them to another scenario? Why did I feel it had to be more than one person? I hoped no one followed me from Sommerstein's office. I couldn't figure out what was going on.

I opened the door to our room with caution after I glanced up and down the hallway. At first I thought housekeeping hadn't been there because the bed was still unmade, but as my eyes adjusted to the darkened room, I realized our room had been rifled.

A cold feeling crept up the back of my head. I stood in the doorway unsure whether to enter. I could see the bed was torn apart, drawers left open, a light left on in the bathroom. Thank God I took my briefcase and laptop with me when I left. The drapes, pulled shut, moved a little.

My heart pumped.

Was someone in here?

Immobile for a few moments, I couldn't decide what to do. Go in? Shut the door and leave? Report it to the house detective? But I didn't even know if anything was missing. I was checking out no matter what. As I debated with myself, the air conditioning turned off. The rustling drapes stopped moving.

I slammed back the door so it made a noise crashing into the wall and stepped inside. I walked across the room to pull the drapes open. Light flooded into the room. No one could be hiding in this small room. I spun around to examine the closet, door open, some of our clothes dropped to the floor.

With caution I checked the bathroom, its opulence undisturbed. Whoever it was came after the maid service because the towels were clean and displayed where they should be. But what were they looking for? Maurice's paper? Mine? No jewelry or cash. It stumped me for a few minutes until hairs went up on the back of my neck.

Sandrine's passport.

With dexterity I opened the safe hidden on the back wall of the closet with a number we had agreed upon earlier.

Whew. It was there. Why would someone risk a burglary charge when there were no valuables? They must have run out of time if they hadn't jimmied the safe. Unless what they wanted was information. Which I had with me. It didn't make sense, but it had to be connected to Sandrine's mishap in the subway. If they were trying to rattle me, they did. I wanted to get out of there.

Should I report it? Nothing was missing. What would be the point? Besides, it would waste more time and I wanted to get back to Sandrine. It also might draw more attention to us.

After gathering our clothes and toiletries into two suitcases, I checked out, patting the inside of my coat for Sandrine's passport. Poor kid. She's had a rough day. And it's not over yet.

I changed cabs twice as a precautionary measure, checking in at the Bermonte Hotel on the Upper East Side, one I was familiar with from previous stays, located near the Ninety-Second Street Y where the symposium would be held.

The hotel, advertised as a chic boutique hotel, was anything but with its shabby lobby. It wasn't the Pierre. So much for good impressions. The rooms, however, appeared similar, only a bit more miniscule and musty, minus the elaborate bathroom. I set our suitcases on stands, searching Sandrine's for a blouse and sandals. I found a plastic laundry bag in the closet, patted my pocket to make sure her passport was there, followed an exit sign to the stairwell that took me to the ground level and departed through a side door. I had to get back to Sandrine.

When I arrived at Sommerstein's office I glanced around the waiting area for Sandrine, my hand touching my side pocket for the missing beeper.

"Where is she?" I asked Heather, an uneasy feeling rattling around in my head.

"Talking to the boss," she said, not taking her eyes away from her computer screen. "I have your briefcase right here under my desk."

"Good," I said, reaching for it.

I rushed down the short hallway. The open door revealed Sandrine sitting on an old sofa, her legs crossed, barefoot, her expression intent.

Sommerstein was speaking. "Maurice was one of the few scholars who actually saw them during the examination period. We were all scrambling to be on the team. Got verified by some heavy-duty experts worldwide. But Maurice had some connections. It got all the academics growling."

He stopped when he saw me, his hand in midair motioning toward Sandrine. "Your friend asks very insightful questions." I released an audible breath of relief.

Sandrine reached up to hug me. In her hand wa a plastic bag with ice dripping condensation on the floor. A bruise saturated the clear skin on her cheek. She was wearing a dowdy sweater buttoned to the neck.

"Michael," she said, saying my name with joy.

"Come on. Let's go. I've gotten us moved into our new hotel." I tipped her chin back and forth with my hand comparing the two sides of her face.

"I have some pain meds. That looks nasty. You could use a stitch or two."

"No. No doctors. I will be fine." Sandrine touched the damaged spot. "One minute," she said. "The professor is answering my question." She sat down in her spot while I leaned in the doorway, arms crossed.

Sommerstein, unshaven and rumpled, jumped in. "So basically a spokesperson for the Vatican leaked knowledge about the artifacts to a reputable Rome art dealer who created a buzz about them. Then the whole archaeological community went on alert, especially the Israelis. Hey, they're my people, but when it comes to their sliver of land, they'll start a nuclear war to authenticate their right to it. Not that they'll acknowledge any weapons of that caliber.

"Anyway, the pope must've plastered twenty layers between the church and whoever represents them. Lot of substratum as we say in our field. A maze of connections too. At first the specimens were under heavy guard at a vault in Rome, and the Vatican disavowed any connection. But who could believe that with all their secrecy? No one knows what the hell they've got stuffed in their basement. Or for how many centuries. Or how big it is."

She frowned.

"Hope I haven't offended you. Are you Catholic?"

"No. I go to Catholic school as a girl and attend Mass sometimes with my *maman,* but I am not a true believer."

"What does that mean?" I asked, my natural skepticism pulling me into the conversation.

She squinted at me. "It means I am realistic about flaws and respect tradition. How did they come to be here?" asked Sandrine.

"Appropriate channels to get them into this country. Can't imagine how much underwriting the insurance is costing." Sommerstein pushed some files aside on his messy desk. A Styrofoam container with the remains of his lunch hung on the edge.

"They don't tell me much. I'm just in charge of the platform for the events. But I can tell you one thing. Everyone who's anyone is going to show his face on opening night. And there's a lot of people, museums and governments scrambling to own them. Bernard from the Louvre,

Easton from the National Gallery, Beyer from the Met. Even the Saudis are sending a rep.

"Michael, did you know the Chinese are coming in for this?"

"I understand major museum collections wanting them and of course, the Israelis, but what significance do they have for the Chinese?" I asked.

"Beats me. Except they love power and control. Another way to show everyone up. I don't trust them. The buzz is they put a syndicate together for this. Look how much the Van Gogh went for at auction recently. Eighty-two million, but if the buyer hangs onto it for twenty years, with inflation and the rarity, it'll be worth in the neighborhood of a hundred and fifty million."

Before Sandrine lay down on the bed and closed her eyes, she swallowed a pain reliever I gave her. I sent the bellman for more ice and fashioned a poultice with a washcloth. I sat on a chair next to the bed and watched her doze off. Shopping would have to wait. With my feet propped on the bed, I skimmed through a few abstracts of papers to be presented at the conference.

The one of most interest to me expounded on the latest discovery of a lavish, four-hundred-seat theater at King Herod's palace outside Jerusalem. I visited the excavation site a few years ago with a colleague who specialized in biblical discoveries, a testament to the king's extravagant taste in fifteen BCE. No one's disputing this find. Herod, Jewish proxy leader of the Holy Land under the Roman occupation, a stronghold for Jewish rebels, was all powerful. Were the God's Gold artifacts ever held there?

My eyelids fluttered down with my mind dancing between the twilight of the academic world and the intensity of a new situation. I drummed my fingers on my knees. When I opened my eyes to Sandrine's steady breathing, I observed the bruise commencing its rainbow of colors. My situation became a reality.

I felt awkward displaying her to everyone. She was someone people would notice and now the shiner would prompt all kinds of questions, drawing attention to me. The academic community, a nosy one, generated gossip, damaging reputations with impunity. It rivaled their published papers, which inspired unwelcomed critiques. Like Brooks White. Then I stopped to ask myself, "Why do I give a shit what people think?"

Anxiety elbowed its way into the front of my consciousness as Sandrine snored softly. Why did someone want my contacts? Or was it a fluke that my beeper was stolen? I missed it buzzing in my pocket, someone trying to reach me. Usually it was a doctoral student or my mother's doctor, until recently. It had to be coincidences, all coincidences.

Sandrine turned on her side, hands tucked under her chin in a prayer mode. Poor kid.

I wrote a note on a piece of hotel stationery and left it on her pillow. "Be back soon. Buying a new beeper and treats."

When I returned Sandrine was awake but groggy. I had coffee, Danish and Moleskin for her foot. Maybe I should have insisted she go to the emergency room. I voiced my concerns.

"No. I do not want to talk to anyone else."

"Listen, Sandrine, I don't know what's going on here. I'll understand if you want to leave. I can get you a flight tonight or first thing tomorrow." I plopped into the upholstered chair next to the bed in the tight room. She rose to sit on my lap, placing her arms around my neck.

A pressure in my head exacerbated spinning snippets of images: Maurice's superiority, Sandrine's doe eyes, Brooks White's grin, and Yossi Farber's antagonism, all waiting for me.

"Look, there's something strange happening around the artifacts, the auction. Maybe someone wants them very badly and they think I know something, although I can't imagine what, except I believe they're authentic. And so did Maurice."

"Do I have to worry?"

"I don't think so, but when I went back to the Pierre, someone had been in our room."

"What? Did they take anything?" Sandrine's body turned rigid. "This gives me chicken bumps. I do not like someone looking through my things."

"Nothing's missing. Just be aware."

"I am not afraid. I do not want to leave you," she said, heading for the bathroom.

I finished my coffee and stretched out on the bed.

Sandrine curled up next to me, her forefinger stroking the dented line between my brows.

"My face and tooth hurt. In France we get drunk at lunch for a day like this."

In moments her steady breathing created a rhythm for me, one where I let go of my puzzlement of the past or the present. I shut my eyes and drifted away.

Chapter Eighteen

New York City
September 22, 1993
5 p.m.

Sandrine readied herself with a long shower and a brief application of makeup. She attempted to cover the bruise and cut on her face. A shadow marred her clear skin. A cigarette sat near her purse. She didn't want to light it in the room. In front of a full-length mirror on the back of the closed bathroom door, she pulled her wet hair off her face into a chignon that emphasized her bone structure. I waited in the chair, observing as she transformed herself into a fashion model. In a lacy black strapless brassiere and panties, she lifted the dress we purchased that morning from the bed and slipped into it. Smiling, she walked toward me, stopping to turn around so I could pull up the zipper on the midnight blue silk sheath from Lanvin. I stood up and spun her shoulders to face me.

"*Oh là là.*"

Sandrine beamed a wide smile, her lips a soft pink. "*Merci.*"

She returned to the mirror to attach shiny drop earrings to her lobes. "I am a bit nervous to meet your colleagues who are so educated." She pinned a coral silk flower into the back of her hair, a bold move that added drama to her look.

"Don't be silly. You know as much as most of them. Most academics are very narrow in their knowledge. They're good at one topic but can hardly hold a conversation about anything else." I hesitated.

"I don't mean to say they're not smart. Some are brilliant. But many aren't well rounded. They can't talk about anything except their subject matter. And they do seek to intimidate."

I turned on the television to a local news station, muting the sound, finished dressing and turned up my collar to drape a bowtie around my neck. I softened. "You handle yourself very well. Just be charming. And, by the way, you look beautiful. How's the tooth?"

Sandrine rotated away from the mirror to face me. "I am fine. The two ibuprofen did the trick, as you say.

"But I have a more important question: Why do you have so much opposition to these pieces that are up for auction? They are authentic, no?"

Pulling at the studs that were not cooperating on my tuxedo shirt, my voice sounded far away as I grappled with them, my chin tucked. "I believe they are. Keep in mind I haven't seen them yet, but from everything I've heard and read, they're an extraordinary discovery."

I glanced in the full-length mirror attached to the bathroom door and saw a Chinese face fill the TV screen in the reflection. I dove for the remote I had tossed on the bed, my thumb anxious for sound. I caught the end of an interview.

"So how do you know they are real?" Sandrine leaned in behind me to examine her cheek from a few angles.

". . . to see these priceless objects. Wen Yee, Chinese entrepreneur of the emerging capitalism, is here to bid on them, along with celebrities, heads of government and biblical aficionados. Apparently, the recent international incident involving the ship Yinhe—or Galaxy—did not keep his contingency home. And now, for the weather. . . ."

I exhaled, reaching for the remote. The Chinese had their hand in everything.

"The factors involved for authenticating a piece have to pass three tests. First, there's provenance." I looked down at my shirt. "Damn. These things are too small." I lifted my eyes, making a plea for assistance.

"Let me help you." She stood in front of me. I inhaled her perfume, the same one that enticed me in her shop a little over a month ago. I could feel her breath as she worked smaller fingers through the button holes.

"What's provenance?"

"The paper trail, where the objects came from, how they showed up at particular locations. These artifacts passed through many hands once they were brought back to Rome after the defeat of the Jews. My research leads me to believe these artifacts were the spoils of war, passed and hidden many times, starting with the barbarians. Then the Vandals took them, an Eastern Germanic tribe from the third century, and established themselves in Africa, perpetuating Roman culture. Through war the Byzantines gained control in the fourth through sixth centuries and almost to the Middle Ages when the Persians and Islamists hid them. My theory is they reached safekeeping at the Vatican around 1377 when the popes came back from Avignon."

I felt I had to share more.

"There's a Princeton scandal that involved their curator, the Cultural Ministry of Italy and wealthy patrons who made purchases of sold or donated artifacts from other museums that lasted ten years. Then the Getty Museum's former curator, who shuttled all over the world from New York to Paris to Switzerland, was in a five-year trial with the Italian government when she was accused of acquiring pieces through nefarious channels to make it a world-class institute."

"This sounds like a good job for me," Sandrine teased.

"Trust me. You don't want it. Five years is a long time to be in the company of aggressive attorneys. The curator's downfall was that she accepted Greek, Roman and Etruscan masterworks collected by a few wealthy patrons of the arts."

"Who were they?" asked Sandrine, her expression that of a child listening to a storyteller.

"Affluent collectors. No one took responsibility. The Italians stopped the case because the statute of limitations ran out."

"So the curator lady is free?" She stepped back to admire her success with the studs.

"Yes. But who knows how much she knew about the origins of pieces when she was purchasing them for the museum. If someone told her it had been in their Lake Como villa for a few centuries, who's checking? Or, even in another case, who knew what they were acquiring? Hey, there are a lot of phonies out there, especially in the art and academic worlds.

Healthy skepticism is good."

"Are you skeptical about me?" she asked, leaning forward to assist with my bowtie.

I met her eyes. "No. I think you are exactly who you say you are."

She placed her arms around my neck. "You are my truth."

I turned away. After the conference I needed to consider where this was going. And share more about my mother, what she meant to me, how she surprised me on a few counts.

Sandrine sat on the bed watching me, listening, her heels tipped on their sides. "Next time I make you a custom tuxedo shirt from the shop from the best soft cotton."

"I'll take it," I said, bending back starched cuffs. I approached her to help with my cuff links.

She looked at my watch, a TAG Heuer similar to what many of my students wore.

"I think we will be a little late, Michael."

"Okay, I'm almost ready. Besides, it's good to be fashionably late, whatever that is."

"I have one more question. How do you know your treasures are legitimate? I do not want you to get into trouble."

I smiled at her naiveté. "In this case we have provenance for the God's Gold items because they're from the catacombs of the Vatican, and even though they're not adjudicating it, they're not repudiating it either. A Vatican official signed off on it and the pope had no comment. So I'd say that's a pass." I pulled braces over my shoulders and adjusted my shirt, a bit unsure she grasped the explanation.

"But who believes this?"

"There's a second test they have to pass. It's called connoisseurship, the opinion of experts. We've had some discrepancies, particularly with Yossi Farber's team, but on the whole, these artifacts have passed that test too. Every top archaeologist from Athens to Stanford has weighed in, especially after the carbon dating. I'm not sure there's not some type of conspiracy with Farber and the Israelis and even the Chinese to discredit the findings, but the science is sound after years of examination."

Sandrine got up, slipped on her shoes and faced the mirror, adding gloss to her bottom lip with her pinkie. She wiped it on a tissue and returned to me, pulling at my shirt sleeves, rotating the cuffs to show off gold links. "*Magnifique.*"

"Am I boring you?" I asked, placing my hands on her waist.

"No, I am very interested. I ask the questions." She paused and took a deep breath. "I want you to be proud of me."

I kissed her nose, stepped back and shrugged on my jacket, taking her in. Breathtaking. Every man in the room will notice her. So much for keeping a low profile.

I got back on topic as she flicked off imaginary lint on my shoulders, pulling at my lapels.

"Finally, science has to come into play. In this case the carbon dating has been repeated numerous times. It proves these are from AD 50 to 80. I expect there to be some controversy brought up at the auction, but I can't see how anyone can make a case that these aren't legitimate."

I held her hand to stand in front of the mirror for a moment of admiration. "Let's go, kiddo."

"Kiddo? This is something good?"

I held the door for her before it slammed behind us.

In the cab ride to the Judaica Cultural Museum, Sandrine stared out the window. "New York is spectacular at night. So many lights, sounds, pretty people."

I reached for her hand. "Gritty too." My apprehension about recent events ransacked my mood—Maurice's death, my beeper, the rifled room, Sandrine's black eye. I glanced at the cheek that she skillfully covered with makeup. Maybe it was nothing. But something bubbled inside of me.

Chapter Nineteen

New York City
September 22, 1993
7 p.m.

After passing through security doors at the Judaica Cultural Museum, a renovated mansion built by a successful German immigrant in the 1880s, guards checked Sandrine's clutch and the contents of my pockets. Similar to airport screenings since the bomb placed on Pan Am Flight 103 in 1988, security had tightened up. The bombing last year in Buenos Aires of its Jewish community center had all its organizations on alert. We lost part of the elegance of the evening.

"Michael, this is necessary?" I knew it was and ignored her question. A phalanx of uniformed and plainclothes officers observed facial expressions, body language and demeanor, lessons learned from the Israelis after all the airplane hijackings in the eighties.

I whispered to Sandrine as we gathered our belongings. "I wouldn't be surprised if half the guests are law enforcement. Keep your eye out for women with gun holsters in their arm pits." I decided not to mention the World Trade Center truck bombing last February in the public parking garage underneath the North Tower that killed six people and injured more than a thousand.

"Really?"Sandrine stroked a few loose tendrils into her chignon.

I held her arm as we gave our names to two guards at a desk.

"Would I kid you?" She smirked at me.

Two men standing near the entrance admired her as she glided by.

We entered a museum-sized room with decorative high ceilings, a buzz of voices, the clink of glasses and the sparkle of diamonds. Overwhelmed at the sight of so many people and the enormous bullet-proof glass cases displaying archaeological treasures, we paused near a wall to take it all in with an inhaled breath.

The sounds of a string quartet playing classical music floated on top of conversations. The stage lined with American and Israeli flags stood at one end, a lone microphone in the center.

A tuxedoed waiter passed with champagne flutes on an ornate silver tray. He offered us one with a cocktail napkin. I tipped my glass toward Sandrine's.

"To our adventures," I said, lifting the liquid higher. As I sipped I observed cameras near the ceiling sweeping the room.

"*Oh là là.* This is Moët. I know my champagne from the Loire region."

Brooks White caught my eye across the room, holding up his glass as a greeting. Damn. I was not in the mood to talk to him, especially at a social event.

Sandrine was quiet, enjoying her champagne, staring at the display cases staggered throughout the room, the pinpoint spotlights focused on each rare object.

Heather, Dr. Sommerstein's assistant, approached us. Dressed in black, wearing worn cowboy boots and a multicolored scarf, her unruly hair was slicked into a ponytail. A pinpoint nose diamond sparkled as she greeted us warmly.

"Boy, you two cleaned up great," Heather said, touching Sandrine's arm, examining her face. "Feel okay? You look good."

"Yes, thank you. I am well." I observed Sandrine's self-conscious discomfort with reference to the incident. Maybe she thought she hadn't covered the bruise with enough makeup.

Sandrine searched my face. "Can you see it?"

I examined her by tilting her chin toward me into the light. "No, it's fine."

"Boy, will I be glad when this is over," a woman said, sidling next to Heather.

Heather introduced her partner. "Marianna Hodges. Michael Saunders and Sandrine–I'm sorry. I don't know your last name."

"Agneau."

Marianna, a wispy blond, offered, "That's lamb in French, right?" She elbowed Heather. "I told you I took French in high school."

"Yes. And my first name means protector of men."

She gave me a sly look. Ironic since I was supposed to be protecting her. So far I hadn't done a stellar job.

Heather and Marianna looked at her with admiration.

"The boss is on the other side of the room. He'd like to introduce you to some people when you make your way over there. Don't miss the chopped liver on the buffet table." Heather addressed Sandrine. "The very best fake pâté New York has to offer. No shrimp. Strictly kosher at this event."

I perused the room with a new awareness. Indeed, there were skull caps on a few men as well as some Orthodox in their black hats and long somber coats. However, most of the crowd was well dressed, international and academic. Thank you, Ma, for preparing me for anything.

"Keep your eye out for celebrities. I hear Annette Bening and Warren Beatty might show," said Heather.

Marianna remarked, "Oh, I'd love to see them. She's my heroine."

"Enjoy yourselves. The Prof wants me to greet the academics participating in the symposium tomorrow. But don't leave until they do the official opening from the stage," Heather reminded us as she trailed off with Marianna, looping their arms together.

We wandered around the perimeter of the room to examine the rare auction items. Years of excavated treasures were displayed—bullae, ostraca and other pottery from the Holy Land. Explanatory plaques on the walls gave more information.

"In 1870 French diplomat, scholar and archaeologist Charles Clermont-Ganneau excavated a partially destroyed tomb high on a cliff overlooking the Kidron Valley and the City of David in Jerusalem. Without the ability to read the inscription over the door, he chiseled it out of the rock and sent it to the British Museum where it resides today."

"See? A Frenchman did a good thing," said Sandrine turning to me.

I touched the small of her back. "He did. He inspired many more excavations of the site and that's what we're looking at tonight, most from the late eighth or early seventh centuries BCE."

"You mean BC, before Christ?"

"Yes, however, the Israelis and many archaeologists use BCE, before the Common Era." The explanation tugged at me with a new realization. I added, "In this area of biblical study the Israelis rule. Most of us have had to learn the Bible and some ancient Hebrew."

"This is fascinating. I have always been drawn to this although I don't know much about Bible studies. A Catholic school education is narrow. It's more about discipline and staying away from boys." She smiled at me. In her heels she was almost eye level.

I leaned toward her. It wasn't a place for a kiss. We meandered through the cases stopping to view displays of pottery, juglets, *shekel* weights, more ostraca, ancient notepaper and bullae, the clay impressions with Hebrew inscriptions used to seal documents.

"What are ostraca?" asked Sandrine pointing into a case. "It looks like broken pieces of pottery to me."

I was ever the teacher with a willing student. "They are pieces of pottery with writing on them. In ancient Greece the citizens wrote the name of the person on a pottery shard to ostracize them. This one was discovered by an Israeli archaeologist from Hebrew University. He believes this shard dates to the time of King David from the Old Testament, about 3,000 years ago. Carbon dating has it at about one thousand years before the Dead Sea Scrolls." I read the inscription. "'As yet undeciphered, some words, such as *king*, *slave* and *judge* have been translated. Not for sale.'"

"I don't understand how someone could gather all of this. It is so vast. And now they sell it. Why?"

"This one is for display only, but it could help an archaeologist or museum raise money for the next dig. Other items are sold because some want to share them with the world. Still others are greedy. There's a lot of competition as to who has the best collection. Prestige is a commodity in the business of archaeology."

"Did you ever think to go to the museum side?" She glanced around. "It has some glamour."

I laughed, straightening my bow tie. "So you don't think I'm living a glamorous life after seeing my New Haven apartment?"

"Of course. But this has so many facets—professors plus elegance with excitement. What makes this so special," she said, glancing at photographers taking pictures, "is that it seems as if the whole world is watching."

"This collection is significant because they can trace the inscriptions and names back to Isaiah in the Bible. It's been collected over eons, switching hands, being hidden, looted, sold again. Each piece is a story. People have died for it. Like this British archaeologist." I pointed to an explanation of jug handles with writing on them as we stopped in front of a display.

"'In 1938 J. L. Starkey was murdered by Arab marauders on his way to the dedication of the Palestine Archaeological Museum in Jerusalem, now known as the Rockefeller Museum.'"

"This is so fascinating. Not just the objects. But to be here with the people who discovered them. Thank you, Michael, for bringing me."

I squeezed her hand, embarrassed at her adoration. People acknowledged us as we sauntered by, making our way to the other side of the room, winding through the crowd of accomplished academics, city officials, dignitaries in sashes, socialites wearing their coveted jewels and small knots of people crowded around Hollywood collectors. A group of Asian men and a tall exotic woman gathered in a corner. The man I had seen on TV stood in the center.

"Michael! I've been looking for you." Dr. Sommerstein reached for my arm to pull me into a small group of men while leaning into Sandrine's ear. "Is everything all right with you?"

She nodded.

"Michael Saunders, the Honorable Yusef ben Doron, the Israeli ambassador. And his lovely lady." Sandrine supplied her name in the awkward moment as they shook hands.

The ambassador, a balding man with a thick silver fringe of hair and a beefy body, responded in unaccented English. "I have heard so much about you and your academic prowess, Professor." He sounded sonorous in the space, enunciating every word with the hint of a broadcaster.

"Thank you. It's an honor, Sir."

Sommerstein interjected, "Ambassador ben Doron is a Yale graduate."

"Really? We are honored to call you an alumnus. May I ask how you found your way there?"

"Of course." He paused to take in Sandrine, his grey eyes focusing on the splash of color in her hair. "My parents made *aliyah* to Israel when I was a teenager. They survived Auschwitz, a rarity. They were originally from Krakow in Poland. I was educated in the states for college and graduate school after my stint in the army." Israelis give their pedigrees based on where their family was during World War II and their military service.

Sommerstein, infused with pride, said, "He should brag. He went on to become a decorated pilot in the Israeli Air Force."

"Everyone serves in the Israeli military, even the beautiful young women." He glimpsed at Sandrine again. "Our *sabras* are among some of the most accomplished in the world. Israel is about defense first. We are small and powerful."

"Ambassador, do you think the God's Gold objects will serve your history, your country?" I asked.

"Well, they will serve a purpose to many; however, with our claim to disputed territory, it adds credibility. After all, we have five thousand years of history to justify our right to a small strip of land. And, I might add, if they are returned to Israel it is a fulfillment of biblical prophecy."

"Is your government bidding on the rare objects?" I set my glass on the tray of a passing waiter.

"I cannot say at this time. We want to see more provenance, authentication. biblical treasures flow in and out of our culture. Pardon my skepticism. I am not at liberty to say."

I surveyed the room and then asked Sommerstein, "Where are they? I thought they might be in a separate area. I'm anxious to see them."

"Security. You have to go through that door over there. They're in another room and they only allow four people in at a time for less than a minute. They hired extra guards, cameras, the works. No one's taking any chances. It took a phalanx of armored cars to get them here. We almost didn't put them on display because of all the issues. I've been working with the NYPD, the FBI, the National Guard, you name it."

Sandrine shifted closer and whispered, "Oh, Michael, we must see them."

"Better get in line," said Sommerstein. "You've got Sharon Stone ahead of you."

"A pleasure to meet you, Ambassador," I said. Sandrine gave a demure smile, lowering her eyelashes.

She held my arm as we made our way to the other side of the vast room where a line formed. "I didn't know Sharon Stone was interested in this."

I shrugged my shoulders. "When you're voted the sexiest woman in Hollywood you can be interested in whatever you want."

Chapter Twenty

New York City
September 22, 1993
8:30 p.m.

We entered the darkened artifact room, ushered in by armed guards. Other personnel surrounded the perimeter. Small pin lights illuminated the greatest treasures to have survived biblical times, the holy instruments of Jewish worship. Observing a sacred quiet for a few moments, each person emitted a gasp as they circled the room to stare into three large glass cases. First, we approached two silver trumpets suspended in midair. Nicked and battered, a testament to their journey through time, they were larger than expected, their patina worn down to a dull shine.

Sandrine placed her hand to her chest with a sigh. I lost my clinician eye and stammered, "Oh, wow. They survived the Romans, the Vandals, the Byzantines . . ."

"Please move along. Do not touch the cases," a guard's steady voice repeated.

We rotated in slow motion to the next display. A gold candelabrum with seven arms, not unlike the menorahs I had seen in homes and museums, displayed itself in elegant simplicity. I saw a woman's reflection across from me through the case. Tears rolled down her face.

"Please do not hold up the line. Others want their turn too." The voice broke my introspection. I slid Sandrine's hand into mine.

"Never in my life do I think I will see something like this, feel so close to God. Thank you, Michael."

The final display showcased the largest artifact, the Table of Divine Presence. I was well acquainted with the statistics. It was twenty inches in height, octagonal in shape and made from gold hammered onto ancient wood. The gold had worn away in some places, but it appeared in good condition considering the eons it had survived.

The borders, decorated with eggs, rope, fruit and precious stones, led the eye to the surface with its grandeur of onyx, emeralds and carbuncles in a meandering design. A rhombus placed in an open network design in the middle sparkled with amber and crystals.

The four stone legs in the shape of lilies were reminiscent of the architect Antoni Gaudi's nature shapes he added to his designs in Barcelona. They bent underneath the table with pointed leaves enticing the viewer. Ivy and grapevines grew out of the stone until they met the top.

I was speechless, overwhelmed, after so many years of studying the artifacts. I inhaled a deep breath, placing my arm around Sandrine's shoulder to guide her out of the room.

As we exited into the glitz of the main room I heard people behind me say, "Ingenious. Incredible. Extraordinary."

"How 'bout another glass of champagne?" I asked Sandrine.

"*Oui, oui.* I have never experienced anything like this in my life. I am breathless."

After we exited the dimly lit room, I scanned the room to get my bearings. My eyes gazed over the small knot of Asian men with the tall, slender woman in a red dress. Ah, the Chinese contingency I've been hearing about, I thought. The man in the center is the face I saw on TV.

A man in a rumpled tuxedo approached us. Unshaven, with a motley attempt to grow a goatee, his unruly hair sparked around his head.

"Well, well, well, don't you look spiffy tonight? I suppose I'll have to introduce myself to your stunning companion." He reached out his hand toward Sandrine with unattended fingernails. "Yossi. Yossi Farber, archaeologist extraordinaire and academic nemesis to your friend here."

I stiffened as Sandrine, a bit confused, propelled herself to make room. Yossi stepped closer, the aroma of cigarettes wafting around him.

"Yossi. Can't say that it's good to see you. I see you overreached in your wardrobe for tonight." I perused his unpressed shirt, ill-fitting collar and brown shoes.

I turned to Sandrine. "Yossi is very bright and accomplished." I waited a beat. "Just ask him."

My sarcastic humor amused her. She peeled away to peer at another exhibit piece and inspect the buffet table in the awkward silence.

Yossi moved closer to me and gritted his teeth before speaking. "Yes, well, the shallowness of your comment is only matched by my astute humor. The reality is you're attaching yourself and your reputation to artifacts that are not authentic."

"I'm not going to get into a dispute with you here. Save it for the symposium. The facts are there. I don't have to prove anything."

I shifted my eyes to look for Sandrine, easy to spot with the coral flower in her hair. As she read another of the explanations attached to the wall, a man moved over next to her.

"Yes, it would be to your advantage to promote the authenticity and get cozy with a wealthy buyer, wouldn't it? Even a foreign government." Yossi raised his salt-and-pepper eyebrows with a knowing look.

Infuriated, I opened my mouth to say something inappropriate, but stopped myself. Yossi Farber, known for being antagonistic, creating challenges where there were none and getting in the last word, folded his arms across his chest.

In a low voice I said, "You are not going to insinuate me into an altercation on a night like this. I'll see you at the symposium. Be prepared for the facts."

"Ha! You, my friend, are going to lose. We have evidence the authentication is bogus. Glad I haven't staked my reputation on it. A damaged academic can't publish papers or do keynotes. And, just in case you think I'm jealous, check out the next issue of *Archaeology Journal*. I've got the lead article."

A nagging uneasiness hunkered down on me. What did Yossi mean about wealthy buyers and foreign governments? Did he know about Brooks White's mother? Israelis? Chinese? What does Sommerstein know? I wandered over to Sandrine, glaring at the man vying for her attention.

I whispered, "I'm going to be near the exhibit of small sculptures." I wandered away sipping my champagne, brooding.

"May-may I have your attention please?" A female voice broke through the buzz of murmuring in the room. The music ceased with a grand finale and a flourishing of bows. A slim woman in a black dress standing behind a microphone on stage repeated her request two more times before the room turned its attention to the riser. Nervous, she slapped a small piece of paper against her thigh. A small crowd gathered near the front of the makeshift stage, a few sipping champagne.

"Thank you all for being here tonight. My name is Bernita Goodman. I'm the curator of the Judaica Cultural Museum and the exhibit you're viewing tonight." The crowd applauded with enthusiasm. A few yelps were heard from the back. "Thank you. It has been years in the making and I probably have more than a few grey hairs to prove it."

A group of younger people off to the side held up their champagne glasses. One shouted, "Bernita is boss," a comment greeted with a few laughs.

Bernita leaned in sideways to the microphone to acknowledge her fans. "My staff. I also want to thank the Dobbins Quartet for our lovely musical interlude this evening." They stood, instruments in hand, taking small bows.

She righted herself to look out at the crowd. "Obviously one doesn't bring objects like these to the public without years of preparation and the enormous support of many people, including benefactors who have sponsored and underwritten this evening. Mrs. Luisa Phillips White, where are you?" A white gloved hand, the wrist wrapped in a cuff of sparkling jewels, appeared. I stretched to see a petite woman swallowed by the crowd.

"Thank you, Mrs. White, for your generosity."

More clapping. This part could be boring.

"I want to take a few minutes to acknowledge our honored guests. Ambassador Yusef ben Doron from Israel, Mayor David Dinkins of New York City, the most extraordinary city in the world, and Professor Seymour Sommerstein, department chair of Roscom Liberal Arts College.

This would not have been possible without them." Their hands waved as they turned to greet the crowd.

"There are dozens of others who worked on this project. I cannot recognize all of them, but you know who you are. I speak for the board, its trustees, the dignitaries attending tonight and the city of New York. Welcome. Thank you from the bottom of my heart. And now, a few words from President of the Board of the Judaica Cultural Museum, Mr. Jonah Goldstein." Bernita stepped off the riser and walked toward her staff who were buzzing with excitement in the corner.

A portly gentleman took the microphone, adjusting its height. "Thank you all for coming this evening and making this extraordinary event happen. The museum is honored to have been one of the sponsors.

"Most of you know there are many coveting these rare artifacts. We are grateful to have been in their company for a short space in the eons of time they have been on this earth. I want to share the appreciation of the board that tonight's fundraiser will assist the museum in bringing in more exhibits like this that share our cultural history. The exhibition will be here until the twenty-fourth, but sadly, the pieces of God's Gold will be leaving us shortly for Shropshire Auction House. And new owners."

I edged next to Sandrine who hovered near the food. "Ready to go soon? Big day tomorrow. Maybe we can have brunch without damaging a tooth and read the *New York Times* in the park."

She smiled.

"Michael, you must taste the *pâté*. Almost as good as my *maman's*." She picked up a piece and put it in front of my mouth. I leaned in to taste the elegant spread on a piece of bread.

She pointed to a tiny beetroot macaroon on her plate. "*Délicieux*. You must try it," she said, munching on the *amuse bouche*. Her voice rose, "Look at the desserts. I cannot leave until I taste the foie-gras crème brûlée with pink grapefruit, and the profiteroles with whipped vanilla cream drizzled with Tainori chocolate sauce and fresh mint. I ask the caterer many questions, but most important she tells me these are milk substitutes so it can be kosher. She trained at the *Institut Supérieur de Gestion* in Paris. This haute cuisine I did not expect."

With a sweet tooth larger than my appetite, I wondered where she put it all. Thank God I have her to distract and delight me. I wandered away.

A nagging uneasiness slid down my spine. I can't get a vision of the larger picture. Was Maurice's death an accident? What about my beeper? Is Yossi a threat or just a pain in the ass? What did Yossi mean about wealthy buyers and foreign governments? Does he know about Brooks White's mother? There's an undercurrent I can't identify. I'm a player without a rule book. Or maybe it all doesn't add up to a damn thing. What I can't figure out is–

A hand traveled across my back. "Why so glum?" Brooks White positioned himself in front of me. "Glad to see you here and not holed up in your room preparing for the symposium."

"Oh, Brooks. Well, some of us who aren't legacies are bright enough to only need a short amount of prep time."

Brooks ignored my comment, motioning with his chin to where Sandrine was standing. "I see you brought your lovely French cup–companion with you."

I reached out to shake Brooks's hand pulling him forward. In a low tone with a smile on my face, I murmured, "You sexist bastard. Women are not cupcakes."

"Don't tell me. You're the one who brought the date with a shiner," responded Brooks, raising his eyebrows. "Testy, aren't we?"

Brooks stepped aside to include a petite angular woman dressed in an ivory beaded cocktail gown with a small fur wrapped around her shoulders. "I'd like you to meet my mother, Luisa Phillips White."

Mrs. White extended her gloved hand to me with a firm shake. The stacked diamond cuffs encircling her wrists shimmered in the light. Compact with regal bearing, she appeared to be in her seventies, silver hair coiffed into a modified French twist. Around an elongated nose her face was mostly pale and unlined, a slash of pink lipstick emphasizing her uneven, thin lips. With incisive blue eyes that were similar to her son's–intense, focused and steely, they communicated, "I suffer no fools." She wasn't beautiful with her irregular features, but she made an elegant statement. She held a jeweled evening bag in her hand.

"Brooks has told me about you." She squinted at her son standing next to her, his hands crossed in front of him. "As well as some of his other Yale compatriots. My late husband and I were quite proud when he chose academia. We're horse-and-mill people so an indoor activity is a shift from our interests. If the goal isn't financial reward, why not contribute to the young minds of America?" Her voice rattled with the opinionated pronunciations of old money.

"It is my pleasure to meet you."

"I understand you are delivering the keynote after that terrible tragedy."

"I am. Will you be there?"

"I will not. I am saving myself for the auction the next day. I have great interest in the God's Gold items. It is a rare occasion that allows the public to bid on such treasures. I was quite impressed viewing them this evening with the drama of display and lighting, although I have seen them before."

Damn. How did she witness them and I never laid eyes on them until tonight? "So may I be so bold to ask how you arranged that? Most archaeologists haven't examined them because of security issues."

"Well, I do have a few connections."

Mrs. White must have observed my frustrated expression.

"I don't mean to be flip, but as the sponsor of this evening, I have been intimately involved with bringing them to the States. I saw them the first time in France. I admit there's been quite a bit of subterfuge surrounding them. In reality we all know they arrived on the open market through releases from the Vatican. It is my understanding the pope himself had to sign off on them." She seemed self-satisfied with her unknown sources.

"So then you know where they've been. I'm amazed some clever reporter hasn't tracked their trail," I said.

"Darling, if I haven't shared what I know with Brooksie here, I doubt I would spill the proverbial beans with you." Disappointed, I looked at Brooks, seemingly chastened, standing next to his mother.

And then, unexpectedly, she offered, "What I can tell you is that a priest has stated he witnessed some of the Temple relics in a vault four stories under the west wing of the Vatican."

"How did he get access?" I asked, moving a step closer. This is odd. She has more information than anyone else I've spoken to.

"I'm not telling you anything that is not common knowledge. Visiting US priests are housed in the west wing. Let's face it. There have been things going on in the Vatican for centuries that we know nothing about. I have made a study of the Catholic Church."

"And your conclusion, Mrs. White?" I love amateurs with opinions.

"The pope is a fence and the Vatican is filled with ill-gotten gains stolen from cultures around the world." She stopped herself. "Especially the Jews."

Brooks stood immobile, mortified.

Her frankness surprised me. But then again, when you have millions of dollars behind you, you can say whatever you want. To anyone. At anytime.

"So may I assume you are a fan of the Chosen People?"

"I wouldn't say that. I do have enormous respect for the persecution they have suffered and their survival skills through the centuries, but personally, no, I am not fond of them."

Appalled by her comment, I shifted my stance. And I'm the one who's supposed to be *schmoozing* her? My best bet is to change the subject.

She continued, a small package of opinions and prejudices. "I think the Israelis are very smart with a right to defend their land, but I have reservations about the way they do business."

Uh-oh. I'd better get her off this topic. "May I ask if you will be bidding?"

"Professor Saunders, I like bold men. Yes, as you can see I have an avid interest in the stars of the show. I have been anticipating their arrival on the open market for many years."

"Would they be for your private collection or are you bidding for an as-of-yet unknown buyer?"

With a coquettish smile, she said, "My, you are strident. As you know, it is a competitive market. The Chinese, Saudis, Israelis, world-class museums, governments around the world, educational institutions and your Dr. Sommerstein have been breathing down my aristocratic neck to find out my intentions."

Her confidence was unnerving, but I regained my footing.

Brooks gazed toward Sandrine, standing alone devouring another dessert.

"Mrs. White, I don't have to remind you of the emotional value of God's Gold besides the historical significance. I'm sure you wouldn't want them to be purchased by those who are not willing to share them with the rest of the world."

"Of course not. On the other hand, my responsibility is to my foundation and heirs. Brooks? I'm feeling fatigued. I think it's time to go."

Brooks reached into his pocket for a small phone and dialed a number. "Ernest, bring the car around."

"Hey, where'd you get that?" I asked, ruminating about my beeper.

"Oh, latest Nokia technology. Good for emergencies. And to keep in touch with Mother." Luisa White appeared pleased. "Holds up to ninety-nine contacts."

"May I see it?"

Brooks passed the phone to me. I clicked it open, turned it over, shut the device and pretended to put it in my jacket pocket. I'd hadn't seen anything this efficient. I only knew a few people who bothered with those clunky devices attached in their cars.

"Hey, these cell phones are running sixteen hundred dollars. Get your own—if you're not too wrapped up in Mesopotamia," Brooks smirked at me.

"Brooks! We never quote the price of anything. Ever," said his mother in a hoarse whisper.

Brooks turned away.

"It was a pleasure to meet you, Mr. Saunders. I'm sure our paths will cross again."

I walked over to Sandrine, deflated. She held out a spoon for me to taste what she was sampling. "Was that Brooks's mother? She carries a Judith Leiber Swarovski-encrusted minaudière in her hand."

"And this has significance because?"

"Michael! The one-of-a-kind minaudiéres are worth thousands. Women covet them all over the world. Carrying one is not only a status symbol; it is a work of art. All your first ladies hold them when the president makes their inauguration."

"I had no idea. How do you know this?" I asked, once again enchanted by my Paris lamb. I disposed of her empty plate and placed it on a waiter's tray.

"You forget I am a Parisian in the fashion business."

I kissed her lightly on the cheek.

Chapter Twenty One

New York City
September 22, 1993
11 p.m.

Back at the hotel I peeled out of my clothes while Sandrine retreated to the bathroom. Tonight created more tension for me. Yossi, Brooks, his mother, a Chinese entourage—all breezed by me. I had that creepy feeling everybody knew something I didn't.

I propped up against the headboard on the bed and turned on the TV. A blonde woman was reading the local news. After a few stories about mayhem on the streets and charitable needs, she turned to the next story.

"Dignitaries from across the globe gathered tonight for a view of biblical artifacts at the Judaica Cultural Museum to be auctioned at Shropshire's this week. Rumored to be worth close to a billion dollars, security was tight. A Chinese delegation headed by Wen Yee, an industrialist of the new pioneer capitalism . . ."

A photo of the man I saw tonight flashed on the screen.

". . . is in town to bid on the rare objects."

A brief clip of the Chinese arriving at the museum, lights popping and a view of a red dress splashed in front of the camera. A microphone was shoved at them by an aggressive reporter. Two of the larger men with Wen Yee stepped out to interfere, allowing him to enter the doors with ease.

As a picture of the three God's Gold items took up the screen, the newscaster read, "These rare objects are coveted by many across the world.

We'll keep an eye on this story and let you know who goes home with the prize. And now to our great fall weather. . . ."

I clicked the remote to turn off the TV as Sandrine emerged from the bathroom, her face clean of makeup, hair falling around her shoulders, steam following her. Her robe fell open to reveal she was naked underneath.

"I took another shower to get rid of hairspray, makeup and perfume. Now it is just me and my black eye."

"It doesn't look so bad."

She turned to the dresser to comb out her hair.

"The Chinese made the news tonight. They showed the delegation we saw at the event."

She turned toward me. "I wonder why they get so much publicity."

"I think it's a big deal that they're here. It's only been a little over a year since they loosened restrictions on business transactions. They're making billionaires over there almost overnight, but I'm not sure how legal it all is."

"Tell me something else," said Sandrine, weary from a long day.

I picked up a folder on the bed filled with information I put together before I left New Haven a few days ago. While Sandrine napped from jet lag, I met with my favorite librarian at Yale. I spent a few hours going through microfiche files of old newspaper articles and copying them. I was curious after my encounter with Brooks. I didn't find much on him, but his mother spawned interest from the press.

I read aloud as Sandrine curled up next to me.

"'Luisa Phillips White, part of a turn-of-the-century oil family in Tulsa, Oklahoma, comes from "black gold blue bloods," and is financed by East Coast mills and manufacturing.'"

I read about her foundation and donations to conservative causes. One of the articles revealed a society photo of her in a younger incarnation wearing a tiara on a yacht.

"Sandrine, do you know who the Vanderbilts are?"

"They are rich, right?"

"Well, they were. They've lost most of their money. The last of the Vanderbilts' ten great mansions in New York was torn down in '73. They have a university left but that's about it. Someone in the White family knows how to preserve their fortune."

"What does it say about Brooks's *maman*? Her cuff bracelets were real diamonds."

"His great-grandfather was a US congressman from Oklahoma who built a fifty-five-room mansion with a leather elevator. It's in a small town. Supposed to be one of America's castles built in the Italian Renaissance style." I looked at her lying on her side, hand under her cheek. "You thought only Europeans had old money?"

"We have chateaus in France, but the people owning them? How you say—bankrupt? We don't have so many rich people. Most lost everything in the wars, taxes and from our laws. Or maybe bad management. Who knows? All gone. Now they open on the weekends for the tourists to walk down drafty hallways. What else about Madame Brooks?"

"'The castle is filled with sculptures of jackals, coyotes, gargoyles and owls.'"

"Howls? What is this?"

"Come here and I'll tell you." I held her arm as she scrunched toward me. "It's a large bird that goes, 'who, who.'"

She play-slapped my chest, cuddling into me to see what I was reading.

"How do they get to have so much money?"

"Self-made men with a talent for acquisitions. Entrepreneurship. Harvard educations. Family started with oil then went into mills and manufacturing. They reside in an insular community with private clubs where they meet other wealthy people. Brooks and his mama are ranked on the Forbes list as the eighty-fifth richest family."

"I am not interested so much in a rich man. I like a smart one better." She grabbed the folder and papers out of my hands, tossed them off the side of the bed, threw her leg over my lap and began to make swirling motions on my chest with her hands. I closed my eyes in arousal.

I knew Brooks came from money. I just had no idea how much.

Chapter Twenty Two

Miami, Florida
June 17, 1993

I thought my mother would never get it out. I can't say I wasn't getting depressed. This was a long unwind. Yes, I loved her, but the exit was painful on so many levels. What could be so terrible to keep locked inside for decades? I was losing patience, my foot rattling against the silver metal chair in the cloistered hospital room.

"My mother and I lost our jobs when the troops came home. My mother had bad varicose veins so she couldn't stand on her feet much. Even though we had a small army pension, it wasn't enough. The war left my mother and I bereft.

"When your dad offered to marry me, I wasn't madly in love, but he was going someplace. Big, good-looking guy with a cleft chin like Kirk Douglas and a job, and me without prospects. My mother said to do it even though there were problems."

"What kind of problems?" I hesitated a moment. "Were you pregnant?"

"Heavens, no. That was a fate worse than death. If a girl got pregnant and she wasn't married, she had to give the baby up for adoption or get an illegal abortion in Harlem."

"So what was the problem?"

"My last name was Epstein."

She paused while I digested that information. The words hung in the room and collapsed on the floor.

"You're Jewish?"

"Yes."

It hadn't taken me but a minute to make the connection between a last name ending in *-stein* and its ethnicity.

I hadn't had much contact with Jews until I got to college where they were segregated into their own fraternities. A beautiful girl named Rebecca Cohen was in my poli-sci class. I mentioned to my big brother that I wanted to invite her to one of our parties. I'll never forget his response.

"Stick to your own kind," he said to me.

"Why didn't you tell me I'm Jewish?" I sat back in the chair, my mind racing.

"You're half. Jewish law says if the mother's Jewish, the children are too. I even had you circumcised. That was an issue for Gentiles after the war."

In a college history class I learned about the Holocaust and what they did to the Jews. The Nazis found Jewish men by pulling down their pants.

"Why didn't you tell me before now?" Anger made my voice rise.

"Shh. Because Byron didn't want me to." She played with a ribbon on her nightgown.

I stood up, the chair falling back.

"You kept a secret all these years? What kind of a person does that? I missed knowing my grandmother."

My fury was palpable. I felt cheated, shorted, like a child abandoned in a dark alley. I headed toward the door, a sharp jab of a headache pulsing at my right temple. I had been plagued with migraines for years. This was going to be a doozy.

"Michael, let me explain. You don't understand the times." Her hand reached toward me, the rings loose because she had gotten so thin from treatments.

"In the fifties, even the early sixties, there was a lot of antisemitism."

"Who was antisemitic?"

"Everyone. When the war started in '39, they couldn't even get the Wagner-Rogers Bill passed to let German-Jewish orphans into this country outside the quota system. I'll never forget the quote from Laura Delano, President Roosevelt's cousin. 'Twenty thousand charming children will all too soon turn into twenty thousand ugly adults.'"

"What does that have to do with me?" I wanted to walk out, but it was my opportunity to find out more. I righted the chair and sat down, a scowl passing across my face. I folded my arms across my chest in anticipation of her explanation.

"After the war, people felt guilty they hadn't cared about six million murdered. Roosevelt knew about the camps and refused to bomb them. I'd go to the movies and come home hysterical from the newsreels. President Eisenhower made the Germans go into the concentration camps and clean up the bodies. They took photos so no one could say it didn't happen. It didn't matter. Soon it was all swept away. Americans wanted to move on."

"Wait. Did you have family in Europe?"

"Maybe. I don't know. My dad–your grandfather–died in Normandy trying to storm the beach. He was buried there, a Jewish star marks his grave. The army sent us a picture. I was a teenager and my mother was left alone with two daughters to raise. The army didn't give you much if you lost a spouse."

"I have an aunt?"

"Yes. Unfortunately she's passed too, at a young age from this terrible disease. Now they're learning about the BRCA gene that plagues Jewish women of Eastern European descent, but in those days there was no information. You just suffered and died without fanfare while people whispered around you about the big 'C.'"

"So get back to the story." I got up to lean in the doorway, still angry, but not willing to leave now that she was talking. It was an outpouring that had been locked up for decades, a cleansing of the soul. I wondered if I had cousins, but it wasn't time to ask.

She began to cry and reached for more tissues, patting her eyes and nose. "I didn't want to marry out of my faith, but we were poor and your father pursued me. My mother said to do it even though it would be a *shanda* for the family. She didn't want anyone to know."

"What's a shanda?"

"A shame. Jews were always self-conscious in front of Gentiles. We didn't want to do anything that would embarrass ourselves or that would reflect on our people. We felt like guests in this country and didn't want to provoke our hosts."

"What do you mean?" It's not that I hadn't heard of antisemitism before. It's just that I had never thought of myself as a possible recipient of someone else's prejudice.

"Anything that happened that became part of the public manifesto raised the question, 'Is it good or bad for the Jews?' We didn't want to do anything to bring attention to ourselves. When Bess Myerson won Miss America in 1946 that was thought by many as our reward. Now we were supposed to be quiet.

"I was young, scared, without any college and a successful man wanted my attention. What else did I have? He was going someplace with his career. What did I know except I wanted a comfortable life and to help my momma?"

"So you married. Then what?"

"Well, Jews and Gentiles didn't marry much in those days. We talked about it. He had something to hide too, coming from a poor family. The guys who advanced the corporate ladder came from good backgrounds, wealthy ones with Mayflower ancestors, university credentials and country club connections. Your dad never finished college. He ran out of money and started working at Sears. But he was ambitious. He knew he'd get a promotion from assistant manager to manager someday. Maybe we could move someplace where no one would know us."

"But why did you have to hide?" I eyed her with suspicion. I asked again, "Were you pregnant?"

"Michael!" Her eyes started to water.

"For God's sake, Ma, tell me the truth."

Her hands started to wring the sheets. "I was. I had only missed a month. Maybe too soon to tell, but as soon as I found out he said he'd marry me.

You can't imagine what it was like telling my mother. She cried and cried. It was such a horrible thing in those days. A shanda. I wanted to kill myself."

She paused and closed her eyes. As angry as I was, I wanted to hug her. "I could have gone away and given you up for adoption. A few girls in my high school 'disappeared' to an aunt's house in the country and then came back. But I couldn't bear the thought of not seeing you. Not after six million murdered. Byron was good to me. My dad was gone and he said I could name you after him."

I didn't know what to say. Was I going to judge my own mother for sex before marriage? My God, people bragged about it on TV nowadays and had their babies out of wedlock all the time. It was the secrecy of it that infuriated me. Feelings burst into my head. A migraine started a steady drumbeat. I felt nauseated. I got up to close the blinds.

"Why are you doing that? I like a little of the outside world in the room."

"Ma, I have a headache starting. I feel a little dizzy. The fluorescent lights bother me. Go on." I couldn't allow anything to halt her story.

"Of course there was another alternative. A girlfriend from the store slept with one of the married men and became pregnant. She couldn't tell her family. I knew he wasn't going to leave his wife. It was sordid. I was the one who took her up to Harlem on the bus to get rid of it. I still remember bundling her into a seat next to the window and wrapping a shawl around her shoulders. She leaned on me to get up the steps of her apartment building. I lied to her mother and said she got sick at work. I never wanted to go through that."

A tic started near her left eye. I could see she was agitated with the memory.

I persisted.

"Why couldn't you be who you were? Why the secrecy?"

She answered me, her voice impatient. "Michael, Jews didn't get promoted. Even if they were married to one. There were quotas in colleges, especially the Ivy League, law schools, medical schools. Jews couldn't live in certain neighborhoods. A friend had to get an attorney to buy them a house and then transfer it into their name in the small town where they lived. Clubs, hotels, certain restaurants were restricted. You couldn't just go and do what you wanted."

"So you disappeared into Saunders." I was trying hard to understand my mother's confession, her motivation, the times. I uncrossed my arms and sighed at the subterfuge. Another pulse localized itself on the side of my head with an irreversible pounding.

"Yes. Byron didn't want me to tell anyone I was Jewish because it would hurt his chances for promotion. Only a few girls in the hat department knew my last name. I was panicked at leaving my family behind. But my mother told me to do it after she got over the shock.

"Byron wanted me to marry him and make a life together. He came over with flowers and pulled up a chair so he was knee to knee with my mother in our tiny kitchen. He promised to help support her. I knew she would welcome that. He was so sincere, his six-foot-plus frame crammed into our space. She cried again and gave us her blessing. I reminded her she'd be a grandmother."

"She was happy about that."

I felt a sense of relief that I was here, that my mother hadn't chosen another alternative.

"We went to city hall after work one day and just did it. I felt cheap. Like I had sold myself out. But I didn't have a lot of time to ruminate. My belly was going to get bigger and the world was changing fast.

"Levitt bought 400,000 acres and started building homes in New York. GIs were going back to school. There was opportunity. Byron promised me a house with a yard for you to play in, with swings and a real kitchen. I saw us as a family, like in the ads." She paused to reflect, her lids closing for a moment.

"I don't want you to think I was just some empty head. I was a girl with principles who got caught. I weighed my options and made the best decision I could. Yes, I could have given you up. All I had to do was sign a paper that you could be raised as a Catholic and the church would have taken care of everything. But I couldn't do it after the pope turned a blind eye to the Jews during the war. I wanted my own baby. And Byron wasn't religious. He didn't care as long as I passed as a Gentile. I even had you circumcised in the hospital." She started to cry a little.

"I felt awful about abandoning my faith even though we weren't religious. All Jewish baby boys have a *bris*, a ceremony that signifies the oldest covenant between man and God. I couldn't do the ceremony part, but my father would have wanted it."

"Good thing. Most of the boys in the locker room were circumcised, Jewish or not."

She paused when a tray of food was brought in.

"It reminded me of those stories during the Holocaust where women passed as Gentile if they had blonde hair. My mother's family was from Hungary near Budapest. Everyone had light eyes and hair. A blue-eyed brunette could be a blonde with what was available in every drugstore. I thought about Jews who tried to pass during the war. I did it anyway. All the movie stars were light-haired like Marilyn Monroe, Lana Turner and Kim Novak."

If I walked across the room and hugged her, it would be a fountain of tears so I crossed my arms across my chest again and waited. She sniffled and grabbed a tissue. The pulsing in my head was steady.

"You'll never know the guilt I felt. It wasn't easy keeping a secret but Byron insisted. He promised to give me money to send my mother every month. My sister moved away with her honey and she was alone. If we sent a little she could survive.

"We moved to Florida when he was promoted, joined the country club. I let him fill out all the paperwork about our backgrounds. He's the one who took the *h* off the end of my name. Too biblical he told me. I'd cringe when I'd hear antisemitic comments or jokes making fun of us. I drank a little to ease the pain. So did Byron.

"One time we had his superior from the home office for dinner. I worked for days getting everything ready so it would be perfect. So much was about likeability. Estelle stayed to assist."

"Was I there? I don't remember any important guy coming for dinner."

"No, I don't think so. You were probably at a friend's house." She peered down and adjusted her blanket. When she raised her head, her eyes were teary.

"Look, Michael, this is hard. I haven't thought about it in years."

"What happened?"

"Oh, God. I can't do this."

"Mom, you have to tell me. Was it the dinner?"

"No, no. Everything was fine. In that respect. "

"What?"

"They had a few drinks before dinner in the living room while I got everything ready. When we sat down to dinner, the guy, his tie loosened, was already a little sloshed. I made small talk asking about his wife and family. He was complimentary to Byron about the store. And that's when things shifted. I can recall almost every sentence. We had finished the main course and were eating dessert. I had made a chocolate cake, your favorite, because I knew there would be something left over.

"'Byron, you have no idea what a pleasure it is being down here. Not that crazy about travel but this is a plum job for me.'"

'That so?' Byron leaned back in his chair. 'Our numbers look good compared to the competition?'

"I knew he didn't mean other department stores. He was always gunning the managers against other store managers in different districts." My mother stopped and started to worry the blanket with her fingers.

"'Naw. Just happy to be down here away from the Jews.'

"Byron saw me freeze and leaned in, his expression blank."

"Then what happened?"

"Well, the guy went on about how he wished things were more restricted where he was, how he didn't like Jews. And then he dropped a bomb. He leaned forward and looked around as though someone else was listening besides us.

"'Truth is, Byron, couple of people in our top management have a policy that no Jews get promoted.'

"'And why is that?' I asked. I felt my lip trembling and tried to seem casual, but I was appalled. I'm sure my voice went up a notch."

I didn't want to interrupt her. My mother was repeating the incident as though it was a vision, a movie slowing, hacking through an ancient reel.

"He said, 'Cause we don't want them in the organization. Too difficult to deal with. Always asking for more. Lot of us think we didn't gas enough of them.'

"I couldn't take anymore. I got up and went into the kitchen to serve more coffee. After I cleared the dishes and served the cake, I went back into the dining room and told them I had a sudden headache and had to go to bed. After an apology I disappeared into the bedroom. I heard them talking and laughing until past midnight. When Byron finally came into the bedroom he was furious with me.

"'What's with walking out? Like that's not a signal.'

"'I thought I covered it quite well.' I remember I was sitting up in bed with a magazine, my hair in pin curls. Byron came around to my side of the bed. He'd had quite a few and was pointing his finger at me, his face dark with anger.

"'You signed on for this. There's no going back now. You have to do this. You could have jeopardized everything we've worked for tonight.'

"At first I tried to shrug it off with, 'Men always think women get headaches. It wasn't a big deal. He was too drunk to notice I wasn't there.'

"'No, he isn't an idiot. He knew something was up. I saw the way he raised his eyebrows when you took off. You made him suspicious.'

"'Oh, please. The guy is an avid antisemite who advocated murdering more innocent people.'

"'Yeah, and he's my boss. You almost killed it for me tonight.'

"That's when I started to cry. The tears flowed and my nose ran. I couldn't stop. It was like a wave crashing through my head. I really did get a headache."

"What did Byron do?"

"He brought me tissues, got undressed and fell asleep snoring in minutes. The last thing he said to me was, 'Sara, get a grip. Maybe what he was saying was true. Don't blow it. You like living here? Shopping? Driving a nice car? Next time I'll take him out to dinner alone.'

"But his words stung and I bottomed out with my lack of power. I didn't think about equality like the women do now, but I knew somehow I had lost. It was a damaging turning point. I stayed in bed a few days and then life had to go on. But I knew my husband wasn't on my side. And I knew that it didn't take much to know what people really thought about Jews."

My mother sighed, a signal that this story was over. I walked over and hugged her. We stayed like that for a moment. "That's enough for today. I feel weak."

"Eat your dinner. Will you tell me more tomorrow?" I was finished too.

I needed to take an Excedrin for my migraine and lie down in the dark.

"Oh, I don't know. There's no point in dragging all this up. Maybe."

With that her eyelids lowered. I saw from her steady breathing she was asleep.

Chapter Twenty Three

Miami, Florida
June 18, 1993

My migraine subsided after I swallowed some extra pills I traveled with, but I had spent a sleepless night searching through childhood memories in my head. Oblivious, as most kids are to their environment, I missed the nuances of my parent's relationship. Normal was what everyone strived for in our neighborhood—no avant-garde artists or eccentric professors, only working dads, stay-at-home moms and all of them smoking and drinking.

I returned the next day to hear the rest of my mother's story. It wasn't hard to get her talking again. Once you open a dam the water gushes forth, especially if it's been bottled up in an explosive basin that springs a leak.

"My mother passed away. I didn't know she was that sick. I had never let her know you. She only saw you a few times when you were a baby. I'd clip one of your school pictures and mail it to her, but I was too embarrassed to have her visit. She had a Brooklynese accent, wasn't always well groomed. Someone would know she was Jewish. And, after the incident with Byron's boss, I was terrified someone would find out."

"What happened to your sister?" I could tell she didn't want to answer this question because she shut her eyes for a minute as though she could erase a blackboard.

"My sister stopped speaking to me. We were never close even though she was only two years older than me. As kids I was the younger, prettier sister. She was jealous. When I moved to Florida, she left home too. Her death came as a shock to me. It didn't occur to me that this type of cancer ran in families."

"But how did you live a lie every day?" She didn't like this question. Her voice shifted to a harsh tone, one I rarely heard.

"Listen, I carried it off very well for a long period of time. I was comfortable. If I had stayed in New York I'd be standing on my feet as a salesgirl and you'd be someplace else in a different life. Or not at all. We all make choices. Then we have to live with them. Don't be so quick to judge me. Your life has been a privileged one. Besides, some things wouldn't have changed. This disease still would have wracked our family."

Annoyed at her comment, I didn't express it. I wanted to know the rest of the story. I sat on the bed and held her hand. The truth was exhausting. She looked paler than usual. I patted her hand for a while and then moved to the chair.

"Remember your piano teacher and little Ivy who was sent home from the Halloween party? I was mortified. I told the Rosenbaums what happened when they picked her up. Embarrassing, but they were gracious."

"Why did you say anything at all?"

"Because Ivy would have told them about the incident. Such a sweet girl. I'm sure she'll never forget it."

"Mom, get to the point."

"Anyway, about a month or so later, while you stumbled through your music lesson—I think we can both agree that it wasn't your forte—Ruth and I sat in the kitchen smoking, sharing an ashtray and drinking hot tea in a glass the way she liked it, with lots of sugar, which was very Old World—she called it Russian style—I blurted out to Ruth that I was Jewish. My mother had died a few weeks before that and I was so overcome with grief and guilt, I just regurgitated my life.

"It was the first time I had spoken about being Jewish in years. I made her promise she wouldn't tell anyone. I don't know what triggered it. It could have been the intimacy of the moment—it doesn't take much for two women to open up—or the fact that I had my secret tightly bound inside of me, like a concubine's feet. It just came pouring out. What a lovely woman. She looked shocked at first. Then she got up, bent over and hugged me while I cried into her shoulder. It's what my mother would have done.

"My façade of secure housewife went spinning into the smoke twirling around our heads. Maybe it was her sympathetic interest. Or the fact that I had turned away from my people, my history, my family. Or the reality that I could have been sitting where she was, the wife of a schoolteacher, embedded in the middle class.

"I had denied who I was for so long, that homey, empathetic, we've-had-troubles-too depth I had been lacking. She started speaking Yiddish to me and I understood every word. An outbound ship moved off my chest, flinging tethered coiled ropes into dark waters. I took a deep breath to compose myself and released some pain. In a flash I was back in my New York neighborhood speaking in my *mommen loschen.*"

"What's that?" I shifted in my hard chair. This was the most she had ever shared. I felt like a new being had emerged to mess up my image of the magazine mother who raised me.

"My mother tongue."

I couldn't sort out my feelings of confusion and betrayal. "So you're Jewish now?"

She looked uncomfortable. "Well, I haven't been to a synagogue for years but yes, if someone asked me right now if I was a Jew, I'd say yes."

"But how did you keep up the deception? It takes a lot of effort to live a lie."

My bewilderment manifested itself in a creeping wave of tension in my head. I leaned forward as though I could absorb more by transferring into her space. The scientific part of my being screeched with questions, more questions, proof, documentation, the realities that make a hypothesis true.

"Look, to me it wasn't a lie. It was survival. I came from nothing. If I had to keep my mouth shut to send my mother money each month and be comfortable, then that's what I did. After 1945 when the war ended, there were new rules. People were antisemitic before, but now they blamed the Jews for drawing us into another European war. Some said we should all be dead." Her voice rose with a quivering throng, a defense and justification for her choices.

"Okay, okay, I didn't mean to upset you. It seems incredible to me how you kept it up for so long."

She sighed before starting again. I was opening a raw wound.

"I just did. Byron was trying to get the numbers up in all the departments so he'd get another promotion. That Sears in Coral Gables was one of the top stores in the country. A plum job. Miami was growing, people had homes, needed appliances, lawn mowers, back-to-school clothes. Business was good. After the war people wanted families, guys took advantage of the GI bill, Miami had sunshine."

She stopped to take a large gasping breath, the top of her body urging forward with a slight bend.

"Mom, wait. Don't push yourself. Breathe normally."

I reached out to touch her leg through the white woven blanket, the antiseptic aroma of the room making my head spin with searing pain. A tear slid down her face. She wiped it with a crumpled tissue in her hand. I poured her a glass of water from the nightstand.

She knew I hated it when she cried. I felt it was a guilt trip, a ploy to make me uncomfortable. Was she trying to manipulate me with emotion? She started up again after another gulp of air.

"You didn't work if your husband had a good job. The ladies in the Junior League, the women at the Coco Plum Women's Club, the moms I met through PTA, were part of my social milieu. I played along. I had to ignore comments, but, on the other hand, I thought a few of them might have been in my situation too. Although I never asked. I minded my own business. Until Byron blew it all up."

"What do you mean? What happened?"

My brain, on high alert because I had so little information about my father, raced to military attention. My spine stiffened.

"I caught your father having an affair with my friend . . ." She trailed off.

"Louise? Arthur Brady's mom?"

I knew there had been an affair. I never had any details. Incredulous, I flashed back to Louise taunting me one day when I came looking for Arthur, yelling "Come in!" when she was near naked. Thirteen and big for my age from my father's farm stock, I headed toward the back of the house and walked past the bathroom looking for Arthur's room.

"Michael, c'mere." Her words were a little slurry, like she'd started early. A lot of adults had Bloody Marys for breakfast, vodka tonics for lunch and martinis with dinner, then drank until they fell asleep. Maybe she'd welcomed the day with a drink. The women must have been so bored.

I stood in the bathroom door. Mrs. Brady was in a see-through black brassiere. I couldn't see much but the shadow must have been her nipples. She wore a garter belt attached to her waist. My mother wore them too, rubbery fingers holding up her hosiery, an uncomfortable-looking contraption that required dexterity. Arthur's mom had on underpants with a leg propped up on the toilet seat to roll up her opaque stockings, the black rubber talons dancing between her legs.

"Michael, I sure could use help with this," her fingers grasping at the hanging straps trying to get the thin fabric of stocking between them and the metal latch.

I ran. I ran down the hall, past the living room, through the front door and didn't stop until, heaving, I sat down on our front steps near my mother's potted plants.

A nurse in mint green scrubs pushing a tray with miniature white paper cups interrupted us. "Mrs. Saunders, it's time for your meds and blood draw." She turned to me. "Excuse me. We need a little privacy now. My patient looks very tired."

In the few moments she had bustled in with her rolling metal cart, I saw my mother's eyes were closed. I stood up, kissed her on the cheek and left.

It was a lot for me to digest. I headed for the hospital cafeteria and bought a coffee. I drank it black sitting at a table in the half-empty room. It would be easy to judge her. My logical mind went to the blame side first, but on the ride down in the elevator, watching a few elderly people enter in wheelchairs, walkers or slump-shouldered from age, the soft side jump-started.

True, my mother wasn't who I thought she was. It was easy to criticize her life as a sham. But, now that it was coming to a close, even though she dumped it on me, I had empathy for her. She had been a good mom, loving me unconditionally, patient with my moods and headaches, encouraging my education. As an only child, my bond with her was enduring. I loved her. There was no doubt she had provided the best for me, although her self-protection created such a dichotomy. I missed an entire legacy, one she deemed unworthy.

I knew my father was a shithead. I learned he was unfaithful because Arthur knew the story. He stopped speaking to me as though my mother was the hussy and not his.

In those days a divorce was a town scandal. Rumors reverberated through the halls of school. I was humiliated. While his parents reconciled, my father moved out to a hotel near Sears on Douglas Road. He'd come on his day off to see me, picking me up in a new Lincoln he had purchased. I'd sit silently in the front seat until we got to a luncheonette. For the most part I gave monosyllabic answers while I ate my grilled cheese. Yes, school was fine. I still liked swimming. No, I wasn't mad at him.

But I was. I knew it was his fault. It didn't take long until our financial circumstances shifted. The house went up for sale. My mother, now a divorced woman, was no longer welcomed at the club.

The common notion was that you couldn't have a single woman around because they might steal your husband. Ha! So Estelle disappeared along with the Cadillac and a few other niceties, like piano lessons. My mother didn't want me to have to change schools so we stuck it out in Coral Gables until I graduated. Then we resided in a pink stucco duplex off LeJeune and Hardee Roads.

Byron drank more, got fired and moved to another city. I know she fought him for the alimony and child support, but he didn't have it. At least he said he didn't.

I was angry. Furious was more like it. I was an adult years ago. Why didn't she share all this then? I missed so much—relatives, stories, history. What happened to her sister? Even my small civil-ceremony wedding that dissolved later seemed pathetic in retrospect. No wonder I had no family there. Never mind my holy skepticism about religion. I was a Jew. Or was I? The thought raced around my mind like a trapped mouse. If I am a Jew, I don't know a damn thing about it.

Chapter Twenty Four

Miami, Florida
June 22, 1993

Subsequent visits with my mother didn't yield much more information other than she tried to absolve herself by saying other people did the same thing in those times and she did it for me.

What kind of people hid where they came from? Denied who they were? It got my gall every time the topic came up. I kept searching for reasons, something that I had missed. I tried to be sympathetic to her illness, the indignity of creeping death, her sanguine demeanor, but the truth reverberated around me. Now it came up every time I visited her. I had opened the porthole on a submarine and the ship was filling with water.

My mother defended herself by saying, "Oh, you'd be surprised. Jewish men couldn't get ahead on Wall Street, in banking, law firms or get loans to buy a home or start a business. Jewish boys went overseas to attend medical school. There were quotas. That's why Betty Blumberg, who I worked with at Sandra Post, sent her Teddy to Scotland. People changed their names all the time. Greenburg became Green, Raskowitz became Ross. If your first name was Irving you changed that too. You don't understand how pervasive antisemitism was.

"People wanted to know what church you went to before they wanted to know where you lived. We were called a lot of names besides being accused of being communists. Of course the Rosenberg trial for espionage in '49 didn't help that. Those people didn't deserve to die and leave two orphans."

"But you had a voice. There was injustice all around." I was frustrated with her complacency.

She mustered a tone of anger in her voice when she responded. "Look, I couldn't do a damn thing about it. What about the blacks? Poor Estelle took three buses to get to our house and couldn't use the bathroom until she got there in the morning. You don't remember separate bathrooms and water fountains but I do. The bus station where she transferred had no facilities for 'colored.' She couldn't even buy a snack. Carried her lunch bag with her in a faded cloth tote. She'd get to our place and change into her uniform, put on a hairnet and start to work. I wasn't like some of our neighbors who put a toilet and sink in the garage. She used our facilities.

"I don't remember that."

"Oh, yes. A few people on our street did just that. Enclosed a corner of the garage. I didn't understand it. They were preparing their food, bathing their children, but they couldn't use the bathroom. Ridiculous.

"I grew up in New York where black people or African Americans or whatever the appropriate term is now–I know it's not Negroes, although that was a respectful term then–they went to school and worked in offices and rode public transportation, sitting in the front if they wanted to.

"I was shocked when Byron first took me to the South. He warned me not to say anything when he saw how upset I was at their situation. Black people had to be off Miami Beach by sundown. They lived in their own neighborhoods so unless you had contact through servants or gardeners, there was little interaction. All the schools were segregated.

"The few times I drove Estelle home, because it was bad weather or she stayed late to help with a party, were a revelation. I couldn't stand the thought of her sitting on a bus bench in the rain or the dark. She lived over in Colored Town, an all-black neighborhood on the edge of Coconut Grove, in a small house with a fence. Byron thought it was too dangerous for me to drive there at night.

"But one Christmas Eve it had been drizzling all evening, and the buses didn't run that late so I drove her home." Byron was snockered and I wouldn't let my worst enemy get in a car with him. Besides, I needed a break from all the gossipy chitchat of the evening.

"The relationships were so superficial when I look back. A few of the people read books or talked about politics, but mostly it was nonsense. It galled me that the few I knew to be prejudiced considered themselves good, churchgoing Christians. But I had learned to keep my mouth shut. I also relished a little time alone in the safety of my car with the windows rolled up and the doors locked. I knew by the time I got back Byron would be passed out with his clothes on, collar undone, in his favorite chair in the Florida room.

"Estelle arrived that morning and we prepared the meal and house together all day. Some of the people from the club were coming over. Boy, could that woman cook! Do you remember her chocolate seven-layer cake? It was like something you bought at Andalucía Bakery, only better. The house was all decorated and I had a six-foot spruce in the living room picture window. You helped with the ornaments. I admit I loved that part and you did too. It was something we did as a family. I never had any crosses around, but I bought a big gold angel for the top. It symbolized someone was watching over us."

When my mother drifted off into her memories I became a little impatient. I had to allow her the wandering time but I was interested in her motivation. If I had been raised a Jew, would I be teaching at Yale?

"Mom, get back to the story."

"Estelle's neighborhood was so dilapidated. It made me sad and guilty when I saw the conditions on her block. It's amazing how a neighborhood can be a few miles away and not part of your world because you drive around it or by it, windows rolled up, doors locked so nothing seeps in. "

"'This is where I live, Miz Saunders,'" she told me as I drove up to her place on that Christmas Eve.

"We sat in silence, the rain pounding on the car. What could I say? 'It ain't fancy but we's own it, Foley and me.' I could see there had been an effort made in the yard with a few planters sectioned off with railroad ties. The flowers were bent in the deluge.

"The rain had been steady but suddenly, one of those cloudbursts exploded that slams your windshield with such a force of water there's no point to the wipers. The car rocked a little with each thunder clap. Then we were illuminated by lightning. I watched her face and could see she was terrified. She reached across the seat and grabbed my arm. We had touched before because we often worked side by side, even hugged on occasion, but this was different. The urgency of her contact jolted me.

"When she realized what she had done, she pulled away, embarrassed."

My mother paused to reach for a cup of water. Her lips were dry and cracked looking. I thought this might be too much for her, but she seemed ready to continue.

"Mom, did it bother you that black people were treated so badly?"

"You know, Michael, it did. But what was I going to do about it? My own situation was precarious. I was grateful to be where I was in life. I cried when I saw the beatings with Bull Connor on TV and what was going on in Alabama. How horrible to use water hoses on innocent people. Byron told me to shut it off. It was none of our business. But that flame of injustice burned way down in my belly. Maybe that was the Jewish part. Those young people who went down to the Deep South to help with voter registration? A lot of them were Jewish. Like Michael Schwerner and Andrew Goodman who were murdered with James Cheney in Mississippi in '64. I'll never forget it. You were a young teen. I tried to shield you from the violence and racism."

She seemed to be digesting the information as though it had all been recently presented. Had she become complacent after all these years?

"The separation between blacks and whites in the South was strange to me. I could never wrap my head around it. In New York we didn't mix socially, but we weren't cruel either. There was an appreciation for their culture, the jazz clubs up in Harlem, an acknowledgment of respect for what they'd been through. Although, like antisemitism, no one talked about slavery. We swept it under the rug. Oh, of course there were a few firebrands who tried to mobilize them, but for the most part no one brought up a war of the last century. We all just wanted to eke out a living, spend time with our families and not rock the boat."

"So what happened that night in the storm when you drove Estelle home?"

My mother closed her eyes. "Well, she couldn't get out of the car for a while, even though she always carried a black umbrella. I took her hand in mine with the next clap of thunder that hurt our ears. The lightning was right behind it so I knew it was close. I couldn't recall whether it was safer to be in a car or under a covering. The porch was further than it looked and treacherous to get to with a few broken flagstones and up some steps. Getting soaked or falling or even being struck by lightning didn't look like a smart decision. I patted her hand to soothe her. Her body jolted with each noise. I wish I could have taken a snapshot in the eerie light when the car was illuminated. Our hands, hers rough and worn, fingernails clipped short, dark against my white skin and oval manicured pink nails. I guess my brain snapped a photo anyway."

"So what did you talk about?"

"The things women talk about—us, recipes, family. She had a few kids and grandkids but was very proud of her Marvin who had gone north for school. She was telling me about her 'woman's troubles' when a clap of thunder was so loud, I jumped. Hail started beating down bouncing off the hood of the Cadillac. I said a silent prayer that it wouldn't be dented because Byron got upset about anything that had to do with that car. We glanced at each other, fear in our eyes. She couldn't get out of the car and I couldn't drive. So we just sat there, the inside steaming up with our breath.

"'Oh Jesus. I'm 'fraid of thunder and lightning. My momma tole me we is being punished for our sins when God makes this kind of noise.' She pulled her hand away, patting her heart in a steady rhythm, like I had seen the black ladies do on TV with their fans in un-air-conditioned churches.

"'Oh, Estelle, do you believe that?'

'Miz Saunders, I just know my people are poor and have suffered so much. We been slaves in this country like them Jews in the Bible for so long. My great-great-great grandmomma didn't see freedom 'til she ran away from Mississippi after the Civil War. And I ain't so sure we seeing it now.'

"I had never had a frank exchange with Estelle about race, although we chatted about you and the house and 'Mr. Byron' every time she came. In the intimacy of the car I wanted to confess that I felt oppressed too, but

I knew how ludicrous that would be in her eyes. Me living in a big house with fancy clothes and a nice car. I had no room to complain.

"But I knew what she was talking about. In her position a life was prescribed. She wanted to survive, even if it meant cleaning someone else's toilets and cleaning up their messes. I made an extra effort to treat her with fairness, be kind, but I knew that wouldn't change anything.

"When some of the ladies from the club started to put them down or make derogatory remarks, I'd excuse myself. Once, I heard a particular woman I didn't like call me an 'n-lover' behind my back.

"It was okay for black women to prepare our food, handle our bed sheets, do our laundry, even suckle our children, but not okay for them to eat with us or use our bathrooms? The hypocrisy of the relationships was absurd to me."

"So what happened that Christmas Eve?"

"It took forever, but finally the rain let up enough where she could consider making a run for it. I couldn't get any closer to her front door. She took out a bandanna from her bag and wrapped it around her hair. 'No point ruining my 'do before church tomorra.'

"She opened the door to make a run for it, her umbrella ready to snap open. 'Goodnight, Miz Saunders. Thanks for the ride. Y'all have a Merry Christmas.'

"Wait." I clicked open my purse to search for a fifty-dollar bill I had stuffed in a special side pocket. I had already paid her for the evening and had given her a Christmas bonus—I have to say Byron was generous about those things—but I wanted to do something more. 'Buy some new porch furniture for you and Foley.' I knew it was pure guilt but it was on so many levels.

"'Oh, Miz Saunders, I can't take this. You already paid me.'"

"'Never mind. This is different. It's for you.'"

"'Oh, I don't need nothin'.'"

"'No, I want you to have it. Buy yourself something.'"

"'That's why I can't take it. I get paid a fair wage. I don't take no money for no work.'"

"My eye caught the dilapidated chairs on the porch again. 'Buy you and Foley some new rocking chairs. Mr. Byron will give you a discount at the store.'"

"'Oh no. We's happy with what we got. Besides, around here, those bad boys see you got somethin' nice and it's gone.'"

"'Well, then it's for Marvin. He could use some cash for school or books.'

"She hesitated, then took the folded bill from my hand. 'Okay, for Marvin. Thank you, Miz Saunders. I'm going to cook you and Mr. Byron up somethin' special next week for New Year's Eve.'"

"Later, when I asked her how Christmas had been she said, 'Me and Foley bought us some catfish to grill with collard greens and my special cornbread. We celebrated the Lord real quiet.'"

"When I got home I was so annoyed with Byron for drinking too much. He was in his chair, mouth agape, chest heaving, legs splayed with his shoes still on. If I left him there, he'd wake up in the morning, his body stiff, breath reeking and head pounding, cursing me for not getting him to bed. And you'd find him on Christmas morning.

"I felt sorry for him, the lie he lived pretending to be someone he wasn't. At least I knew who I was down in my soul. I didn't think that was pretty either, by the way, but I had made a choice of survival in a world more comfortable than what could have been my fate.

"Now I was going to have to struggle to get him upright after slurred objections, propel him toward the bedroom with urgings of 'Don't let Michael see you like this,' untying and pulling off those huge Cordovan wingtips he wore. But I did it. He was a big, uncooperative man, his dead weight leaning into me as I forced him down the hall. I pushed, guiding him toward our room as he grumbled. In minutes he was flat on his back on top of the spread, letting out a snoring racket that competed with the window air conditioner and the storm outside."

Chapter Twenty Five

New York City
September 23, 1993
9 a.m.

The cavernous room buzzed with the movement of chairs, the screeching of sound checks from the stage and academics greeting associates. The university world is a concise, tight one, especially in the field of archaeological discovery. With the hierarchy of Ivy Leagues at the top of the list, the prestige shifted to smaller private colleges with endowments for excavations in remote places at the bottom of the list. Big-name credentials were not as necessary as funding. Rich benefactors who wanted recognition on buildings, scholarships, or grants wielded power.

I eyed the draped tables with notepads and plastic ballpoint pens, sweating pitchers of water and folded cardboard signs with professors' names. Alphabetical by university, I was usually seated toward the back; however, today my seat was on stage as one of the first speakers.

I handed my carousel of slides to the audio-visual attendant, watching as a few images flashed across the screen as a test. He offered me a remote with a few instructions.

Sandrine remained at the hotel stretched out on the bed. She moaned a few times as I got ready. Maybe it was the champagne from the preview event last night to ease the dental pain, or maybe nightmares. After we returned she mumbled that her tooth still hurt, so I fashioned an ice pack from cubes retrieved from the icemaker down the hall. The liner of the bucket worked well.

She wanted to be at the symposium this morning, lifting her head off the pillow in an attempt to show she was willing, but I convinced her it was better to arrive in the afternoon. By then I'd be on the panel talking about my own research. As I left I glanced at her through the crack in the door, eyes shut, a new ice pack held tight against her jaw. I really like this girl. I really like her a lot.

"Will the symposium please come to order? Professors, take your seats." A few minutes passed as the noise started to subside.

"I'm Dr. Seymour Sommerstein from Roscom Liberal Arts College, your host for this week's events. Please take your seats," he repeated to the unsettled room. I observed that most of the male professors were dressed in jackets and ties, while the women wore dresses, some with jackets. A few professors of both sexes showed up in T-shirts with jackets, long hair pulled into pony tails. Two professors in white short-sleeved shirts and bow ties shook hands in the front row and continued chatting, finding their seats in slow motion.

"Welcome to the École Biblique et Archéologique Française and Scholars Symposium, affiliated with the Sorbonne and sponsored by Roscom College. If you check your agenda you'll see we have three papers to be presented before lunch, including our keynote. Please save your comments for the panel discussion after lunch on the God's Gold discovery. I know there's controversy about this topic, so I'm asking you to be respectful of others' opinions.

First, we have a short tribute to Dr. Maurice Dubois, the esteemed professor from the University of Paris. Most of you are aware of the sad circumstances surrounding his death."

Murmurs floated across the room.

"Please, professors, let's keep comments to a minimum. I know that as scientists many of you view religion with a jaundiced eye; however, I ask that we observe a moment of silence to remember our esteemed colleague and his accomplishments."

"What's happening with the investigation?" one of the professors in the short-sleeved white shirts in the front row shouted out.

"Yeah, we have no information," echoed another. "Was it an accident?"

"Gentlemen, ladies, scholars, this is a police matter. I have nothing to share with you. At the moment Dr. Dubois's death is being investigated as an accident."

Noise enveloped the room. People commented among themselves and a few shouted out more questions. "Is someone targeting us? Was it random?"

Dr. Sommerstein tapped on the microphone with a metal pen. "You're an unruly bunch, aren't you? Attention. We must move forward with our speakers." The room settled down again.

"Many of you knew him personally and we understand your grief and concern."

The guy was a prick so I can't imagine anyone saying a good thing about him, but I didn't like the idea of someone possibly targeting academics.

"We welcome any personal remembrances submitted in writing to publish in our next journal. Dr. Dubois was an established academic who pioneered the use of carbon dating in the field of biblical archaeology. As an author of more than a hundred articles and a groundbreaking textbook on the topic, he was revered and respected by many students and authorities all over the world."

Sommerstein paused to inhale, a relief that he could move forward.

"A moment of silence, please."

People stopped shifting in their seats. The whirr of the air conditioner, the rifling of a few papers, someone writing pervaded the quiet. A few people bowed their heads, others doodled on the pads in front of them and the woman next to me slurped her coffee from a Styrofoam cup and set it under her seat.

"Thank you. I know Maurice would want us to continue. And now our esteemed colleague, Dr. Michael Saunders from Yale University, will deliver his paper, 'The Journey of Sacred Biblical Treasures from the Essenes to Their Hiding Place at the Vatican.' Let us begin our program. Dr. Saunders?"

The room exhaled a collective sigh and got back to business.

I approached the podium adjusting my blue blazer, tucking my tie inside and opening my folder. A spray of nervousness coursed through me.

I started with the journey of the priceless treasures—a golden candelabrum, two silver trumpets and the Table of the Divine Presence—beginning with the sacking of the Temple in Jerusalem in 70 CE by the Emperor Vespasian and his son Titus, and their arrival in Rome.

I looked out at the audience. "To clarify, throughout this paper I will be using BCE, before the Common Era, instead of BC, before Christ, and CE instead of AD, the *anno Domini* designation.

"First, the Essenes were a sectarian group of Jews who inhabited Khirbat Qumram, a plateau in the Judaen desert near the Dead Sea, after abandoning Jerusalem because they did not approve of the way the Temple was being run. They flourished from second century BCE to first century CE in large numbers throughout Roman Judea, adhering to voluntary poverty, eschewing slaves, refusing animal sacrifices and observing celibacy in some places. With their abstinence from pleasures and personal property, the Essenes remained socially segregated and antagonistic toward Romans.

"They did, however, respect learning. The Dead Sea Scrolls are attributed to part of their library."

Once I established who the Essenes were, I purported my theory that they were the beginning of the journey for God's Gold, as they were entrusted with valuables that resisted the elements in their caves. The only way these artifacts could have survived is if they were hidden by the Essenes, or a particular family, for a long period of time.

"The Arch of Titus in Rome is offered as proof that the spoils existed, as did the memorialized history written by Flavius Josephus, a Jewish priest of royal descent who wrote his account in 37 CE, after he switched sides to be a military advisor for the emperor." A few photos of the Arch of Titus flashed on the screen with a click of my thumb.

I read the account in a professional voice with new reading glasses perched on the bridge of my nose, recounting the journey of the artifacts through barbarians, Vandals, Byzantines, Persians and Islamists. Corresponding slides of the treasures as well as history book sketches depicting various marauders put visuals to the words. Adding the slides was my idea to enhance the paper. Heather, Sommerstein's assistant, pulled it together for me, although we hadn't had much time.

I read another eight pages, including a view of an unpublished inscription from a mosaic in the chapel of Saint John Lateran in Rome dating to 1291. It commemorated the Roman fleet under Vespasian, founder of the Flavian dynasty, who sacked Jerusalem.

I continued, "There is also evidence from Istanbul that includes a message from the Emperor Procopius in 534 CE about the Byzantine Empire receiving spoils from the barbarians. On a marble slab commemorating a victory, the following is written and I quote, 'There was also silver weighing many thousands of talents and all the royal treasure amounting to an exceedingly great sum and among these were the treasures of the Jews, which Titus, the son of Vespasian, together with certain others and captives, had brought to Rome after the capture of Jerusalem.'"

I reiterated the theory that once the artifacts arrived in Rome, they never left the Vatican basement. With acknowledgments of popes, eyewitnesses and numerous historical references, I said, "While the world searched, they were in the safekeeping of the Catholic diocese all along.

"How these treasures reached the open market is speculation. I do not want to express any definitive information on their pathway from the bowels of the Holy See, which, we are all aware contains seven and a half miles of meandering bookshelves in the Tower of Winds from the Papal collection, some of which have never been viewed by their keepers. Yes, these are mostly manuscripts, but it makes the point that the church has never released an inventory of its contents." I peered out at the audience over the top of my new glasses.

"I quote from a noted archaeologist's work, 'The Tower of Winds staff has no knowledge of what documents reside behind a heavy door at the end of a corridor on the lower floor. It is always closed, and its key never leaves the side of the chief prefect.'"

I turned over more pages in my stack of twenty. "It is my theory that if the priests inside the Vatican do not have an inventory of what is there, it is possible that not only were these treasures hidden, but more may be there as well."

After a succinct summarization building my case for the Essenes, I closed.

I appreciated the applause.

Sommerstein took the stage. "After a short break, Dr. Saunders will return to read Maurice Dubois's paper." The room erupted as people headed for another coffee or the bathroom. A few people approached me for details while I sipped water for my dry throat.

Ten minutes later I was back center stage delivering an abbreviated version of Maurice's paper, "Radiocarbon Testing in Relation to the High and Low Chronology of the Temple Treasures Looted from Jerusalem in 70 CE."

It was strange reading someone else's words and research. At least Maurice and I agreed that the artifacts at the center of the controversy were authentic. After a brief introduction, Sommerstein and I had agreed I would skip to the important part of the paper.

"I want to address the carbon dating of the artifacts in question."

Although I read the treatise aloud a few times at the hotel so the words would flow, I hesitated before I laid out Maurice's hypothesis. I took a deep breath and launched into the most difficult part.

"Scholars utilize three independent methodologies to analyze discoveries: radiocarbon dating, which is regarded as the most scientific and precise that involves analysis of frost-damaged tree rings and acidity of polar ice. Radiocarbon dating can be performed on any organic substance including wood and other organic materials; however, it cannot be done on metals. It is in contrast to the old cultural and historical methods utilizing strata, which I deem inaccurate based on intuition." I shifted my weight.

"My hypothesis examines the radiocarbon dating and its accuracy of these treasures. The archaeological era of 70 CE, which involves a lightning rod of debate about low and high chronology, has created controversy over the years. Low chronology suggests we lower the date of eleventh century BCE to the tenth century based on assemblages fixed there. High chronology occurred around the time of King David, 1000 or 980 BCE." I tried not to drone on with the explanation in a monotone, but I had to cover the didactic material for another page.

I thumbed through the corners of the pages to see how many pages I had left to deliver. I was almost finished with the defense of radiocarbon dating of the God's Gold pieces. "In conclusion, whereas a radiocarbon dating of sixty-six percent—as previous artifacts have received—is not reassuring, our particular artifacts have received a sixty-seven percent rating, verified by the team headed by Dr. Jason Herbert, the Jonah B. Finklestein Professor of Archaeology at Harvard."

I sighed, turning over the last piece of paper, removed my reading glasses and returned to my seat in the back of the room. Silent for a moment, applause broke out for the dead man's paper.

Chapter Twenty Six

New York City
September 23, 1993
10:30 a.m.

Dr. Sommerstein stood behind a podium leaning into the microphone.

"Thank you, Dr. Saunders. For those of you who want the annotated footnotes, we have copies of Dr. Dubois's paper in its entirety up front, although obviously, he is not here to defend his research.

"Now we'll hear from Dr. Thomas Stevens from Georgia Southern University about ongoing disputes at the site of Jericho. His paper is entitled, 'Jericho: Biblical Fact or Fiction?' Dr. Stevens?"

After brief applause I tuned in for the beginning of the talk. We all knew the biblical story based on the Israelites following the deity's words, Moses leading them out of bondage in Egypt and Joshua guiding them into the Promised Land. The controversy had moved past the discovery of large storage jars filled with grain, an inscribed clay tablet and excavated human bones. The main question was whether the radiocarbon dating shifted from the Late Bronze Age.

Dr. Stevens's sonorous voice filled the room. "The controversy around Jericho centers on three areas: the time period the event occurred, whether Jericho was a city or a series of twenty small settlements, and the occurrence of a natural disaster. The idea of the walls tumbling down is a myth. An earthquake destroyed Jericho, not the shouts of Joshua's army.

"Today, with research near the Jordan River, Jericho has been renamed Tell es-Sultan and is under the dispensation of the Palestinian Authority in the West Bank. I purport to prove the demise of the walled city located above the Dead Sea near so many springs, also known as 'The City of Palm Trees,' is being debated because so many believe the biblical story as truth. These less-informed . . ."

After ten minutes my mind wandered and I lost interest in the slides of pottery shards, iron vessels and small pieces of silver. I pushed back my chair to go outside for a bathroom break.

Preoccupied with the conference and the upcoming auction, I drifted to Sandrine, how responsive her body was to me, how well our rhythms blended, how relaxed and compatible we were together. We needed time to sleep late, eat brunch and wander gardens, the things lovers do. Paris had been our aphrodisiac.

Did Sandrine fit into the larger picture of my life? I wanted more time to explore a future with her. The good news was she hadn't put any pressure on me. With this kind of synchronicity most women would have dropped a few hints about what was going to happen next. Most didn't take me seriously when I told them I was a no-more-marriages-no-kids kind of guy.

My mind jogged a step further. What would she do in New Haven? She asked about my mother yesterday, but I wasn't ready to open up yet. I told her that she passed away from breast cancer and that I was close to her, but the other part would have to wait. When? Would it change anything?

With so much discussion about Jews and the artifacts, I asked her in one of our hurried conversations while we were getting ready what she thought about people of the Jewish faith. What if she were prejudiced? Her response settled me.

"In France the Vichy government during World War II collaborated with the Nazis. Even our own French police. Many children rousted from their schools were taken away. It was wrong. An embarrassment, how do you say, a stain on all of us. When I walk in the Marais *quartier* I see the plaques on the walls saying what happened. It makes me sad."

I thought maybe that was the moment to tell her, but I could see she was upset. And we were rushing. Would it make any difference? It made sense to tell her later.

My feelings about my mother shifted from clear and uncomplicated to puzzling and complex. Her choice of living a lie for so long disturbed me. I knew I'd get over it soon, but I wasn't ready to let it go. I kept trying to find a reason other than what she told me. Would an earlier confession have changed anything?

I was jolted back to reality standing in front of the urinal. Seymour Sommerstein was at the next urinal.

"Fancy meeting you here," the professor said, meeting my eyes. "That's a rowdy bunch to control in there."

I acknowledged him with a grunt.

He continued, "This symposium has been difficult from the beginning. Maurice's demise added an extra level of tension."

I commiserated with, "Maurice created hostility walking into a room." I zipped my pants and checked the top.

"I'm not going to argue that with you, but the guy had charisma with all his awards, TV appearances, and scholarly recognition. Academics get jealous too."

Seymour followed me outside. I wanted to ask him what he meant by the jealousy comment.

"Michael, just a minute before you go back. I was going to talk to you anyway. As with most acquisitions there are politics involved. I need a favor."

What was the point in scurrying around for prestige and money when we're supposed to be concerned with intellectual property in the academic world?

"I'll be blunt," said Sommerstein, plunging his hands into his pockets. "I need you to schmooze Mrs. White, Brooks's mother. She has tons of dough and will be a high bidder for God's Gold. You saw the pieces the other night and they're spectacular. Priceless since the carbon dating of the table. She wants to purchase them and donate them to the college. A real coup for a small place like ours. We could loan them out around the world and make a fortune. I need you to convince her that it's worth putting her money into them."

"Wait a minute," I said, motioning Seymour closer to a wall so no one could overhear our conversation. "Why can't Brooks schmooze his mother?" I flashed to how easily the Yiddish word for chatting someone up rolled off my tongue. Ha. The gene pool.

"He and the mother have their differences. Who isn't trying to get their hands on a relative's billions? Look, I need you and the French cutie pie to charm her. These rich people feel they need a purpose, that they're making a contribution. Never mind she inherited it from her third husband's oil fortune. This is a coup for a small college."

"Just a minute. She's not a cutie pie."

"Okay, sorry. Maybe she's got a doctorate, which are in great abundance here. I don't care. I need you to make nice. I've arranged for you and your *lady*," he said, putting the emphasis on the last word, "to sit in the private chamber upstairs at Shropshire tomorrow. You can watch the auction through the tinted glass. Champagne. Hors d'oeuvres. Might even be a few others in there with you. Heard Streisand is supposed to show."

"What if we don't want to sit up there? Besides, I have to be on the floor for my verification speech. And, I don't like using my friend for spurious purposes."

"Whoa. When did you get so touchy? Damn. I forgot about that. Okay, sit downstairs. But you're missing a great opportunity."

Being in the same room with Brooks White was not a gift.

"So how does one bid from up there?"

Seymour pulled out a cigarette. "All done with a special telephone to the agent on the floor. Eventually it'll all be done with computers and instantaneous, but for now this is the system in use. Winners and bidders don't want to get mobbed at the end of the auction by the press or anyone else." With a tone of sarcasm he added, "In case you haven't noticed, we have worldwide attention focused on us right now because of the pieces themselves and Maurice's accident."

"Listen, I don't feel right about this. I don't want the notoriety. Between Sandrine's mishap and my stolen beeper, I'd like to keep a low profile. You know we moved out of the Pierre."

"Yea, I know. Heather told me." Sommerstein lit the cigarette, sucking a drag. "My wife would kill me if she knew I started again." He stared at the lit end as though it was the culprit. "I know you can add the credibility Luisa White needs to make her final decision."

"What about Yossi Farber and his objections? And the Israelis who want the antiquities?"

"Fuck Yossi. He can't fight carbon dating and the Israelis don't have the money. Although, there are a few consortia pooling their resources together."

"Like who?" I asked, aware of the hostility in my voice.

"Like the Saudis and another Arab prince who want to keep them off the market. Or the Chinese and an anonymous backer—"

"What the hell are the Chinese going to do with them? They're all atheists."

"How do I know? Prove to the world they can buy whatever they want? Destroy them so there's no idolizing any religion? The Arabs living with eleventh-century ideals would love to pulverize them. You've heard about that crazy bin Laden guy in Afghanistan preaching *jihad*? They're all nuts."

Sommerstein paused for a moment. "Michael, just help me get these for the college. It would bring us untold cachet as we loan them out around the world. Plus, money for our endowment. Luisa White's our only chance. I'll owe you one."

If I had a choice I'd say the artifacts belonged in the States, maybe at Sommerstein's college where the world could have access to them and not in some museum on foreign shores where academia wouldn't be able to touch them.

Sommerstein smashed his half-finished cigarette into a metal container near the elevator, sucked in his belly and wandered back into the symposium room.

I slipped around a corner to call Sandrine from a pay phone. "*Bonjour,*" I said with aplomb after the operator connected us.

"Ah, my Michael. I am fine. You don't need to call. I'm resting. I will call room service soon."

"No." I almost shouted into the phone. I lowered my voice. "Don't open the door for anyone. I'll come back during the break and bring you soup." Maybe chicken soup now that I have my new identity. I acknowledged how someone could be a food Jew.

"Why? I am hungry now. I hardly ate much yesterday. Except for the desserts."

"I know. I'm going to stay for one more lecture and then I'll bring you something. I have to come back for the panel this afternoon. Feel up to coming with me?"

"Maybe. I will see. Maybe you have time to rub my shoulders?"

I smiled. A euphemism for a quickie.

I walked back into the seminar when the last professor finished his talk before lunch.

"To conclude, the mosaic floor found in the remote Turkish area of Selçuk proves that Ephesus stands as one of the most outstanding finds for the 20th century. My thanks to Drs. Vivian Porter, Angus Scott and Peter Blair, with assistance from doctoral candidates Helena Bronstein and Trevor Howard."

Chairs pushed back before he concluded his last sentence. Clusters of professors gathered together discussing the lectures. I overheard, "And Schmidt's find trumps anything that's been found in the area near Potbelly Hill in Turkey. Forty Kurdish diggers uncovered a temple complex that can change the history of evolution. I have three published papers about it, so why wasn't I asked to be on the panel?"

I turned to exit. A hand on my shoulder stopped me mid-gait. "So what's the rush? Have to read over your paper again?" Yossi grinned at me.

I didn't return the smile, facing him.

"What's the matter? You know this discovery is bullshit too. How can you propagate the untruth of this? It's not possible these artifacts are from the Temple. They never could have survived. And the church has had them hidden for centuries? Who believes that?"

"Look, Yossi, you're a smart guy and I respect you. But you don't know what the Vatican's hidden in their basement over the centuries. I was skeptical too, until the carbon dating of the table, but this is the real deal. We have testimony from Rabbi Eleazer that the pope showed him the candelabra and the table for sacrifices. Who are you to dispute it?"

The conversation became heated. A few people leaving the room glanced at us, although disagreements among various factions were common at these seminars. Academics had passions too.

Yossi's voice rose. "I did the research. The Syrians never escaped with them. Maybe they made it to Rome but there's no way they survived. They were probably unloaded in the water."

"What about the carbon dating? How do you dispute that?" I replied.

"Look, Michael, don't be naïve. Anyone can be bought. How much would it take a scientist to alter a piece of evidence? It happens in police departments all the time."

"Are you saying someone bribed Maurice Dubois? Out of the question. Academic integrity, of paramount importance in our field, guides our principles. Without substantiation, it's heresy to say the artifacts aren't real. There were too many scientists on this project. But, okay, let's say I buy your theory for a moment. Why would someone jeopardize their academic career?"

"Why? Because there's so much money involved. Dubois wouldn't be the first professor to fudge data. Millions of dollars at stake plus worldwide attention? He'd be foolish not to give it a passing glance. Besides, it lends credibility to the claim of Jerusalem.

"I'm an Israeli and I know every artifact shown in a museum isn't authentic. You've wandered the city. There are dozens of small museums with pieces on display from 'biblical times.'" He leaned closer to me, shaking his finger at my chest. "There's a conspiracy behind this one. I'm telling you the Chinese are behind it."

"Can you prove any of this?"

"Unfortunately, not yet. I'm not a detective, but I know something is not kosher here. Too many discrepancies, moving of laboratories, scientists shifted around . . ."

"You've been reading too many thrillers—or comic books." I turned to go, saying over my shoulder, "What if it's you clever Israelis who have cooked up a scheme?"

"Harrumph. You'll see I'm right. Be ready to be confronted with the facts this afternoon."

I walked a few blocks ruminating over Yossi's statements. Were the Israelis trying to manipulate something? I wasn't swayed by his claims, although there were lingering suspicions with recent events.

I stopped into a neighborhood delicatessen to buy soup and a few chocolate and cinnamon *rugelach* for my Paris lamb. I hailed a cab looking over my shoulder and arrived at the new hotel.

I knocked three times in succession. "Sandrine?" I called through the door.

She opened it with the chain, a slice of her face visible.

"Come in," she said, closing the door to slip off the chain. "You make me nervous. I shouldn't call room service? Who wants me? Besides you?"

"No one. Only me." I put my arms around her waist, the white deli bag gripped in my fingers. Even without makeup and with bed hair she looked beautiful. I smoothed the lines between her brows with my thumb. "No frowning."

She giggled. "First, soup. So I have strength for your fun and games."

I set the bag on the writing desk near the window and unpacked our lunch. We ate while I explained what the morning session was like and told her about my confrontation with Yossi Farber.

"Listen, at the auction tomorrow, Sommerstein wants you to sit in the room upstairs with Mrs. White, Brooks's mother." Sandrine made a disappointed face, the corners of her mouth turning down. "I told him no, but maybe you can stop in and use your Parisian charm. Tell her I'm a good professor, that my credentials are impeccable."

"Why do I do this?" She twirled a piece of hair around her finger.

"So she buys the artifacts and donates them to Sommerstein's college."

"But why? I like this *patisserie*." She nibbled a rugala, bits of chocolate sticking to her lips.

"It'll make him famous. Or at least his college."

"But you tell me the Israelis want this."

"I know. But she'll win. She has more money. Remember the guy from lunch at Yale? And we saw him last night?" She nodded." It's her son."

"Oh. I don't like him. No *savoir faire*." She licked the ends of her fingers.

"Never mind. You'll have a glass of champagne and enjoy the show. Might even be a movie star in the private room with you."

"What? Who? Sharon Stone? I like Julia Roberts."

"No. Not her. Maybe someone else."

"But where do you sit? I do not want to be alone with these very rich people."

"I'm supposed to be up there too, but I have to sit in the front. I'll come up after I speak."

Sandrine got up to sit on my lap. I slid her bra straps down, massaging her shoulders for a few minutes. I felt some of the tension in her neck area melt away.

"No, I don't want to sit away from you. I want to sit close to what happens. I have never been to this kind of auction before. Besides, how does this help if I talk to this lady?"

"Never mind. Come to bed. I can do a better job at the massage. And I don't have much time. My panel starts at two." As we moved toward the bed, she reached for another rugala.

"Very good. Not the same as French macaroons, but delicious."

I fell back onto the pillows and pulled Sandrine on top of me. Her large brown eyes were so trusting. My hands roamed her back, unsnapping the lacy brassiere. "Good thing I had lots of practice doing this with one hand in high school."

She smiled. We laughed as she stuffed the rest of the pastry in her mouth, rolling off me for a moment. I unbuckled my belt and slid down my clothes, kicking them off the bed.

"Take off your shirt," she said.

"No time. Just a quickie. I promise a magnificent replay later."

"Michael, you make me happy," she whispered in our post-coital embrace.

"I could get really serious about you," I said, coming out of the bathroom and buttoning my pants. I took her face between my hands and examined the bruise. "Sure you want to come for the afternoon session?"

"Oh yes. I am most interested to hear you. I was reading an article in your magazine this morning." She tossed one of my academic journals across the bed. "Ask me questions. I know the difference between a reliquary and a memento. The reliquary is the receptacle for the relics, homage to the saints, and the memento is a souvenir."

She surprised me. "And what else did you learn?"

"That I would like to see this exhibit of medieval religious objects at the British Museum. Most of the gold pieces came from the Vatican." She grinned with her knowledge.

"Hmm." Sandrine got better every day—smart, sexy and an advocate for obscure archaeology. I knew she was someone special. And then I beamed to my mother's memory. Boy, I wished I could take her home to hear what she would say. She'd love her.

Sandrine disappeared into the bathroom. "I will be out soon."

Chapter Twenty Seven

Miami, Florida
June 23, 1993

When I arrived at the hospital my mother was sleeping. The story about her and Estelle in the car on Christmas Eve got to me. My mother was a good person. I just didn't understand her motivations.

I sat down in a chair near the window watching the traffic. After a bit I wandered downstairs to buy a *Miami Herald*, catch up on the ball scores, read a few editorials. I waited in the cafeteria with my paper and a cup of coffee. Hospital eateries aren't a place of joy. The few other tables that had occupants appeared glum. No good news unless you're having a healthy baby or test results are negative.

I wasn't really reading, just letting the words float by me while my distracted brain tackled all the issues being thrown at me. Cancer. End-of-life. Antisemitism. Blacks in the South. What else could paint its way across my psyche in lime green and turgid yellow like the graffiti on the wall across from the hospital?

After an hour I made my way back to my mother's room. She was sitting up in bed, her head covered with a bright scarf.

"Oh, Michael. I was just thinking about you. The doctor was here. She says she wants to speak to you."

"What about?" She must have seen my face collapse. I had been waiting for this.

"She didn't say. Maybe I'm improving and I can go home."

I perched on the end of her bed. "Mom, your apartment's not available anymore." I understood the chemotherapy she had been through made her a little fuzzy.

"I can't go to hospice and be with people who are dying."

"Mom, we're all dying a little every day. These are end-of-life issues everyone faces."

Worry fleeted across her visage. "But I'm not ready yet."

"No one ever is. We all have to leave the party sometime. Some of us just make an exit a little early."

"Michael." She closed her eyes.

"Let's not deal with that now. What about a ride in your chair to the courtyard? Get you some fresh air."

Why hadn't the physician told her the next stop was hospice? Was I going to have to do it?

"That sounds good." She shut her eyes as though not looking at me could block out the pain.

"I'll get the nurse."

I returned with Susanna, an LPN who had been especially kind to my mother, a Jamaican lilt in her voice and an abiding nature. She assisted my mother into her robe and the wheelchair, a light woven blanket around her legs.

I took over wheeling her on our short expedition. My mother reached out to pat Susanna's arm.

"Reminds me of Estelle. Sweet like that."

We made our way to a respite spot in the garden. The smooth paths were laid out through the Saint Augustine grass lined with hibiscus bushes blooming red and white flowers. The clattering noises of the hospital gave way to birds chirping. Some families huddled on wrought iron benches, voices low, bodies bent forward to catch the words of their ill relative or friend.

I pushed my mother over to a quiet place in the corner. I had a bag with two bottles of cold water and a few contraband chocolate chip cookies from the cafeteria, probably the only decent thing I had tasted. My mother had lost so much weight I thought they might pique her appetite.

"It feels so good to be outside." She took a deep breath, even though the air was heavy with humidity.

I waited until we settled in and offered her the cookies before asking, "What happened with Arthur's mom?"

A different expression washed across her face. Suddenly, my mother was tired, the bags under her eyes a light blue. She settled her hands on top of the blanket. She shook her head no to the cookies. I wasn't going to mention Arthur's mom tried to seduce me.

"Do we have to talk about this?"

"Mom, if we want truth between us, if you want to feel complete—" I choked a little—"with us, it's important to me. I want to know everything." Susanna, sensing we needed privacy, moved a little bit away and felt for an apple in her pocket.

My mother released a sigh of weariness, as though talking about anything was a chore, especially if it was personal. "I can't just start with Arthur's mom. We didn't have all this self-examination in those days. If you went to a psychiatrist, you were tainted. It meant you were nuts."

"That's not true. Lots of people see a shrink."

"In those days if you had a problem, you kept it inside. Or drank. There weren't all these psychologists or family counselors hanging out their shingles. It wasn't until the seventies that I heard of people going to take workshops to 'find themselves.'"

"So what did you do if you had a crisis or your marriage was falling apart?"

"Gentiles didn't take out their family issues and scrutinize them. They avoided unpleasant topics, especially at home. A lot of thoughts went unsaid.

"I'm not sure how to explain this, but in the culture I grew up in we had arguments, discussions, and disagreements, all dissecting who said what and how they said it. Sometimes there were feuds and people didn't speak, sometimes for years, but for the most part we expressed ourselves openly. We didn't keep our feelings locked up.

"The story of Arthur's mom is painful for me." She glanced away past the wall and the highway, as though the unpleasantness would disappear.

"Why is that?" I felt a pang pushing her to remember the past.

"Michael, believe me. WASPs were living in one world and we lived in another." She paused to reflect. "I chose their scenario for most of my life. It looked simpler."

I sighed with so much to absorb, revisit, reinvent into something comprehensible. Without urging, she returned to my original question about Arthur's mom.

"Their attraction to one another was unmistakable. One evening I watched your dad dance with her at the club and knew something was up. It was the way she lifted her eyes to him. She had a bit of a reputation as a party girl. He was a big, good-looking guy, but my feelings for him had withered. Her husband traveled a lot. 'Doing business out of town' was a euphemism for 'fooling around.' A strange premonition wriggled up my spine as she cuddled close to him while they danced. I wasn't the only one who saw it. It had been going on for months. I couldn't ignore it anymore. And, I had a few drinks too, for bravery.

"I confronted Byron that night when we got home. It was a horrible fight where he said things that couldn't be taken back." Her eyes welled up with tears with the memory. "It was over."

"Where was I?"

"Spending the night at Arthur's house." That stunned me. I was there so often, but it never occurred to me my parents' marriage was unraveling while we were pilfering building supplies for our fort.

"What did Byron say?"

She gazed down, almost ashamed. "It doesn't matter."

"You said you'd be truthful. Tell me." I urged her, knowing I felt raw inside.

"He called me a 'Jew bitch' and a 'dirty Jew.' My stomach sank. I knew I couldn't love him anymore. Those words stung like spots of grease when I fried chicken. I shut down inside.

"His drinking had escalated to the point that he was drunk every night. In those days corporate started imbibing martinis at lunch and continued until bedtime. The culture of the country club didn't help. Plus, he tried to deny it."

She paused to take a deep breath. I knew this was painful to relive. I sat back on the iron bench, my body sticky with humidity. I wiped the back of my neck with my hand.

I too felt sick inside. The disintegration of their marriage and the subsequent financial strain roamed around my head. Not only did I have to examine my parents, but I had to look at where I fit into the world. Had I ever uttered a comment that was anti-Jewish?

In the fraternity house there were guys who were obviously prejudiced. What if they knew about me? And was it only a faith? Or something more? A race? A people? Where was I on that spectrum?

"So when I found out she wasn't the first, I had to leave. I had to maintain some dignity. I mean, there were other women who looked the other way as long as they kept their perks and weren't humiliated too much. I kept up appearances for a while, even though we barely spoke. Later that year when we found out Byron was getting transferred to company headquarters in Chicago, supposedly a step up on the corporate ladder, I surmised they wanted to keep a closer eye on him.

"I made up my mind not to go and fight the windy cold. I told him to go ahead, that I'd think about things and probably follow. I didn't want to interrupt your schooling, your life or move you away from friends. We agreed to sell the house, which sold quickly. I moved us to an apartment in Coconut Grove and served him with divorce papers. He was shocked. Women didn't initiate legal proceedings. I didn't have my own bank account. In those days, a woman couldn't get a credit card in her own name.

"Maybe it was wrong, but I stocked up on underwear, socks, school clothes for you and some Saks dresses for me before he knew. We weren't going to be shopping for a while. Later, I found the duplex in Coral Gables. I didn't want to go back to work because the judge took the man's side. He'd think you didn't need the money. I wanted alimony. Child support was only going to be for a few more years until you turned eighteen. I hadn't considered what it would be like to be a divorced woman, that my friends would abandon me, how tight money would be. I just did it. I felt strong inside, like I had some power. I felt I was in control."

I understood she had stretched to find a core of strength so she wouldn't feel defeated. Her hand tried to make a fist, but she was too weak.

"What happened to the Bradys?" I asked.

"She denied it at first, but when I confronted her in her kitchen one afternoon, she confessed. We both cried because it had been a friendship. She was a lively sort, always coming up with ways to have fun. They got a divorce too, but much later. It destroyed both of our families."

I remembered the awkwardness of the separation when I was fifteen and pimpled. My mother dropped me off in a used Dodge a few blocks from Coral Gables High every morning. It felt weird knowing my parents weren't together. Kids whispered at school. I lost myself in study. All I could think about was graduating and going to college and starting out fresh where no one knew me.

"Why did you insist I go see Byron in the summer? You knew I didn't want to."

I leaned forward to hear her answer. A few times my father shuttled me off to his parents in Wisconsin who had abandoned their farm to Byron's brother. They were living in a small apartment in town. A Miami kid had nothing in common with the teenagers who joined Future Farmers of America. I was bored out of my mind talking to goats. I couldn't wait for that part of my life to pass. I had blocked most of it.

"Because he was keeping up the alimony and child payments. It was only a matter of time before he married again, started another family and forgot about us."

The story reminded me of why I wanted to forget. How much had influenced me without my even knowing about it? I didn't know what to do with these details. Did they matter after all this time? As a professor I was used to having organized thoughts, a secure belief system, a logical way of dealing with bureaucracy and the world. I didn't know how to digest this information, where to file it.

Susanna walked over to us, her apple core wrapped in a napkin. "It's time for your momma to go back upstairs. She's getting tired."

In the last few minutes my mother's neck and head had fallen forward. She dozed to the musical sounds of birds hidden in the canopy of red-orange blossoms of a Poinciana tree above us.

Back in the room my mother slept. I sat in a chair near the window, my thoughts unspooling over my memories, hers and the reality of who I was—a half-Jewish professor with new revelations that made me infinitely more complex.

The door opened. A phlebotomist entered the room pushing a cart. "Time for a blood draw, Mrs. Saunders." She turned to me. "If you'll excuse us."

Before I left to call her doctor, I leaned over and kissed my mother goodbye on her papery cheek.

"See you tomorrow."

Her fingers lifted off the blanket in a goodbye gesture without opening her eyes.

Chapter Twenty Eight

Miami, Florida
June 24, 1993

My mother's doctor suggested hospice.

"She doesn't have long. It's metastasized to her lungs. By the time you make arrangements for hospice it might be too late. I'm so sorry. She's been a cooperative patient."

It was a lot to digest. Even knowing it was coming, it was difficult. The final stretch. I didn't want to move her again so I delayed making the call. I had so much to sort out.

At first I regretted not pursuing my father when I could have, maybe by staying in contact with his family. The kringle cookies I made with my grandmother—that aroma stayed with me. When Byron moved out, all his striving for success seemed useless. The last time I saw him he was living in a dumpy apartment drinking a fifth of whiskey a day. He'd been divorced two more times, dropping kids and wives along the way. I never considered contacting my half siblings.

From a practical point of view I was glad my mother was first and got her share. I had nothing to say to him and he never had much to say to me either, especially as a kid, asking superficial questions about school, which I answered politely. It had always been a strained awkwardness between us. It's not that I didn't feel he loved me. He didn't care enough. No sharing of feelings, motivations or inner thoughts. Once, he said to me, "Michael, get a good job with a corporation like Sears and Roebuck, stick with it, advance up the ladder and they'll take care of you. It's a good, solid life."

Maybe it was the times. So much was for appearances in the fifties. In their heyday they seemed to be enjoying themselves with friends, dinner parties, trips, the club. No one could have guessed they were having trouble. Even me. Life was a sitcom with corny dialogue and prescribed roles.

No one could have predicted the end of the sixties and the beginning of the seventies when cosmic shifts altered everyone's universe. Neither of my parents got into drugs; alcohol was the preferred choice for most of that generation. I grew my hair long and smoked pot a few times in college, but it wasn't my bag.

My mother changed her style of dress to some gauzy blouses and a headband once in a while and my father let his hair grow out a bit, sideburns creeping down his cheeks. For the most part, though, they were straight arrows. They stayed insulated in their upper middle class world, ice cubes clinking in their glasses through John F. Kennedy's assassination, hippies, and Vietnam War protests. They said little if anything about the riots in Chicago or Black Panthers. A few people from the club had sons who served in the military, but if there were discussions, it was who had connections to get into the Coast Guard or how to get a deferment.

In the next few days my mother's physician pulled me aside and said she couldn't do much more for her, reminded me that it was time to move her to hospice, start a morphine drip and complete any unfinished business. She told me in a sensitive way, something I surmised she'd done many times before, but it hit me hard. I didn't want it to end. I felt she still had secrets.

I broke down in the visitor's lounge. So much grief poured out of me, it was an explosion, like a veteran with post-traumatic stress syndrome. How was I supposed to process this? Where did this part fit? I never thought much about brothers or sisters, but now I realized how alone I was. I had to get a grip for her sake.

After that I left the rest of my search for family stories alone. My mother slept a lot and appeared drawn, her pretty looks faded away forever. What was the point of causing her more anguish? I had the truth and it was too late to do anything about it. I was finished with dissecting why my mother kept her story for so long. It's not like I was to going to start tracking people down, digging up the past, investigating a new religion. Nothing changed for me. I was still an atheist, a cynical one at that, who knew his roots.

"Mom, when the time comes, where do you want to be buried? Should I contact a minister or a rabbi?" I couched the questions as though it was only a possibility.

"Oh, Michael, I don't know. I haven't given it a lot of thought. I intend to hang around and play with grandchildren."

"C'mon, you know I'm not the kids type." She responded with a slight smile because we had teased back and forth so many times about expanding our family. "Mom, I have to know what you want. Cremation?"

"Yes, that's fine. I don't like the idea of you having to come down from Connecticut to visit a cemetery. Now let's talk about something else."

"What kind of ceremony?"

"Oh, I don't know . . ."

With my mother's agreement to cremation, she added, "I know it's not popular after so many were murdered in the ovens, but I don't want you feeling obligated to visit a grave site. Just do the efficient method and be done with it."

I protested, but she continued. "Honor me by having fun, making some good choices and eating a gourmet meal with a great bottle of wine." Her weak smile let me know she meant it. "Maybe say a prayer even if it isn't part of your realm. Think about me once in a while."

The martyr response zapped me. I would think about her the rest of my life. She had been a good mother, albeit with a few gaps in judgment. She was already maudlin so I had better ask another question while I could. Her face was expectant, pale with an absence of lines.

"What am I supposed to do with the ashes?"

She waved her hand in a noncommittal motion I interpreted as "whatever."

Chapter Twenty Nine

New York City
September 23, 1993
2 p.m.

The symposium room was only two-thirds full after the lunch break. "Typical for the afternoon session of a conference," I told Sandrine who took an empty seat next to me in the back. With her hair in a ponytail and no makeup she could pass as a student assistant. A few more people wandered to their seats with cups of coffee, available outside the door.

Dr. Sommerstein opened the session. "Will the participants on our panel entitled 'God's Gold: Fact or Fiction?' please take the stage? Let's welcome Dr. Michael Saunders, professor of archaeology at Yale University and visiting scholar at the Sorbonne; Professor Yossi Farber, head of the antiquities department at Tel Aviv University; Dr. Ehuda Yanger, international director of biblical archaeology at Hebrew University, and Emily Woodruff, senior specialist of antiquities at Shropshire Auction House."

I squeezed Sandrine's hand underneath the table as I pushed back my chair to make my way to the front of the room. We were lined up in chairs behind long tables with two microphones stationed in front of us. Emily Woodruff, the only female member, dressed in a tweedy jacket with pearls, sat at the end shuffling through papers. I was closest to the podium with Yossi seated next to me. I cleared my throat. All the action will be on this end, I thought as I caught Sandrine's eyes in the back.

Sommerstein began, "With the controversy surrounding the objects known as God's Gold exploding worldwide, what do you see are the issues?"

Yossi raised his forefinger, leaning forward to pull a microphone toward him. "I'd like to speak to the question." He pushed his glasses up on the bridge of his nose.

"I am an Israeli as you can tell from my accent. The objects in question—the silver trumpets, the candelabrum and the ceremonial gold table—could not have survived two thousand years. When you examine the history, it is obvious these fragile objects, which we have all viewed by now, could not have been transported through so many centuries without being destroyed. The theory that the Vatican had them in its basement is a plausible one, but bogus. That is the first issue. The second issue—"

I interrupted, "But what about the carbon dating?"

Yossi shifted his body to face me. "Carbon dating can be wrong. There are experimental errors, spectrometer discrepancies, differing philosophies and imperfect scientific techniques. Despite what the media promotes, radiocarbon dating is an imperfect science. I'm disputing that these are objects of religious significance and the fervor created around them, as well as the carbon 14 dating, are hype. I contend there is a conspiracy to verify them so that some can enjoy financial gain."

"What?" asked Professor Yanger. "Do you have proof?"

Infuriated, I slammed my hand on the table. "That's ridiculous! Those of us who are qualified in the antiquities field rely on carbon dating—with or without the high or low chronology dispute. If you don't accept these findings, then you're going to have to disqualify most of the museum exhibits around the world."

I settled into my chair, surprised at my vociferousness.

"Yes, and there are those with shoddy credentials who dispute our recent findings of the tomb!" said Yossi, referring to King Herod's tomb and its excavation outside Jerusalem, a known controversy to the academics in the room. "All of the papers about this, including the auction, are built on the theory of one man, Maurice Dubois, who relied on other scientists for verification. It is a house of cards."

"Gentlemen, please!" Sommerstein tapped the microphone on the podium.

I watched Sandrine shift in her seat. She hadn't seen me in this role until now, comfortable yet passionate. This is what my world was about—scientific research, often disputed, academic papers with opinions, teaching with inspiration and knowledge. She told me on the way over that she found me fascinating, that she wanted to know more.

Yossi and I argued our positions. The sole female interrupted us. "Our institutions, as well as the international staff, stand behind the findings. As implausible as it may seem, the spoils from the destruction of the Temple in AD 70 are recognized and the world community acknowledged these objects as original to that time period and—"

Yossi raised his voice. "That is not possible. This is a way to raise funds. Of course the auction house that stands to make millions in commissions would support—"

Professor Yanger, a soft-spoken man, inserted, "I think the greater question is where these artifacts were during this span of time, how were they cared for and who is responsible for their release? Carbon dating hasn't changed much since it was discovered in the 1940s. I agree only the table could be examined because the metal objects are inert, but who's going to take responsibility prior to that?"

"That is of no import to this discussion," shouted Yossi, on fire with rhetoric. He launched into the history of secrets devised by the Catholic Church until interrupted by Sommerstein.

"We have to stay on topic."

I reached across to pull the microphone toward me. "There is far more documentation about the validity of these objects, which have been studied since their release onto the open market fifteen years ago."

"Bullshit!" yelled Yossi.

Insulted in front of my peers, I pushed back my chair in anger. I wanted to punch Yossi out, but I was still bound by a modicum of propriety.

"We are going to have to cut this off if you can't communicate in a civilized fashion," said Sommerstein.

Yossi grumbled something to himself in Hebrew while I slid my chair forward.

The panel continued. "Final comments, Dr. Saunders?" Sommerstein, visibly rattled by the confrontation with accusations of monetary gain, wanted to wrap up. He was used to disagreements, but this had been tinged with hostility. Did his lack of impartiality to acquire the artifacts make him look bad? He asked each person for a brief summary while glancing at a small timer on the podium.

Yossi and I glared at each other as the others concluded, emphasizing their points. It was obvious to me that there was a serious question of validity to God's Gold, along with political insinuations. This could be a long few days.

As we left the stage a collective sigh exhaled from the participants. I made my way back to Sandrine.

"I'm ready to get out of here," I whispered.

"You do not need to stay for the rest of the program?"

"I'm done." I gathered my belongings and papers to stuff into my briefcase. "Let's have some fun before the auction tomorrow. Interested in the Museum of Modern Art? No artifacts there."

Sandrine smiled, touching my arm.

Chapter Thirty

Miami, Florida
July 8, 1993

When my mother passed away on July 4, I was relieved she had shared her truth with me. Her candor gave me a lot to contemplate, but that's what I do anyway, ruminate about my world–research, competition, students. It wasn't a holiday for me, but she would have enjoyed the fireworks exploding in the Miami sky. It meant I'd always remember the anniversary of her passing. Just like her to have a little glitz and glamour on her way out.

I consulted the clergy associated with the hospital. The Jewish custom was to complete burial as soon as possible. I called the recommended place and with sanitary efficiency her body was picked up. Cremation was not customary; however, the ashes were returned to me in a small wooden box in three days. I was struck by how light they were. The human body doesn't take up much space when reduced to ashes.

I spent the next few days completing paperwork, taking most of her jewelry to a store for resale, saving a few expensive pieces from Byron that had appreciated over the years, and going through her address book to call friends. No one was from the old crowd. They all disappeared into the ether after the divorce, but she had a cadre of girlfriends she shared time with–movies, theater, meals. Oddly enough, she joined a mah-jongg group near the end, a Chinese tile game Jewish women liked to play. They were the most responsive.

I wanted a reading of the *Kaddish*, a Jewish prayer for the dead. I figured if she told me about her religious beliefs this late in life, they meant something to her. I couldn't do it, but a volunteer came over to my motel the day after the ashes were delivered to read it with me. Three friends from her weekly mah-jongg game, the manager from Sandra Post as well as a younger woman who lived in her building showed up with Danish and a tray of fruit in the dated lobby the following day.

An older woman, who didn't look familiar, also came. She reached out to put her hands around mine. Petite with silver hair and a fashionable shawl wrapped around her shoulders, the double handles of a purse hung from her wrist.

"I don't know if you remember me. Ruth Rosenbaum, your piano teacher's wife, Ivy's mom." It clicked into place. "I saw your mother's obituary in the paper and called the hospital. They gave me your information. I'm so sorry. Your mother was a wonderful woman. And she loved you very much. We lost touch after the divorce with so much tumult. And of course the piano lessons ended. I'd stop in to say hello to her at Sandra Post on Miracle Mile once in a while. She had such class."

"Wait a minute. You used to sit with my mom in the kitchen during my lessons. You and your husband stayed with us while my parents traveled one time."

"Yes, such a beautiful home on Greenway Drive. They went on a business trip, a real treat for us to stay at such a lovely place. One time Ivy stayed with you while we went to Cuba. My husband loved the Latin rhythms." She stepped aside as another woman approached to murmur her condolences.

I touched her arm. "Wait. Please don't go." My head whirled with bits of information. Maybe she could answer a few questions for me. Did she know about my mother?

"Oh, I just wanted to offer my sympathy for your loss. I took the bus here and I don't want to miss it." Her eyes watered. "Mr. Rosenbaum of blessed memory passed a few years ago and Ivy lives in Atlanta with her family. I'm a grandmother," she said with pride. "I never learned how to drive, the New Yorker in me. I just came to wish you well. You were a nice little boy."

"I'd like to ask you a few questions. I have a few confusing memories."

"Oh, I couldn't answer anything. We were friends for a period of time. You know how that is. People pass through your life. Now that I'm older I do my best to keep life simple."

"But I want to talk to you. Can I buy you lunch or dinner tomorrow?" I didn't want to sound desperate but a montage of photos flipped past me: my mother giggling with her in the kitchen, an ashtray full of cigarettes, the two of them sitting next to each other listening to Mr. Rosenbaum play show tunes or Gershwin, the Halloween Ivy spent the night, the time they came out with red-rimmed eyes.

"Oh, I don't think so. It's really not necessary. I don't go out much in the evenings anymore."

"I'd be happy to pick you up and take you to lunch in the Gables. How about the Biltmore?"

Ruth hesitated, conflict clouding her face. "I don't really remember so much. And I don't want you to go to any expense. Besides, I have my mah-jongg game tomorrow."

"No. It's my pleasure. My mother didn't share a lot and I'd like to know a little more about her when I was growing up. A cup of tea after your game? I remember the two of you drank a lot of tea."

She smiled. "Sara made it for me Russian style in a glass with a lot of sugar."

"So I can come at three?"

"Oh, I don't know. I take a nap in the afternoon."

"Please. I really want to talk to you about my mother."

"Well, okay, but not tomorrow. The day after is better. But my mind clouds up sometimes."

She left after she gave me the address of her apartment building close to Miracle Mile. I watched as she walked with a deliberate slow gait through the door to sit on the bus bench out front.

Chapter Thirty One

Miami, Florida
July 9, 1993

It was a sad goodbye to a complicated life. I felt empty inside, considering it may have been a completion for my mother. But it wasn't for me. It created a void that I couldn't fill.

What was I supposed to do with the ashes? I didn't want to take them to Connecticut with me. My mother had no connection to Yale. Then I got the idea to take them over to Biscayne Bay.

The next day in the early morning hours I found a dock that stretched out into the water, a few dark-skinned fishermen slumped over their fishing lines. Next to them sat brown paper bags with a possible lunch, bait lined up and metal tackle boxes distressed with use. A bevy of seagulls circled overhead.

I opened the box from the mortuary at the motel, so I only brought the plastic bag tied at the top with a small wire, a round metal tag with numbers attached. I carried it in a paper grocery bag. No name, nothing. How do I even know they're her remains? I shrugged my shoulders and exhaled. This is what it all came down to—a bunch of ashes. Tears squeezed into my eyes. Was I sad because her life didn't turn out the way it was supposed to or did I feel despair because I didn't really know her? How could you be in the same house for eighteen years with a parent and not have a clue as to who they really were?

It was illegal to dump anything in public waters, especially a body, but I surmised she'd be happy overlooking Biscayne Bay, the lights of Miami

Beach twinkling at night, the breeze of palm trees calming the air. I turned my back away from the others, opened the twist tie and slipped the tag into my pocket. I held her on my lap, opened the top toward the water and watched my mother slip away into the inky bay.

For the second time I cried, sobs and tears flowing through me. I didn't try to stop. I just let it happen, like so much of my life. I felt ripped open, my body, my head, all my guts spilled out. I couldn't imagine feeling whole again.

"Hey, man, you okay?" shouted a voice farther down the dock.

"Oh yeah. Sure." I wiped my face with the back of my hand, stuffed the plastic bag into the grocery one and stood to stroll away with a lighter load. I wouldn't be good for much the rest of the day. The tentacles of a headache started to creep around the front of my forehead.

When I returned to the room, I shut the shades. The migraine seeped in and filled up all the space like a damp cloud. I was drained from allowing my emotions to take over. I never cried like that. I loved her and I knew she loved me. I slept for hours.

When I showed up at Ruth Rosenbaum's pink apartment building the next day, she was waiting for me in the lobby, dressed in a light-colored silk dress, glasses hanging from a pearl chain around her neck. She wore low-heeled black pumps, her handbag stuffed next to her in a flowered upholstered chair. I leaned down to kiss her cheek.

"Thank you for doing this. It means a lot to me."

"I don't know what good it will do. Your mother was a private woman so I'm not sure how much I should reveal. Besides, she was a delightful friend when we were close."

"So you were close?"

"Yes, for a period of time. Can I offer you an iced tea or a lemonade? We have nice amenities in the rec room." She paused. "Once she said to me—I had brought her some *hamentashen* from the bakery—that she never had a friend she felt so secure with. Maybe it was because she could be herself with me. We both came from similar backgrounds. Are you sure I can't get you something?"

"No, thank you. I'm fine. Unless I can get some for you." I'm focused so I don't waste a moment.

"No, I have a kitchenette upstairs. I'm good." She waved at a woman shuffling by with a red aluminum walker, her purse perched in the basket.

"What was the word you just said? What did you bring her?"

"Hamentashen. It's a three-cornered cookie with a filling in the middle. Sometimes poppy seeds, prunes, apricots. Jewish people eat them at Purim. She almost cried. She said she hadn't had any in years."

I shifted in my seat. "What was it for?"

I didn't want to overwhelm her with questions because her demeanor was skittish. She could take off for the elevator in a moment, leaving me sitting in the senior apartment lobby alone. I took an internal sigh.

"Jewish people celebrate everything with food. It all means something. The three corners are symbols of the defeated enemy of the Jewish people, the ears of Haman, the man who wanted to destroy us. Ach, you don't want to hear such stories."

Her eyes fluttered behind her glasses. "One thing I should tell you. She changed her name."

"Yes, I know. It had been Epstein."

"No, not that name, her first name. She took off the *h*. She said it made her sound too Jewish."

"Huh? I don't understand."

"During the war the Germans set up the Nuremberg Laws. They said all Jewish women had to take the middle name of Sarah and all the men, Israel. So she took off the *h*. Or actually I think your father did it. But to tell you the truth, I don't see what difference it made. Sara? Sarah? I never met a Gentile named Sarah anyway."

While I pondered that, she unclipped her handbag, withdrawing a yellowed newspaper photo. "I found this."

She handed it to me. I recognized my mother and Ruth on the street in small hats clutching shopping bags, Ruth reaching out to hold my mother's arm. They were a study in contrasts—my mother dressed in a black sheath, a necklace adorning her pale neck, a hand clutching a white cotton glove, blonde waves tucked underneath the hat, smiling with her complacent expression, her gaze looking off to something in the distance while Ruth wore a printed dress with a bow at the neckline, her eyes meeting the photographer's camera with confidence, dark curls hanging across her forehead, the hat tipped to her crown, brows penciled and lips darkened.

"Where's this from?"

"The *Miami Herald*, probably the late fifties, early sixties. I don't remember."

"Why was it taken?"

"I don't know, really. Two fashionable ladies out shopping. We were so surprised and delighted. It made us feel like celebrities."

She took it out of my hand to fold in half and tuck back into her purse.

"But, wait. Why was it taken?"

"Who knows? A human interest story. Everyone saw it. By then shopping centers were popping up in the suburbs. Maybe it was to keep shoppers coming to downtown Miami. It was still Burdines's biggest department store. Your mother loved Hartley's too."

She reflected for a moment, opening the piece of paper again. "Maybe I shouldn't have brought it downstairs. But it's all I have of her. I knew which album to look for it in. Too many problems. I didn't want to hear about it."

"Problems? Why?"

She shifted, uncomfortable, reluctant to share more.

"No, please tell me. My mother was such a mystery." I gave in to a sense of urgency.

She looked down, speaking with deliberation. "Michael, I don't know how much you know about your mother's life before she married your father. I'm not sure she shared this with you, but she was Jewish."

"She told me that near the end. Why was it such a secret?"

She paused so long I thought she'd forgotten what we were talking about. Then she fiddled with the glasses chain, smoothing her skirt.

"We had a great time together the day the picture was taken, shopping, having lunch. She drove us in her big yellow Cadillac. I loved it because we had a used Olds. I liked a little luxury. After the picture was taken we were exhilarated, like we were movie stars for a moment. Then we went home. We both forgot about the photographer and the picture.

Everything was fine until a few days later when the photo was splashed across the front page of The *Herald's* local section. I was thrilled about the attention in my neighborhood. My friends were impressed or a little jealous, but your mother's group at the country club gave her a hard time."

"What do you mean?" I folded my hands, a schoolboy ready to listen.

"Even though they didn't have our names, everyone recognized us. Her friends wanted to know who the lady was with the dark hair. Did she live in the Gables? She didn't belong to the club. Was she Italian? Greek? Worse, Jewish?

"Ay, it's hard to explain. In those days people didn't mix socially unless they were in the same class, religion, neighborhood. They teased her. At that time no one knew she was Jewish. Only me. And I found out only a few months before when your grandma died. She had to fly to New York. We got very close because I could speak to her in Yiddish. You know what that is?"

I nodded. I didn't want her to stop talking.

"I was the only one who understood her background. Except your father of course, but she had sworn not to mention it. Bad for business. I just wandered into her life. My husband was such a good soul. The man worked three jobs. I went with him when he gave piano lessons to keep him company. Usually I waited in the car with Ivy.

After the second time your mother, always gracious, came out and invited us in because it was hot. I was a teacher's wife. Otherwise, our paths would never have crossed. I remember walking into that great big living room with yellow wall-to-wall carpeting, a white sofa, a baby grand piano at one end, fresh gladiolas on the side table and central air conditioning spewing cooler temperatures through vents in the wall."

I saw Ruth drift away for a moment as elderly people do when they're telling a story. I waited until she resumed. Her memory was remarkable. Our living room was just the way she described it, even the addition of central air when the window air conditioners gave out.

"Anyway, the picture caused a stir with the women gossiping. They wanted to know who I was and how she knew me and what was my name. Your father said to cool it so I stopped coming to the lessons. We talked on the phone during the day. Then she had marital problems and things began to fall apart and—"

"So you were speaking Yiddish in the kitchen when I walked in that time?"

"Yes. More like whispering. She didn't want you to know."

"Why?"

Frustration billowed up again. Why such a conspiracy to not tell me the truth?

"She wanted you to have all the privileges, the best schools, the right clubs, things the other kids did. We were segregated in those days. Like with the blacks."

I sunk into my chair. What a crazy subterfuge to protect me. To protect me from what?

"Listen, darling, I'm getting a little fatigued. I rest in the afternoon. That's all I know. Just remember her as a good person. She had a pure heart and she loved you."

With that, she hunched forward to rock herself out of the chair. She handed me the yellowed newspaper photo. "A memento." She kissed me goodbye, a waft of her perfume leaving a trail.

Chapter Thirty Two

Miami, Florida
July 13, 1993

Most of my mother's clothes and furniture had been disposed of at Goodwill. When you're going into the hospital, you don't pack much. Sad how little was left at the end. I kept a few pieces and photos, but what was I going to do with them? Who was going to clean out my stuff when it was time for my passage? Without any parents, I felt like an orphan.

Her penury surprised me at the reading of the will, a lonely affair at her attorney's office in Coral Gables. I don't know how she saved anything working at Sandra Post on Miracle Mile after the alimony ran out. I thought she spent most of what she made on tickets for the symphony or shows at the Coconut Grove Playhouse or clothes. Always stylish, she wore smart dresses and heels to do errands until the end, when she couldn't keep up appearances anymore.

Once, after she learned she was ill, I flew in one weekend to assist her. She said, "Michael, can you believe I'm going out in sneakers and a track suit? I never thought I'd dress like an old lady." The transition from being independent weighed on her. She grasped she wasn't going to get better.

The attorney, an older man she knew for years, surprised me after some pleasantries. "With the proceeds of half the house on Greenway Drive, your mother invested in some blue-chip stocks after her divorce—ATT, Xerox and the IPO of Home Depot. She had some good advice, always investing her dividends. I spoke to her broker, a man named Fromm when she liquidated everything. She also had an IRA. Your mother was a savvy woman."

He leaned across the desk and handed me a cashier's check for four hundred and fifty thousand dollars.

I was so shocked I sputtered, barely responding. She never said a word. I saved most of my money as a tenured professor, but this windfall opened some other possibilities for a guy without an elaborate plan. The academic world gives credence to published papers and endowments, not small, or for that matter, large in Brooks White's case, inheritances.

What would she have wanted me to do with her hard-earned savings—the trip to Paris we always talked about, a better apartment, another dig? Mostly, she wanted me to find a partner and settle down. She would mention grandchildren, but she knew the possibilities were slim.

Once, in a wistful tone before my mother revealed she had cancer, she said, "I haven't set a good example of familial relationships so I don't know how I'd be as a grandmother. But if there were a surprise, I could figure it out." The truth was my former wife and I had decided not to have a family. I had no intention of any surprises with anyone.

I thanked him when my words returned, took the check he placed in an envelope and regained my composure. With a handshake, I muttered, "How did she do this?" Another secret she never bothered to share.

When I returned to the apartment in New Haven, the rest of the summer stretched in front of me, a long yawn that I needed to stifle. I wanted something to get away from death and dying, something that would make me spin alive like a trip, something different. Paris came to mind because I had been there for a conference a few years ago without much time to enjoy it. And, I knew it was something she always wanted to do.

After days of contemplation, I pursued a lecture at the Sorbonne that I left hanging when my mother and her illness came to the forefront last April. With the September conference in New York coming up, it seemed an interesting place to distract me—museums, food, wine, a chance for anonymity while I examined my life. My plans to leave for a different environment flowed. It was an opportunity to start my year of sabbatical early, a sense of gratitude to my mother with a slice of guilt thrown in, which meant I must be Jewish.

Chapter Thirty Three

New York City
September 24, 1993
12:30 p.m.

On the afternoon of the most publicized auction in Shropshire history, heightened security started outside the grand entrance. Men and women in dark suits with headsets as well as decoy officers tracked the open courtyard in front of the building. Besides the usual guards near the brass revolving doors at the main entrance, a phalanx of police officers was stationed to examine photo IDs and special passes issued weeks before to attendees, with a hologram that could not be copied.

The possibility of terrorism after the World Trade Center explosion in the basement garage in February had all of New York City on high alert. Two helicopters buzzed overhead. Metal detectors had been installed at the entrance for the occasion.

Some attendees approached on foot after manipulating the subway to a nearby stop. With the street partially closed off, others arrived with chauffeurs in limousines that dropped them off at the curb a few hundred feet away. Today, however, since this was a closed auction, no one would be allowed to enter without a pass.

Shropshire personnel had been asked to report at 8 a.m. through the basement parking garage, although the auction wasn't scheduled to begin until 2 p.m. Some employees drove in from the suburbs; most of the upper management, their backs stiff with tension, arrived in chauffeured Lincoln town cars.

Typically employees entered with their IDs at a side entrance of the building, but today that entrance was sealed. The New York City Fire Department objected so personnel were stationed inside the door in case of emergency. Everyone had to enter through the garage and take the elevator upstairs to the main floor.

The garage that serviced the auction house allowed for fifty stacked cars, not nearly enough for the crowd expected for today's event. A dour attendant dressed in a khaki uniform took the cars when personnel or guests arrived, drove them onto an elevator and maneuvered them into tight spots on the upper floors. A female attendant, her picture identification card clipped to her belt loop, asked for names and keys in exchange for a receipt card. The hollow sound of slammed doors, a few shouts and the roar of engines in a closed space echoed against concrete block walls.

The loading dock at the other end of the garage was set up for unloading artwork, large and small, into a freight elevator. Delivery trucks arrived at the same entrance as the cars and then drove to the other side where another attendant in a glass cage checked them. Nothing would be admitted today unless he could pull it up on his computer screen. No deliveries were scheduled; however, this was how the valuable artifacts arrived two days ago.

Inside the main entrance, behind the reception desk of cherry wood that swept across the front entry, five efficient-looking men and women dressed in muted tones examined their computer screens. The main auction room was expected to be filled to capacity, capped at 456 attendees with 310 absentee bidders who submitted forms weeks ago.

Although catalogs were mailed three months ago to potential buyers who expressed interest and paid the thousand-dollar fee for them, a stack of the elaborate magazines laid at the end of the counter. With an abbreviated version available online, most potential clients paid the fee for easy access.

God's Gold items graced the cover, the candelabrum and trumpets suspended above the decorated table. Inside, photographs of archaeological items as well as ancient manuscripts included lengthy explanations of lots displayed. Emily Woodruff, not normally assigned to the front area, paced behind her staff, blond hair slicked into a ponytail, wearing a black sheath dress, matching pumps and the requisite pearls of the well bred.

Lists of attendees, those who would be escorted upstairs to the private room, everyone who had paid the catalog fee plus personal information, remained in reports with security codes. A professional buzz kept everyone attentive and attuned to the rhythm of the day. The standard double check of alarms, air conditioning, generators in case of electrical failure and guards had been accomplished. Emily's posture reflected one of high alert.

Standard auction protocol was to gather credit card and banking information when attendees arrived, unless they frequented with regularity and their account was on file. Certain doyennes, museum acquisitions directors, their designers and assistants as well as eccentric collectors were known to the staff.

Today, however, everyone had to register to establish their credit no matter how well known they were as clients. Due to the extraordinary amounts of money expected to change hands, the objects would not be released until payment was doubly confirmed. Arrangements had been made to transfer the lots from the secure basement parking underneath the building into armored cars for delivery in the days after the auction.

Emily's eyes spun to the left of the front desk where a small anteroom held bookshelves. It too was paneled in cherry wood, the smooth grain a backdrop for catalogs of previous auctions attached in their upright position with small chains. So many tourists wanted to take them for souvenirs. An annoyance on most days, she knew no one would be wandering in today.

At 1 p.m. spectators arrived, some hustled in by their chauffeurs or assistants who handled the details of the front desk. Most received catalogs in the mail; however, everyone needed a paddle with their number to hoist in the air for bidding.

Emily greeted Mrs. Luisa White, dressed in a beige silk suit, a small hat hugging her head and Ferragamos, their distinctive bow a recognizable status symbol to the staff trained to look for them. Her assistant, a young clean-shaven man dressed in black, held her elbow with one hand, a copy of the catalog pressed under his arm. "This is Robert," she said to introduce him, "my secretary."

He acknowledged Emily with a nod.

Emily greeted her by clasping both of her gloved hands. "It is such a pleasure to have you here with us today, Mrs. White. May I personally escort you to our viewing room?"

"Of course, dear." She turned to her companion, "Let me know when Brooks arrives. I'd like him to sit with me."

"May I introduce you to Agatha Spears who will be assigned to you for the afternoon? She will take care of your every need and accompany us to the viewing room." A young woman in a navy suit stepped forward.

Mrs. White examined her as though an unpleasant aroma was in the air. "Agatha? Quite an old-fashioned name."

"Yes, m'am. I am named after my great-grandmother who was a founder of Wellesley."

"Yes, we like to hire young people with pedigrees in education and art," added Emily.

"Might I have an extra copy of the catalog?" Luisa White asked as she turned to look at Robert standing behind her.

Agatha hesitated. "Of course, we are happy to accommodate you, Mrs. White. We placed a hefty price tag on this one to keep out curiosity seekers. Every archaeology student in town wants a copy."

"I can assure you Robert is not a curiosity seeker. He is a qualified personal assistant with a degree in art history."

"Of course, Mrs. White," Agatha said, placing her hand with care on the small of Mrs. White's back to guide her down polished stone floors to the elevator. Robert trailed, unsure if there would be seating for him.

"How lovely. My Brooksie is a Yale man."

I paused at the back of the room to survey the scene, Sandrine by my side. I held a leather briefcase that I purchased after my mother's passing, a rare treat for a frugal guy. On the right side of the room, elevated by a banquette, almost two dozen men and women gathered in front of computers to take online bids. Those who were seated wore headsets for bidders who would call in their offers while others stood behind them. The men, dressed in tuxedos, were serious, lips pressed with intensity. One, a red pocket square popping color on his jacket, exhaled.

The women, mostly in their thirties with refined haircuts or ponytails low at the neck, knit their brows while they stared at their screens. Some were already online, hands pecking with intention. Tension pervaded the banquette of people and computers. I saw one man snap at a colleague while another shifted her chair away from a competitor. Millions, maybe billions of dollars, would change hands today. And, one of them, with a winning bidder, would garner an extraordinary bonus from Shropshire Auction House.

On the empty stage two podiums stood side by side, the name *Shropshire* inscribed with gold letters gleaming, a polished wooden gavel perched across the top. Behind the podium hung a large screen displaying the company logo and the date: September 24, 1993.

The main auction room filled with people. Paddles and catalogues littered the seats, laps and even the floor near bidders' feet.

I had participated in auctions before, but none of this caliber. A battle of millionaires was about to erupt. Why not? It wasn't only politics that brought out the greed in people.

Recognizable from the photo on television, Wen Yee, the diminutive Chinese diplomat, breezed by us with an entourage of dark-suited men that included the tall Asian woman in a yellow silk dress, a slit exposing a glimpse of thigh with each stride.

Sandrine whispered, "She is wearing a cheongsam with Christian Louboutin stilettos."

"A what? How do you know what kind of shoes they are?"

"Because the soles are red and a cheongsam is traditional dress for Chinese women."

According to the report, Wen Yee, was an exceptional businessman with interests all over the world and the most powerful representative of his government.

"Who is she?" Sandrine asked. "*Trés chic.* I have never seen such a tall Asian person."

"I don't know about her, but he's in town to purchase the artifacts."

"What do they want them for?" asked Sandrine, her eyes touring the room.

"Status. Acquisition. He's known for his vanity and brilliance as well as connoisseurship of the arts. It's a coup for his country."

"But what's the motivation? I am trying to understand their power."

I smiled to myself. Sandrine's French accent charmed me, but sometimes her syntax was off.

"I don't know if some eccentric is going to hole them up in his private collection, or a consortium of museums wants to purchase them to share with the world. Wen Yee, with his ruthless reputation, could one-up the Americans and Europeans on this. It's a matter of establishing culture and sophistication." I leaned closer. "They could go home with the prize tonight."

"But I thought the Israelis or Brooks's mother want to buy them. What is 'one up?'"

"Getting the better of someone."

"Oh. In France we say, '*Prendre avantage sur quelqu'un*.'"

I had little hope of French fluency, let alone remembering idioms, but her translation reminded me that I adored her.

We followed the crowd. "The Chinese don't believe in religion. It's a superstition. It would be quite an achievement for them to own artifacts the Judeo-Christian world deems extraordinary."

Sandrine walked ahead of me down the aisle to the front row reserved for experts and dignitaries where they had been instructed to sit. Hair slicked back into a French twist, wearing a black sheath dress on her thin frame, heels and signature red lips, a few heads turned, especially to watch her confident Parisian walk.

She leaned in to say in a soft tone as we sat down, "But where does so much money come from?"

"Industrialization of China, selling arms in North Africa, new businesses. Their booming economy."

Sandrine looked surprised. "Why do they want them without religion?" She adjusted her dress to cover her knees.

"Maybe they think the God's Gold items belong to everyone and want to purchase them as a goodwill gesture, a way to show their dominance." I paused, adding, "Communism doesn't support religion, but it doesn't keep people from believing. They can't eradicate it. Ironically, they're the largest producer of Bibles in the world."

A Shropshire employee went up the stairs at the side of the stage to test the microphones on both podiums. She signaled to the sound booth in the back of the room.

"What's up there?" Sandrine asked, taking the opportunity to twist to the side and look at the VIP room, nodding toward a large dark rectangle that reflected light on the left side of the second story.

"That's the private quarters where Brooks and his mother can view the auction through one-way glass. Sommerstein wanted us up there but I said no. We're better off right here."

Sandrine raised her eyebrows, sitting in repose for a few minutes, head bowed over the catalog. She raised her eyes, slipping her hand into mine.

"Something bothers me. You haven't told me about your mother."

I felt awkward. A flash of dull pain seared my temple, a sharp reminder that I was not in control of my migraines. No, not now. A shimmer of nausea slithered from my stomach to my mouth.

Even during our intimate moments I hadn't shared my mother's whole story. Yet. I told Sandrine tidbits of my childhood in Florida, a sharp contrast to hers in France, but I hadn't tackled the grenade my mother hurled, because I hadn't processed it. I felt guilt reviewing my anger near the end, pushing it down like bile after a bad meal.

"She was Jewish." It wasn't my intention to blurt it out, bursting into the space between us.

Sandrine's eyebrows rose surprise. "Oh."

"I didn't know until the end."

My body relaxed with the relief of the spilled secret as I squeezed her hand. Sandrine, with an expectant expression, searched my face.

"I'll tell you more, I promise. After all this is over. We're going to be together for a long time."

She allowed her head to dip to my shoulder. "Yes, I feel this too."

Chapter Thirty Four

New York City
September 24, 1993
2:45 p.m.

"Robert, my purse. I want my opera glasses." Luisa White, used to issuing demands, sipped a Perrier in a crystal highball glass, lime perched on the rim. She peered at the crowd below on the auction house floor as though they were ants.

"I don't mind sitting on the ground level, but it is so much more pleasant viewing from up here." She spun her chair in front of the glass away from Robert to face Brooks sitting in the row behind her. "And you, dear, how are you holding up today?"

Brooks swiped his bad-boy bangs off his forehead. "I'm fine, Mother."

"You could have worn a suit instead of your university blazer."

"What are you prepared to spend?" He looked away and checked his watch, fidgeting with the delay.

Luisa continued, authority dripping in her voice. "I spoke to the trustees of the estate. They said I can offer as high as five hundred million. Of course I want to donate the God's Gold items with other pieces we acquired over the years to the university. Your late stepfather was quite a collector, with a vivid eye I might add, and quite the hard bargainer too. I used to tease him about Jewish blood on his mother's side."

Brooks bristled at his mother's remark, but it was acceptable in their rarified circles to make disparaging comments among themselves. He glanced behind him to see if Barbra Streisand had heard. Apparently it hadn't registered because she made it clear she did not want to speak to anyone else in the room besides her assistant. As a foremost collector of Judaica, she studied the catalog with intensity; her tinted reading glasses sparkling, familiar graceful hands with elongated nails searching a page.

Brooks rolled his eyes at Robert.

Luisa, oblivious to her prejudices, continued, "The board at the college is quite enthused. It'll bring the donations of archaeological items to one-point-two billion, if I can get them for that price. Dr. Sommerstein promised to name the collection after us as well as put our name on the Arts and Sciences building. They still have quite a bit of work to do on their capital campaign so it might be years before completion." She patted her son's knee. "Might even be after I'm gone."

Brooks stretched his arm across the empty chair next to him. "Mother, why don't you give it to charity or buy a pied-à-terre in Paris or Rome like some of your other wealthy friends?" He shook his head.

Luisa commented on the décor in the VIP room with its somber grey stitched flannel walls, grey upholstered chairs and a stocked marble bar with a tuxedoed bartender in attendance. A red telephone connected to the floor downstairs.

"They could use a few decent antiques on display in here for us to look at," she said to no one in particular.

A wave of relief swept over me. I didn't know what Sandrine's reaction would be. She took it in stride. I did my best to stay focused with the echo of a headache looming.

Soon I was going to be called as an expert so I fussed with my tie, checked the top of my zipper and patted my jacket pocket for my readers. Sandrine, next to me, stayed engrossed in the pricey catalog. The auction began with a voice offstage.

"Welcome, ladies and gentlemen and honored guests. Our auctioneer today is Mr. Royal Dabney, veteran of more than one thousand Shropshire auctions."

The audience delivered scattered applause as a portly gentleman in evening clothes and white bow tie strolled out and stood behind the main podium. He exuded breeding, a double chin revealing how much he enjoyed his meals. He greeted the audience with a nod.

I felt the weight of the event and the circumstances that catapulted me here. If not for Maurice, I'd be a spectator in the back of the room.

"Today, my assistant is Mr. Brian Proctor, who will monitor the audience bids submitted from the floor." He too entered from stage right in a tuxedo, acknowledging the audience with a thin-lipped smile. "A small reminder to staff and audience: Except for our VIP viewers, those of you who have cell phones are not permitted to use them during the auction."

He gave a small wave to the upstairs gallery. "The analog technology is susceptible to cloning, which means they are not secure. We want to make sure everyone has the same advantages so please refrain from using any devices on the floor. That includes beepers." Sandrine knocked Michael's ankle with her foot.

Photos of a tombstone from various angles projected on the screen behind the two men. The audience reacted with a few *oohs* and *aahs*. It may not be what they'd been waiting for, but the enthusiasm meant the auction had begun.

Royal Dabney addressed the audience as they buzzed. "Shropshire Auction House welcomes you. Good afternoon, ladies and gentlemen. There is great interest in our biblical archaeology items. We begin with smaller lots first before God's Gold is brought to the stage. On the block are six tombstones of Jewish and Christian origins.

"I call attention to our screen of lot one, a Jewish tombstone from Zoar, or Zoara as the Greeks called it, from the fourth to sixth century. At eight inches wide and sixteen inches high, it gives a wealth of information including the name of the deceased, the day, month and year of passing and an expression of *shalom*, which means 'peace.'

"I'd like to call to the stage for commentary Dr. Abydos Capaneus of the Hellenistic Institute in Athens, an expert in ancient biblical treasures."

A pudgy man in a shiny blue suit with a bad comb-over approached the second podium. He adjusted his square-framed glasses.

The first object was wheeled out with care, propped up on a steel table by two employees in khaki jumpsuits wearing white gloves.

Without looking at the audience, they exited when the locks on the table legs were secured.

Royal Dabney moved aside while the microphone, adjusted down for the professor's height, relayed a screech. The professor stepped back, his bushy eyebrows rising above his glasses. Dr. Capeneus began with an explanation in a flowing Greek accent, speaking in measured tones.

"This piece of the Byzantine era has the inscription in Aramaic. Ochre red coloring used during that time colors a seven-branched menorah inside the border." He turned to glance at the gravestone, a pin light illuminating the stone, the star of the stage, giving it the prestige of a museum piece.

"I am here to authenticate that the gravestones are probably from people who were fleeing the Romans in the Great Jewish revolt of AD 66 to 70. Although the final Jewish defeat did not occur until AD 73 or possibly AD 74 at Masada on the west side of the Dead Sea, many tombstones have been uncovered in caves from that area." He faced the auctioneer with the expectant look of a student who had finished his test and wanted to leave.

"Thank you, Professor," said Royal Dabney. "How rare are these gravestones for that area?"

"The six that you have today have been authenticated from the Safi region, southeast of the Dead Sea. They were not discovered until the 1980s in Zoar by a construction company putting in irrigation systems. Most were unearthed by Jordanian villagers who took them back to their homes or sold them to collectors or wealthy business owners. Consequently, only three hundred and eighty-six were saved out of seven hundred. Looting was rampant prior to that. Due to the dry climate in that area, the Christian and Jewish gravestones are well preserved. I would say they are rare, and in my opinion, of museum quality."

The auctioneer came back to his microphone as the professor exited the stage to audience applause. He took a small bow before he sat down, his head shiny through the sparse hair.

"And now, let's start the bidding. We begin at twenty-five thousand dollars. Do I hear thirty?"

Paddles raised and lowered, fingers popping up from the employees at their computers. A palpable anxiety stalked the room. "Thirty-five, forty? Can I get forty-five? I see fifty." The auctioneer's smooth patter led to frantic bidding, numbers going up and down.

"This is so interesting," Sandrine said to me.

"Wait. It gets better," I whispered back. A tympani of throbbing pulsed in my temples. Why hadn't I brought a pill with me?

Upstairs in the viewing room, Brooks studied his mother who appeared bored.

To no one in particular she said, "I wish they'd get to the good stuff. I read up on these gravestones. The Christian ones are more valuable because they've been incised instead of painted. They, at least, have some artistic value. I previewed one that had a Christogram with peacocks, an ancient symbol of immortality." She placed her hand on her chest. "I've always wanted peacocks for our backyard but they make that God-awful noise."

Luisa turned to her son. "The Jewish stones are plain, like their houses of worship. Nothing compares to a grand cathedral or a well-appointed church. Brooksie, have you ever been in one of their churches?"

"No, Mother. I don't even go into ones of our faith. And they refer to them as temples."

Chastised, she faced forward.

The auctioneer evaluated the mood of the audience by surveying the room. The success of any auction was determined by the first item, setting the precedent for the day.

"Do I hear two-fifty? Who's going for three hundred thousand? Esteemed buyers, this is from the biblical era. Let me read you the translation from the stone." He put on his reading glasses to peer at the paper in front of him. "Esther, daughter of Levi, died on the third day of Sivan, four hundred and three years after the destruction of the Temple. Peace upon Israel. Peace."

People around Michael and Sandrine hummed with comments.

"Very significant."

"The details make her so real, I have chills."

"Maury, can you imagine the rabbi's face when he sees that hanging in our living room?"

The audience's murmuring stirred me. They felt an emotional connection to the young woman from sixty-six Common Era in the arid land of Zoar. Esther slid down my consciousness. I had a relationship with her. If not for my mother's confession, would I feel the same?

The bidding pumped higher. A few of the amounts brought squeals, nervous coughs or gasps. The audience, a show unfolding, narrowed to a handful of players. I watched as the Chinese group consulted among themselves, leaning in toward Wen Yee who sat in the middle. The auctioneer was lashing them toward a higher number, pursuing eye contact with the final few. Royal Dabney's assistant marked down each bidding amount. Finally, it petered out.

"Ladies and gentlemen, esteemed collectors, an American museum paid one-point-one million dollars for an ancient Judean coin at an auction here two months ago. It was a silver *shekel*, dated to the first year of the First Jewish Revolt against Rome in 66 Common Era, minted as a declaration of sovereignty. This gravestone is from that time period. Four hundred thousand twenty-five seems small. Do I see four hundred fifty? Thank you. And where is five hundred thousand?" His persistence drilled the audience until bidding arrived at eight hundred thousand dollars.

"I must point out that there were only two *shekels* available and we have six gravestones today, but these are exceptional and uncommon. We might not see anything this rare again for decades. If ever.

"Eight hundred thousand going once, going twice, I see a paddle. Thank you, sir, for your bid of eight hundred fifty thousand dollars. Are you going to let this gentlemen steal the prize? The bidding activated again, reaching a cool million. "Going once, going twice, sold! To number two-two-three for one million dollars." He closed it with a slam of his gavel.

"Congratulations on your fine purchase."

"Maybe this is a good job for me with my accent," Sandrine teased Michael. "How much do auctioneers make?"

I thought for a moment, distracted by my headache that ratcheted up a path to my temple. "I don't know exactly, but I think they get seven to ten percent with high-end items. Then the auction house adds on a buyer's premium." I could see Sandrine calculating the amount of money from the first sale.

"This could add up," she said with a smile. "What's the premium?"

"Shropshire will add on an extra eighteen percent for expenses and commissions that the buyer has to pay."

"Oh, that man just spent more than a million dollars."

The sold gravestone, wheeled off stage, lost the limelight as another took its place. The audience, jittery with expectation, grumbled, settling in as the auctioneer began again.

"Our second lot is a Christian tombstone from Zoar, also in excellent condition. Generally they are rectangular and highly decorated by the artisan. This one, made from local sandstone embellished with a large cross, palm fronds and numerous birds, represents an extraordinary specimen. The text of the epitaph written in Greek says this belonged to Petros, Peter in English, a popular name from the apostles . . ." He continued pointing out specifics that were enlarged on the overhead screen.

Royal Dabney recited the background of each piece, where it was found, whether the carbon dating had verified the findings. More experts were called to the stage to comment on the authenticity of the pieces. At a certain point, as he wended his way through lesser items with little drama, fewer paddles bounced up and down. Someone groaned as a catalog slipped off his lap. The audience wanted God's Gold.

The six gravestones sold with a rhythm of enthusiastic purchasing. Several celebrities, including Steven Spielberg who sat off to the side, bid without anonymity. Others, who didn't want to be acknowledged, must have placed their bids with the attendants because the deck was busy. A sluggish buyer risked losing because of the fast pace.

But millionaires and billionaires could be elusive. I dealt with a few at Yale. Squirrelly is how I would describe them. In this rarified world of acquisitions, speculation swam around three art collectors: Bill Gates, Ron Lauder and Steve Wynn. They weren't here that I could see. Maybe they were upstairs or bidding over the phone. Or maybe it would be a hedge fund manager from Greenwich? Or a Russian oligarch? Trophy art had to be better than trophy wives. It couldn't cheat on you.

"And now, ladies and gentlemen, most distinguished members of our audience, this is what we've all been waiting for." The auctioneer raised his hand and motioned to stage left as the God's Gold items were wheeled out on steel tables and positioned under spotlights by three Shropshire personnel in khaki jumpsuits wearing white gloves. A tall, good-looking attendant with slicked-back grey hair positioned himself next to the first display, his plastic ID tag clipped to his waistband.

Photos flashed from every angle of the rare artifacts on the overhead screen. Light applause and expressions of joy with palpable excitement played through the room. The bank of computers with attendants stirred with activity—phones to ears, hands to mouths to muffle conversation, the incessant clacking of keyboards and the restless movement of people who expected big bonuses for assisting their clientele in making the purchase of a lifetime.

The silver trumpets suspended in a bulletproof case reflected prisms of light. The musical instruments resembled what the audience would recognize from symphonies, except for the elongated throat. The instruments used to call the Creator—magnificent and unique with biblical significance—inspired reverence. The audience hushed.

Their obscured patina, black with centuries of tarnish, revolved slowly to reveal a patch on the battered bell of both items polished to dull silver.

"Any alterations to an artifact are rare; however, in this case, we wanted to authenticate that the trumpets were both fashioned from ancient silver. According to our scholars, the precious metal was probably mined in Egypt," Royal Dabney added.

"I don't see any wires," Sandrine whispered to me.

"You won't. These museum and auction people are very clever that way." She gave me a slight push on my leg.

I was blinded by the extra spotlights. If I were at home, I'd darken the room in silence to get past the peak of the headache.

The mature guard rotated the table with caution so everyone in the audience could get a view. I looked around to see their reaction.

People stretched forward, necks craning, while those in the back stood up. Police stationed along the side of the room cautioned a few to step back to their seats.

On the other end of the stage the twenty-four-inch gold candelabrum gave off sparks as it gleamed in the lights. The overhead photos commanded the room as they revealed the pedestal where the seven prongs lifted their arms. The base was encrusted with sea monsters and eagles, ancient pagan images, which were unusual. Research verified the Israelites deemed them acceptable in that time period. The six branches with a place at the top for pouring oil and placing wicks sat on the base, with a center arm that held a spot for oil.

Royal Dabney began again, reading from a card, "As a representation of the Jewish faith depicted on the Arch of Titus in Rome, the conquerors knew the symbolic significance of lighting the world for the faithful when they pillaged this sacred menorah from Herod's Second Temple, halting the vision.

"This precious metal candelabrum stands majestic and proud, a memento of thousands of years that have passed. To note: This is not pure gold, which is too soft. Analysis has shown this has been mixed with small amounts of copper, silver and zinc."

The guard for the candelabrum, a short, stocky man with a moustache, cracked a brief smile. Then he pursed his lips as though he was ready to whistle, hands hanging at his side. He took his cue from the auctioneer and walked the table in a small circle. The audience cooed with excitement.

A slack-faced guard with deep creases on his face lifted his chin, casting his eyes to the audience. In a parade rest pose, his hands locked behind him, he was behind the center display covered in a black cloth. He waited for the audience to settle down at the auctioneer's urging. When the nod came, he slid away the cloth, flaunting the Table of the Divine Presence.

The audience cheered, pulsing to their feet with applause. The guard rotated the octagonal table in a small circle so it could be viewed from all sides. It was, by far, the largest and most valuable of the three items displayed.

The Table of Divine Presence, a glorious representation of what had been used as an altar, gleamed with the admiration of the centuries. The craftsmanship, a breathtaking work of gold and precious stones, brought tears to the eyes of some in the audience, including a man with a black velvet yarmulke sitting a few seats from us. In his long black jacket and pants, he wiped his cheeks with a handkerchief before the tears melted into his wiry salt-and-pepper beard. I felt an emotional connection.

Although many in the audience were in attendance for the cocktail party three days before the auction, viewing the artifacts without tempered glass gave an aura of intimacy. Once again, the auctioneer settled them down with polite pleading.

"Ladies and gentleman, I know you want us to continue. We need your attention. All of these items will be sold as a single lot. The significance of them is known by most of you; however, I would like to share the specifications of the candelabrum given in the Bible from God to Moses on Mount Sinai.

"I quote, with a few exceptions for repetition of our ancestors, from Exodus twenty-five-thirty-one-forty: 'You shall make a lamp stand of pure gold. The base and shaft shall be made of hammered work; its cups, its calyxes, and its petals shall be one piece with it, and there shall be six branches going out of its sides. Three cups shaped like almond blossoms shall be of pure gold.'"

My reaction, subdued on the outside, didn't reflect what I felt on the inside. Somehow, in some distant way, I felt linked to this. Did it remind me of my mother and the denial of where she came from? How far back could I trace our lineage if I tried? The latest DNA research said all Jews came from four women. It meant something to me that each generation passed on their belief system to the next despite the odds of survival. I wanted to examine more when this was over. I shifted with restlessness, tuning into the audience's applause.

After a dramatic pause Royal Dabney continued, "Distinguished guests, we are looking at the result of God's instructions to Moses, an extraordinary theory even if you are not a believer." He used his gavel to calm the audience. The police officers who rimmed the room took a small step forward. The auctioneer sipped water from a glass on the podium's edge.

"For those of you who cannot view details, I want to share with you that The Table of Divine Presence stands at twenty inches in height, covered in precious stones." He read from a sheet of paper. "A meandering pattern decorates the sides of an open lattice network adorned with small eggs, twists of rope and pieces of fruit. It leads the eye to the surface, a grandeur of onyx, emeralds and carbuncles all secured with gold pins.

"The top of the gold table represents the best of precious stones for the time period. A rhombus placed in the middle sparkles with golden amber and reflective crystals. All four lily-shaped legs are identical, the flower petals wrapping to the underside with the base of the legs crafted from carbuncles and deep red garnet stones. Ivy and ancient acanthus leaves, spiny and strong, wind up the legs. Underneath the table, leaves bow out to the viewer. It is a work of art, evoking emotions of the centuries."

As the overhead projector activated another round of photos, I glanced at my watch, reaching for a sheaf of papers in my briefcase. It only took us an hour and a half to get to this point. I knew I would be called to the stage for authentication, a job that Maurice would have relished.

Although I presented information on a regular basis to students and colleagues, I felt awkward. The migraine had taken over. Perspiration popped above my brow, a full marching band of cacophony. I have to do this.

"How's my tie?" I asked Sandrine in a brief retreat into vanity.

"You look smashed," she responded. A quick smile flickered across my lips.

"Would Dr. Michael Saunders please come to the stage?"

"Now we're finally getting somewhere," Luisa White uttered to herself from her vantage point. "Thank goodness I'm up here. Whoever wins will be mobbed if they're in the room.

"Robert, I'm ready for my gin and tonic."

I approached the stairs at stage right. The auctioneer's assistant moved over to allow me to stand at his podium. I placed my papers in front of me, a crutch for a professor who wasn't a professional speaker.

"Please help me welcome Dr. Michael Saunders, professor of biblical archaeology at Yale University, author of numerous scholarly papers on

God's Gold. Roscom College, one of our sponsors, has asked Dr. Saunders to authenticate these treasures in lieu of Dr. Maurice Dubois, who was the unfortunate victim of an accident."

The audience responded with a hum of explanations as stories about Maurice echoed through the room. With the amount of publicity garnered, most had heard the story. The drama of the moment expanded. From the stage I heard a woman in the front say to her partner in a harsh whisper, "People have been killed for these. Do you think it was an accident?"

I watched Sandrine touch her cheek, knowing she must have been thinking about the subway.

"Although this paper is based on the late Dr. Dubois's research, I have incorporated my own theory into it since the professor is not here to present or defend it.

I paused to read, "The overwhelming vision of history catapults our brain to the time of Moses."

I glanced at Sandrine, rapt with attention.

"I appreciate the healthy skepticism of many experts worldwide. In an attempt to answer some of the queries surrounding this unusual offering, it will not be possible to share all of the data required to bring them to this point. I refer you to your catalog and scientific papers for those details. If I share the research scientists have accumulated on this topic, we might be here until next week. I know most of you prefer we start the bidding."

I flashed my best cheesy smile as a few heads nodded at my sarcasm.

"First of all, the artifacts have been through years of rigorous scientific examination. Although I was not there for the original process, it is undisputed by scientists that they were crafted from before the conquest of Jerusalem by Titus in 70 of the Common Era.

"Most likely they were used to celebrate the traditional Sabbath. There is a great deal of conjecture about these rituals and the symbolism of the artistry. I cannot speculate on that. Suffice to say, even when they find a new home there will continue to be worldwide supposition into the future.

"What I can share are the facts. The evidence is manifold from the Arch of Titus in Rome displaying the spoils of the conquered to a dozen scientific opinions about their authenticity.

"Most often I am asked how they survived to be here. It is impossible to trace their journey through time and subsequent ownership by vandals, barbarians and thieves; however, the Catholic Church, one of the most powerful and secretive organizations in the world, gained possession of them, either by purchase or trade, sometime after 380 CE according to the Roman historian Bishop Eusebius of Caesarea, who wrote the first history of Constantine.

"The Vatican, built on one hundred eight acres in Rome in 326 CE, West of the Tibor River, holds artworks in trust for all of humanity, and has stored them in its labyrinth of catacombs for centuries. The Tower of Winds built in 1578 is seven-and-a-half miles of bookshelves that lead to the church's most valuable documents and artifacts residing in a vault at the end behind a heavy locked door. A chief prefect wears a key that never leaves his side. There are no known witnesses that have entered this room.

"The candelabrum was viewed by Rabbi Yitzhak Herzog, chief rabbi of Israel, who met with Pope Pius XII during the 1950s for the purpose of having Jewish children who had been baptized during WWII, then residing in monasteries, returned to their families. It was during that meeting that the pope showed the artifacts to him in a private viewing area.

"The rabbi demanded their return to the Jewish people. The pope refused. Upon the rabbi's homecoming, he launched a campaign to have the children as well as the artifacts restored to where they belonged. It fell on deaf ears.

"In the early 1970s the pieces known as God's Gold were released to cover mounting expenses created by priestly scandals that continue to be brought forward worldwide. The church has never offered an explanation as to their origins."

My allusion to them caused Wen Yee and the Chinese contingency seated in the front center of the room to lean over and whisper to one another.

"At this point in time my duty is to have examined the research completed without speculation as to how these artifacts arrived on the contemporary scene." I paused for a deep breath. "I can verify they are the greatest archaeological treasures from biblical times that have survived to this day."

Applause burst from the spectators in the room, a resounding affirmation of anticipation. A few people stood with fervor.

I gathered my papers, nodded to the auctioneer, his assistant, the audience and climbed down the stairs to return to my seat. I felt self-conscious with the attention. Sandrine grabbed my hand as soon as I settled in, an expression of rapture on her face.

Luisa White with her second-story vantage point said, "Electrifying. They're absolutely stunning. I've never seen anything so extraordinary in my life."

Brooks leaned forward to touch his mother's shoulder. "Mother, stay calm. If you're going to spend my inheritance, at least enjoy yourself. There's going to be a lot of competition." He signaled to the bartender to make him another drink.

"Thought you were on the wagon," Luisa said when she saw the drink being delivered.

Brooks shrugged. "Not today."

Among the other notables in the VIP room besides Barbra Streisand were a Brazilian banking widow who revolved her chair away from them; a dot-com mogul with an entourage of five leaned in for a whisper fest, and a real estate tycoon in sunglasses drinking a cocktail. Everyone stood to get a better view, attentive to the sound piped into the room by small speakers in the corners.

"I know this is an emotional moment for many of you," the auctioneer began, acknowledging a woman crying in the front row. "Due to Shropshire's unique offering, the opening bid will begin at a modest twenty-five million. Do I have thirty?"

Royal Dabney, an entertainer in all respects, knew the psychology of the auction, the ebbs and flows, the drama of a good show. He refrained from the auction chant heard in unsophisticated venues, the patter of "Two thousand looking for three. I have two thousand. Will you be three?" With the practiced art of driving bids higher, the acute sensitivity of freezing at the right moment, sometimes deriding the audience to make a stronger commitment, he never compromised integrity or refinement as a dedicated professional.

The auction began with paddles lifting in the audience as well as surrogate bidders waving from the banquette. The singsong repetition of bids also appeared on the scoreboard above them.

"Do I see seventy-five million? We're just getting started for these irreplaceable treasures. Do I see eighty-five million? Only eight collectors have ever paid more than one hundred million dollars for a piece of art. Will it be you?"

Once the first hundred million was announced the auction thrust forward in twenty-five-million-dollar increments. We watched in amazement. Even at these high numbers very few dropped out.

"Two hundred-fifty million."

"Four hundred million."

Luisa White emitted a sigh from her eagle's perch. It was not going well for her. They were reaching the peak too quickly. She'd be out of the bidding if they kept up this pace. She settled back into her seat.

Brooks touched her wrist. "They're almost at your limit." He sighed in relief.

Luisa leaned back, rigid with tension, her lips tight. "I know. But I thought I might have a chance."

"What if someone must make a pee-pee?" Sandrine asked me, tilting her head.

"There's no getting up at this point," I told her, relieved to be finished. My meds. I can't believe I forgot to add them to my briefcase. How soon could I make an exit?

"Four hundred-fifty million."

The prices reached astronomical levels, the adrenaline of the audience palpable in the room. The bidding stalled. Royal Dabney took a white handkerchief from his pocket to wipe his brow. He sipped water while peering at the audience.

The pause inspired Wen Yee to lift his paddle.

"We have five hundred million."

A standing Shropshire employee held out a finger to signal she needed a minute. Royal Dabney leaned his arm on the podium acknowledging her with a smile and commented, "I've got all the time in the world." The audience roared, breaking the anxiety.

A nod insured the next bid. "I have five hundred-fifty million. Who wants to make it six hundred?"

Another signal from a Shropshire employee, her hair in a tight bun, meant the bidding sailed to the next level. It was the number bandied about internationally and leaked to the press as a possible high bid for the items.

"Six hundred million," said Royal Dabney, his hand cradling the microphone. "I urge you not to stop here. The opportunity to own these objects has not passed. Let me see six hundred-fifty." He stopped to drink water. The break ratcheted up the theater of auction. The audience emitted a collective sigh.

The Asian woman in the yellow cheongsam retreated down the aisle, a momentary distraction, while the others huddled.

I told Sandrine this was the climax, the part when all was revealed in a dramatic play, where the protagonist professed love and the killer confessed.

Suddenly, Yossi Farber, shouted, "Fraud! There is fraud! These artifacts are not authentic. The carbon dating was not accurate. It was tampered with at the laboratory. There must be an investigation!"

Chills ran up my spine. I recognized Yossi's voice and accent immediately. I turned toward the commotion. Yossi was visible in the back of the room standing at the end of a row.

"The carbon dating done on the table is false. The world changed in the 1940s because of nuclear bombs, reactors, and open tests. It changes the results. The carbon dating isn't accurate!"

"Security! We need security," Royal Dabney announced still in control of the microphone. He added in *sotto voce*, "I knew something like this might happen."

An academic difference of opinion had driven Yossi to make a scene? Angst coursed through my body. Who was he to make such an accusation?

Yossi scrambled onto a chair. "The professor, Michael Saunders, does not give you accurate information."

I was shocked to hear my name.

In moments four officers grabbed Yossi's waving arms and legs, pulling him from his perch. They hustled him toward the red exit sign as he struggled against them, continuing to shout with defiance, "If not a conspiracy then shoddy research. Stop the auction! You do not know what you bid on."

Chaos erupted as a few Israeli friends pulled at the officers shouting for them to release Yossi without success. From where I stood it was a melee.

"Please remain calm. This will be taken care of momentarily." The auctioneer, his face glistening with sweat, paused as a man in a suit approached him from the backstage wings. After whispering in the auctioneer's ear, he disappeared.

The hiatus allowed the audience to focus as Yossi's harangue continued. Yossi's diatribe could still be heard among the police shouting to clear the area near the exit.

"Your authentication is false. Why didn't you ask me? The carbon dating is not constant. Investigate the scientists!" he bellowed, a wounded animal fighting for its life. More police rushed toward the back of the room.

"The scientists who worked on this were duped. Or bribed. . . ." Yossi's voice faded away.

"Attention, please. I have an announcement. Please do not panic." Visibly shaken, Royal Dabney said, "I'm sorry. We cannot continue. There is a bomb threat. We must clear the building."

A few women screamed. Chairs tipped over as people headed for the doors, forgetting Yossi who had been silenced as the first to exit. Crackling two-way radios from security personnel zipped around the room. The audience gathered their belongings, panicked.

I stood up to get a better view along with most of the audience, alarmed at the idea of a bomb, maybe under our seats. Sandrine glanced around. She was the calmest one in the room.

Royal Dabney stayed at the podium while his assistant rushed stage left for a better view. Many focused on the disturbance, people craning their necks to see and rushing to leave.

"Please exit with care. We must clear the room." The officers did their best to organize people to depart in an orderly fashion. A door on the other side of the room opened and the audience surged through it.

"Who was the guy yelling?" people asked. Others, pulsing with concern for their safety, tripped over catalogs, shoes, even purses left behind.

The high-pitched shrieks of women pierced the air, drowning out others who urged themselves toward the doors. More chairs fell in disarray as people tried to climb over them. A few people crouched under their seats, blocking the aisles.

The religious man who had been seated near us rocked back and forth in prayer, his eyes shut with intensity.

Why did Yossi wait until now to object? He'd been challenging me for weeks. We had differences of opinion, but what did he think he was doing? Did he plan a bomb scare to go along with his outburst?

The auctioneer, who never lost his cool, did his best to calm the crowd. "Everything is under control." When he saw that it clearly was not, he disappeared behind the curtain.

Chapter Thirty Five

New York City
September 24, 1993
4:30 p.m.

The three Shropshire guards on stage propelled the God's Gold artifacts off to the left, balancing the rolling carts with care. Once back stage in the shadowy lighting, they glided with deliberation toward a large service elevator. The main guard entered a code, inserting a key attached to his belt. As the doors slid open they advanced with caution. Trained for emergencies, they did not speak.

The silver-haired guard rammed a button with his thumb. As the elevator streamed to the basement the shorter man leaned his shoulder against the beige mattress padding that lined the confined space. He asked, "What the hell happened in there?"

"Be quiet. We have a job to do. Just keep moving until these auction items are safe," said the boss.

The basement storage area ran the length of the auction viewing rooms underneath the main structure. In the storage area that equaled the dimensions of two footballs fields, the security guards wheeled the three carts with the artifacts off the elevator. Every aisle's contents, wrapped in plastic, grouped and stacked to the ceiling, revealed a number taped to the wooden frame they sat upon to identify lots. Some included names—Rosenfield Estate, Perth Trust, Ambrose Beneficiary.

Shropshire Auction House, a worldwide consortium of private sales and public auctions, stacked valuable furniture, including rolltop desks, commodes trimmed with gold, antique bed frames, Oriental carpets, bronze sculptures, Ming dynasty vases, clocks, marine chronometers, silver tea services, Tiffany lamps, priceless art, all for future auctions. Hundreds of antiques filled the space grouped by items. Manuscripts and jewelry were stored in another climate-controlled area. Wealthy patrons with multiple homes utilized their services for safety.

The men lined up the carts along the wall next to the elevator where dollies and crates were stored. The veteran guard with the full head of silver hair knew his responsibility, eyes searching for anything amiss. He proceeded to a steel door on the right, entered another code and chose a key. It swung open.

"Move them in here quickly. Be careful."

"In the fifteen years I've worked here, never had to evacuate the stage," said Eddie, the chubby guard." Unintentionally, he bumped his cart against the wall.

"Hey, watch it, goomba. Line 'em up," said the boss.

"I seen a lot of auctions but this one beats everything. My grandma in Staten Island wanted to come in for this, but they wasn't givin' out any extra passes," said Eddie, straightening his cart with the extra weight of a man who enjoys a big plate of pasta. With his smudged white gloves he did as he was told. "You callin' me a goomba cause of my 'stache?" He wiggled his upper lip at his supervisor.

The quiet guard snorted with amusement.

"Shut up. Just do your job. Ernesto, get these carts even."

Slack-faced, void of expression, he stepped with precision.

"Put a tarp over all three of them. Eddie, grab the end and let it float down gently onto the top."

The men grabbed corners, watching as the material settled like a sheet caressing a bed, to cover the God's Gold treasures.

"We don't have time to rewrap them. Place is a bomb shelter. No one can get in. We'll have to come back."

They exited as the code was reentered and the lock turned.

"What's going on in the auction room?" Eddie asked the boss as he re-tucked his shirt.

"Beats me. Some nut started shouting and then the auctioneer said there was a bomb threat."

Eddie said, "I watched the guy who whispered something to the auctioneer. He looked worried. You don't think it's a plot to steal them, do ya?"

"So if there's a bomb threat, what are we doing here?" asked the other guard. "I'd like to evacuate."

"Our job is to insure the safety of the items, keep them from harm. They're secure now," said the guard responsible.

"We'd better get back upstairs." He peeled off his gloves and put them in his back pocket.

"Let's go." A sense of urgency growled in his voice. "Hurry up. Let's take the stairs back up to the stage. Elevator's slow."

A walkie-talkie crackled. The supervising guard responded. "Ten-four. Valuables secured. Returning to upper floor, pronto."

Eddie asked, "Can't understand who bids on this stuff. Millions of dollars too." He tossed aside his spoiled gloves.

"Our job is to protect all of this valuable shit even if we think it's ugly. We have hours of wrapping ahead of us. C'mon. We gotta go," the boss said, pushing the door underneath the red exit sign. They begin their ascent.

"Think there's a bomb in the building?" Eddie asked, his voice echoing in the stairwell, huffing with his extra weight.

"Nah. Someone just wanted to clear the room. Police and FBI went over this place with metal detectors yesterday and this morning," said the boss.

"But why do people buy this stuff? Honestly, it looks like a lot of stuff my grandmother has in Hoboken."

"Hey! Didn't you learn anything in the antiquities training?"

"Yeah, yeah, yeah. But why do they buy it?"

"Because rich people need it. Makes them feel better. We have a beer and a steak for a splurge. They buy fancy stuff. Lot of them are collectors. It's their hobby. Geez, you ask more questions than my four-year-old granddaughter. Hurry up. We don't know what's going on upstairs."

Chapter Thirty Six

New Haven, Connecticut
November 11, 1993

Yale didn't officially let me go, but I couldn't stay. Even though I had tenure, the embarrassment of being wrong about the artifacts had been humiliating. I wasn't the first professor with a bad paper. This could follow me around for at least a decade. Where does a tainted professor go? Some Podunk community college in the Midwest? Thank God my department head thought it a better idea to extend my sabbatical–my mother's death and all–and turn the publicity away from academia.

New Haven with its small town intellectual superiority was not a place for a besmirched professor left out to dry, so mostly I stewed about what I could have done differently. Let's face it, if Sommerstein hadn't asked me to step in for Maurice, I would have been another name on a long list of anonymous academics at the symposium. His fascination with my *savoir faire*, country club background as he put it, catapulted me into the middle of a mess. If only he knew how little of that there was.

I'd have to go back through years of research to see how I was duped by Maurice and try to figure out how he was involved. He wasn't even here to defend himself. Was his death murder? I don't know. It sure looked like an accident when the truck driver's autopsy came back with methamphetamine in his body. He was fifty miles from home after a two-day run. But who knows?

Could someone have engineered it? Maybe. Such a nefarious plot with so many pieces. I won't be the one to find out. The investigation continues while my name is tainted. I was made the fool, even though there's no connection to me as a lowly professor on a long list with others who thought this was the discovery of the century. I'm the one they remember. My demise was that I believed a colleague's data.

What I didn't know when I authenticated God's Gold artifacts utilizing Maurice Dubois's carbon dating and firsthand account, was that he was willing to compromise his integrity. He craved acknowledgment, his outsized ego looking for recognition. He must have been tied to the scientists who were willing to take a bribe from some conniving billionaire.

At first, Yossi Farber became a prime suspect with his outburst. I heard he was detained for weeks. In the end, though, he was the clever one. He exposed the research when one of the scientists left out of the payoff groused to him the items weren't legitimate. The carbon dating couldn't be done on the trumpets or the candelabrum since it doesn't work on metal, so only the wooden table was scraped for a sample from the underside. Enough doubt was cast that Yossi couldn't keep quiet. He was willing to create enough of a stink to cast doubt on the process.

I was pissed at Yossi, but I understand now that when Maurice vanished from the scenario, I was the next target. And the bomb scare? Hardly a coincidence. Whoever masterminded it did not want the items authenticated and wanted the auction stopped. Detectives interviewed me early on, but it was obvious I had more questions than answers. They dropped me. No motive. Or not clever enough.

Secondly, the locations of the carbon dating were kept secret so no one knew who was working on what. I heard they dismantled a lab in Turkey and another in France tracking people. It only took one disgruntled employee to start the rumor, one that turned out to be true. Yossi picked up on it and started poking around. He tried to persuade me, but I put my faith in Maurice. Big mistake.

My reputation, sullied along with others, drew comparisons to other frauds perpetrated on the art world and the public. No one had forgotten Tony Tetro who forged works by Chagall, Miro, Dali and Rembrandt. They hung in museums around the world until a Japanese artist spotted his own copied masterpiece in a gallery in the late eighties.

Shropshire Auction House took some of the heat when they halted the auction, canceling bids, the half-billion dollars hanging in a rainstorm of disappointment and fury. Not the first time an auction house got greedy with all those impressive young people climbing up the scaffolding of the art world. Rumor was they wanted to take the company public and needed media attention to attract investors.

And then there's Seymour Sommerstein, who must have been apoplectic. He thought his small liberal arts college was going to be known across the globe. Yes, but for the wrong reasons. It would take decades to climb out of the hole and get more endowments.

Sandrine took off after the auction. In emotional turmoil and plagued with a two-day migraine when she left, I thought about an intercontinental romance. Long-distance relationships evaporated unless someone advanced, took action. I had never coveted a woman before, but when she went back to Paris after the disastrous event, I thought about her. A lot.

I flew to Paris for a long weekend three weeks after the auction to clear my head and see if there was any steam left between us. She still intrigued me—her thoughtful curiosity, her appreciation of the arts and yes, her sensuality. Another red-eye flight after that wasn't as satisfactory. She had reentered her world of the shop, family, Roland. We spoke on the phone, but conversations were difficult with the time difference and her accent.

Impatience rattled through me. Where was this going? I hadn't relaxed in months. My mother's death, finding out I was half Jewish, meeting Sandrine, replacing Maurice, the confrontation with Yossi, the auction disaster, I had to let it all go. How?

I stewed around New Haven balancing my checkbook, watching old movies and drinking beer until I couldn't take it anymore. It was time to find a purpose, even if my personal life and career fell into a sinkhole of despair.

I couldn't hide in my apartment forever so I ventured out—errands, the gym and a few meals. I had to assume everyone had heard about the *scandale*, especially after a *New York Times* reporter unearthed more dirt in the competitive archaeology departments involved, all vying for recognition. It turned out the independent carbon dating laboratory wasn't so independent.

One evening while I drank a few brews in a student bar with a sympathetic former teaching assistant, a familiar hand slapped my shoulder. Brooks White.

"Drowning your sorrows in drink?" He turned my beer bottle label around. "You'll need more than this."

Damn. Just who I didn't want to see, especially dressed for fall in a herringbone sports coat with a cashmere scarf, while I slouched over a distressed wooden bar in an old long-sleeved Yalie tee shirt. When you're depressed you don't give a shit about weather.

"You slumming now that mama didn't blow your inheritance on some trinkets?" I asked in as surly a voice as I could muster.

"Don't worry. I'm not counting on her. She's off perusing Belle Époque antiques in Prague with Robert. Got to get her name on some building somewhere. So, how are you faring? Busy with a heavy teaching load for the next semester?"

He was goading me, a dig because it was common knowledge I wasn't going to be on the teaching schedule in the foreseeable future.

"I have plans." I wanted to sound confident.

"Do they include the AA chapter for red-eyed un-sober professors?"

I scraped my stool backward, ready to flatten the bastard, but my old TA held my arm. "You asshole—"

"Touchy, aren't we?" He left in his sartorial splendor, leaving me more miserable than ever.

Brooks White remained a pompous annoyance, an over-educated snob waiting for his mother to expire.

What got me was Yossi Farber, who blew the whistle. Fuck that prick too. Bad enough his hypothesis won out, he gloated on top of it. He wrote an article for the *Jerusalem Post* that had been forwarded to me. Yossi was a hero who saved his people from being fools. And I was the schmuck-in-residence. He stopped a fraudulent sale of artifacts while I gave a paper saying they were verified. Shit. The worst humbling I had ever endured.

So it seemed strange to me when Yossi called up one evening as I was researching storage units.

"Michael Saunders? That you?"

I knew from the Israeli accent that it was Yossi. It occurred to me in that split second to hang up. I didn't need another tortuous conversation.

"Yes, Yossi. You must know I don't have much to say to you."

"Of course. But we are still archaeologists who haven't discovered all there is to know."

"Look, my career is in tatters because of you. I'm dealing with some other issues—"

"Michael, Michael. Listen. I want you to come to Israel, see what I'm working on. It's some debris in the Tel Miqne-Ekron region, southeast of here. You can lecture to some of my students."

"You want a disgraced professor to talk to your students?" I asked in disbelief.

"You're not disgraced. You still have a wealth of research and papers that would impress the best in academia. Jerusalem is cold in November but Tel Aviv is warmer. Come. We'll talk."

"You're crazier than I thought. You have financing for your dig?"

"Yes, I have it. Sorry to say, but the money started pouring in after the auction. Once they cleared me. Besides Hebrew University and the Albright Institute, a wealthy evangelical group in your United States sent me a stipend. It comes every month."

"Are you serious? You take money from them?"

"Why not? They want Israel to survive."

"You'll get into bed with anyone."

"Ach, won't you? Didn't I see you with a French *tsakala* in New York?"

"What's that?"

"Sorry. An attractive woman. Never mind. Come. Let's talk."

After examining my options for a few days, I said yes to get away from the whispers, real and imagined. I had forgotten I was an archaeologist, someone who enjoyed going through ancient people's garbage. Israel, a good place to be reminded of that, had enchanted me on every visit.

Yossi, a pain in the ass, garnered respect; I was surprised he wanted to taint his reputation with mine. He wasn't squeaky clean either, with a charge of public disturbance on his record. He had interrupted the auction just as the bomb scare ensued. It stopped the bidding. In the beginning of the investigation he faced a few charges and some restrictions on his travel to America, but later it was all dismissed.

We still don't know who called in the bomb scare. The FBI swarmed the building, but nothing was ever found. I read in the paper it took days to clear the warren of aisles in the basement filled with antiques.

Everyone had a theory, including Yossi. "The Chinese woman signaled someone to trigger the panic so God's Gold could be taken off the market. They wanted to purchase it on the cheap so they could resell it to the Israelis at a higher price. They had to stop the auction. All I did was hasten the event. How would I know what those bastards were going to do? I just knew I had to speak out."

I ruminated about the idea of seeing Sandrine again while I was on that side of the world.

I could stay longer than a few days. Maybe we could examine our possibilities. Or spend some time with her family, find out if Roland with his motorcycle was in or out of the picture, drink some wine. Or perhaps it was time to bring the relationship to a close?

It had been an extraordinary affair, one of the most passionate I had ever experienced: however, it was fraught with a complicated experience and the fact that we lived so far apart.

Sandrine expressed sympathy to me, but she had a life to go back to in a different culture.

As an underemployed professor who couldn't get out of his own way, I needed another journey.

Thanksgiving wasn't a French holiday, the first without my mother. I wanted to be with Sandrine and not alone, or at a table of casual acquaintances. Something about her enticed me, made me feel whole. If it wasn't going to work, I needed to find out now. No point wasting energy on a path that led to a bottomless cave.

Chapter Thirty Seven

Tel Aviv, Israel
November 23, 1993

I flew to Tel Aviv a few days before the holiday. I didn't want to endure another pathetic invitation to join someone else's family. In the past I flew down to Miami and spent it with my mother.

"No point cooking for two people," she'd say, so we'd head for the Biltmore or some other elegant place where she could dress up and run into friends. She liked showing me off.

"My son, Michael, a professor at Yale." As if people didn't already know.

Yossi greeted me as though we hadn't had the confrontation of our lives. Without a hint of awkwardness we fell into easy conversation. He drove me from the airport to the coastal city of Caesarea halfway between Haifa and Tel Aviv, an archaeological site I'd visited before, so I could see the progress that had been made. Built by Herod around 25 to 13 BCE, its history as a seaport and market spanned time. With a nineteenth-century settlement on top of the ruins and after the founding of the state of Israel in 1948, the Rothschild family established a foundation for the excavation.

"When you were last here we were working on the palace, but recently we discovered the amphitheatron. We envision concerts here someday," said Yossi with pride.

He gave me an overview introducing me to the archaeologist and doctoral students in charge. Excavation is tedious work, especially in the sun, although the weather was better than in the summer months. I watched students with their hats and bandannas whisking their small brushes with precision. Back-breaking work. I'm not sure I could do it anymore, except for the thrill of discovery that propelled one forward and compelled one to return. Many of us thought it was magical to be where others had been thousands of years before us.

"We are still utilizing manual drafting, but someday this will all be computerized. Much more efficient."

Impressed, it put me and Yossi on firm ground, sparking a conversation about how the University of Pennsylvania secured the funding for the project. So much of archaeology was about money.

Yossi, more gracious than I expected, drove me around Jerusalem and other sites for the three days I stayed at the YMCA. One day he dropped me off at the Diaspora Museum on the Tel Aviv University campus. I could have stayed weeks absorbing the volume of information.

The lecture to one of his classes at Tel Aviv University went well. He introduced me with a fervor of energy in his voice, reciting my credentials. Did the students know the real story? Who cares? His passion for the history he stumbled into on a daily basis counted for something.

But I felt awkward. On the way home I asked, "About the auction–"

"Must we? I've answered enough questions. I'm a passionate guy. I had an outburst. I apologized."

"No, but did you know when you stood up to make your accusation against me, the bomb scare was in place?"

He took his eyes off the highway for a minute to look at me. "How would I know such a thing?"

"Well, I just thought it odd–"

"Apparently, so did your FBI. But I know nothing. What I think is this Wen Yee and his crew of silk suits figured they would halt the auction. Then they could leak out the results of the carbon dating on the Table of Divine Presence. They knew another auction was impossible."

"But, what's the point?"

"I cannot say for sure, but after the pieces were discredited, they could buy them at a low price. Even elaborate fakes have an audience."

“So you’re the hero in all this.”

“Ach. An accidental one.”

On Friday night he took me home to his small apartment in the south section of the city, a neighborhood of immigrants and small shop owners.

“I am a secular Jew and my wife is observant. She keeps kosher and lights candles on the Sabbath. A mixed marriage, if you will.” He gave me a wry smile.

He placed a skullcap on his head and handed one to me, the second time I had placed one on my head, remembering the volunteer who came to say the Kaddish with me at the motel when my mother died. I felt uncomfortable, but after they dimmed the lights, it became natural.

His wife, Inbal, lit the candles that illuminated our faces. They took deep breaths as she waved her arms in a circular motion toward herself. She began, “*Baruch atah Adonai . . .*” I flowed into the blessing, raising my wine glass when they did. Yossi unwrapped a *challah*, tearing off a piece, and saying another prayer. He explained the braided bread represented the twelve tribes of Israel. It tasted like yellow cake to me.

“*Shabbat shalom,*” Yossi announced, kissing his wife and clinking my glass.

Inbal and I answered in unison, “Shabbat shalom.”

My shoulders relaxed as I sipped more wine, until the realization that my mother’s family had probably done this for generations. Another connection to my history.

As we sat down to a meal of chicken, vegetables and potatoes with onions, Yossi said, “It is our close to the week, a chance to take a breath and reflect. Of course if I’m on a dig we usually work on Saturday, but sometimes I stay home and read. No TV on Shabbat.”

Inbal, a plain woman who covered her hair, didn’t speak much English. She relished putting more food on my plate, refilling my wine glass and nodding with pleasure that I enjoyed her meal preparation.

“So, Yossi, I have to ask this, especially since I’m taking a leave of absence for a while. Why did you invite me here? We haven’t exactly been effusive colleagues.”

“Yes, this is true. I always respected your intelligence, your academic thoroughness. Maybe we might author a paper together at some point, you with American credentials, me with history below my feet. I apologize for dispersions I insinuated on your character with the God's Gold incident. I was out of control.

"I have nothing but respect for you. You were duped like many others by Maurice. Or maybe he fell into a trap. You want to hear my theory?"

"Of course." I had been through the details so many times my head ached with the mayhem of the entire New York City trip. Maybe someone else had a better theory than my obfuscated one.

"Maurice Dubois was the first to be eliminated. He saw the artifacts and swore they were authentic. I believed him at first. I didn't like him, but his reputation as a top-notch archaeologist was impeccable. But, later, I realized it was impractical that they survived. Such delicate items schlepped across countries for hundreds of years? Not possible.

"They had to purge him because his strident attitude would make him difficult to dispute. Poor schmuck never made it to his hotel. They found his briefcase with so much money."

"Ten thousand dollars isn't so much money."

"Oh, another rich American. To an Israeli, this is a fortune."

"Do you think it was a bribe? Awfully small for these stakes."

"More like spending money for New York. He was banking on fame."

I paused, cautious about discussing this with someone who had been my enemy.

"Did you know Sandrine was roughed up on the subway and our room was rifled?"

"No, I did not know this. Maybe they were going to—how you say from your gangster movies—*off* you too?"

"Maybe. I replaced Maurice, although no one could have known that until it happened. I muddied up the scenario by showing up with Sandrine."

"Oy, I'm glad I did not have a stunning Frenchie on my arm."

He saw I looked hurt at his blasé comment.

"Okay, never mind. I was so angry after our argument at the seminar, I did not know this skullduggery. You were frightened?"

"Well, I'm not exactly a tough guy and I didn't know who I was dealing with. Relieved I didn't walk in on them. Still doesn't make sense to me that they would risk burglary to steal my paper."

"But you had more copies?" Yossi switched on the radio and Israeli music filled the car, a jangle of rhythms and tambourine.

"Of course. But the Chinese goons didn't know that."

"So you think it was them."

"Who else could be that clumsy?"

"They tried to scare me away by intimidating Sandrine, or maybe she was targeted as the sacrificial lamb. It certainly would have pulled me off my game if she had been seriously injured."

I remembered how vulnerable I felt at that point. I couldn't have handled another loss. Sandrine was my salvation, my distraction.

"Ah, the Paschal Lamb. An important part of our history. She is safe now in Paris?"

"Yes."

"So what is your theory?"

"Maurice and I were targeted because someone thought if the professors who verified the artifacts could be removed, it would cast doubt over the authentication. But they weren't real in the first place."

"It makes sense. Did you know that a few of the other scientists who worked on the carbon dating have been killed in accidents? These Chinese are like our Mossad."

"Diabolical." Chills scrambled up my spine. "Do you think they'll catch this Wen Yee?"

"I don't think so. I think he has disappeared into the bowels of a country with eleven hundred million people. But we have a connection now."

"That makes me feel better. I have to say I've enjoyed these few days immersing myself in what I've devoted most of my life to exploring. I appreciate you opening your home to me."

I looked around at his modest apartment with shelves of books, artifacts from digs, rocks, a large menorah, reminiscent of the candelabrum, a few layers of random rugs, a sofa that served as a nap zone from the indentations. I don't know what made me do it. Maybe the wine, maybe a chance to unburden myself, maybe because it was Israel, the beginning of recorded religious time.

"Yossi, my mother passed away recently."

"I am sorry. May her memory be a blessing. Inbal and I have both lost our parents. Thanks to God our children are well."

"My mother told me she was Jewish at the end of her life. I never knew. Strange, huh?"

He stared at me for a moment. His wife cleared the dishes and returned with black coffee and a plate of sweets she placed on the lace tablecloth.

"So. How do you feel about being one of us?"

"I don't know much about anything. She thought it was important to hide it from me most of my life."

"Aha. I knew there was something I couldn't put my finger on. You're a Jew." Yossi, amused at my revelation, leaned forward with interest.

"I wouldn't go that far. I wasn't brought up in the faith. It seems complicated with belief systems, bloodlines, traditions. Plus, a few of you are headstrong, I might add."

"Ah, you'll fit right in. Never mind. If your mother was a Jew, you are too. Now you are a real archaeologist," he said with a satisfied grin.

Chapter Thirty Eight

Paris, France
November 27, 1993

Sandrine, working at the custom shirt shop in the Marais when I arrived, agreed to take off a few days to drive me to Provence in her mother's car. After I checked into a small hotel, I stopped to see her, fluttering around a potential customer. Soon he left with a familiar shopping bag, tissue exploding from the top. I'm not the jealous sort, but I remembered how good her attention felt when I came in the first time.

Without customers in the store she joined me on the distressed leather love seat, legs crossed and her arm hung across the back. I stroked her other forearm with my finger. Not an appropriate place for affection, like the French kiss on the Métro or in the middle of the street. I was uncomfortable. I gave her a dry-lipped kiss. She knew I was happy to see her.

"First, I must tell you I think about your mother and why she would keep a secret so long. People in Europe did that too. World War II and the occupation remain a sore place with us. In Paris people are sensitive to thirteen thousand Jews rounded up."

I had shared more details about my mother on a previous trip with Sandrine. She seemed fascinated with Jews and their biblical history. I sensed no prejudice, only regrets people didn't do more to save them, frustration at their persecution. She seemed to think it made me an anomaly—a disgraced ersatz Jewish archaeologist who loved Paris. It put me in a category all by myself.

"When was this?"

"July 1942. My mother was a girl. She saw the neighbors leave. Mostly immigrants from Poland, Germany, other places. She gets upset to talk about it."

"Where did they take them?"

"To the Vélodrome d'hiver outside the city, a stadium with a cycle track. It is torn down. No reminders." She glanced down. "I think people are embarrassed they allow this to happen. The police were—how you say—explicit?"

"I think you mean complicit."

"*Oui.* In the Marais, brass plaques mark the buildings for how many children taken."

"Where did they go?" I knew some of this, but having a French person tell me had more meaning.

"To Drancy, an internment camp. Parents separated from children. My mother tells me forty-two thousand to Auschwitz." She grabbed my hand. "So maybe you forgive your mother. Such fear, *terreur* all over the world."

She touched me with her sensitivity. The fact that she asked her mother about that time period meant she cared. Ironic the country of *liberté*, *égalité* and *fraternité* allowed this to happen on their soil. I let it go for another time.

Even though Sandrine could cheer me, I felt blue, a word my mother used to use instead of depressed. My mother's passing, an academic catastrophe, leaving what was familiar—I was a man in his forties without direction.

Another word hung around, intensifying. *Loser.* What was I doing here? Chasing a woman with a life when I had none? I didn't even know who I was. Might as well have been a refugee. I wouldn't allow the self-pity to dominate, but it was there, a billowing refuse of sewer rubbish.

"So when do we leave for our expedition?" I asked.

Sandrine, a good travel guide, steered us to Avignon where we spent the night at a pension on the Rhône River. She insisted I tour the pope's palace built in the fourteenth century, a Gothic refuge for the Supreme Being who refused to go to Rome. In all the grandeur, what impressed me the most was the secret hiding place dug around the perimeter of his dressing room to store valuables, now covered with Plexiglas.

Sandrine smiled at me, her hands on the wheel of the old Renault, large sunglasses covering her eyes. "From here we go to Nîmes to see the Roman aqueduct, Pont du Gard. It is almost two thousand years old, probably a young site for an *archéologue* like you."

I appreciated her making an effort to enhance my mood, but I got the distinct impression she didn't want to take the relationship any further—an affair, New York City, a fancy cocktail dress, but a life together? I couldn't see it. And neither could she. Most women by now would have dropped a few hints about the future. Not her.

We enjoyed being together and our lovemaking was about the only thing that got me out of my own head—her aroma, the passion, our sensuality blended us together. I had truly never experienced anything like it.

"Now we are off to Arles to see the Théâtre antique d' Orange that the Romans constructed and the Abbaye de Montmajour built by the Benedictines. You will like it, I promise."

It felt good for someone else to be in charge. I had confronted too many decisions lately.

Plus, in my research I uncovered the fact that my favorite evil emperor, Vespasian, after he conquered the Jews, put three vessels of the conquered out to sea with instructions for the captains to abandon them. Despite his instructions, one ship made it to Arles.

Arles turned out to be my favorite place on our tour. We stayed a few nights at the Hotel du Musée, wandering the narrow streets to see the sites, trying a few restaurants, strolling along the Rhône River.

In my network of Ivy Leaguers, Thomas Gaston, a history professor with Southern manners who advised on multidisciplinary graduate student dissertations with me, knew I was having a tough time absorbing recent events. When I mentioned where I was going to be traveling, he insisted I check out a bed and breakfast he had found for sale in the classifieds in one of our scholarly magazines. He asked if I would take a look at it for him. Why not? I welcomed any distraction.

After a day visiting the museum on the Rhône filled with ancient sarcophagi, Sandrine and I traipsed around looking for an address on winding streets not too far from the city gates. A stone edifice with a tacky blue screen door caught my eye. It had some charm in the middle of the block on a one-way cobblestone lane.

Gaston had emailed me, "The chefs are divorcing in an amicable split. It's supposed to have a great country kitchen, but I can't tell much from the photos they posted. Take a look at it for me. Sounds like an ideal retreat or may be right for retirement, although overpriced. It's down the street from the Communist Party headquarters and across from a shop that sells funeral wreathes and statues."

On a brief tour of the six bedrooms that included a musty attic aerie, the owner's private space with a master bedroom and library, the home incorporated three floors of narrow winding stone steps reminiscent of a cheap horror flick. The owner, an American cocooned in sweaters and a shawl, confessed she didn't have the exact date it was built, but that it probably had been a private residence since the early 1600s.

When we descended to the ground floor, she guided us into a large country French kitchen, copper pots hanging on the back stone wall, a communal prep and cooking station in the middle of the room surrounded with beat-up wooden stools and, at the far wall, glass cabinets, the trim painted with a sloppy hand, colors peeking through to frame a brimming pantry of staples and spices.

A sigh elicited from Sandrine who murmured, "A perfect place to prepare a big family meal."

The walls and floor of the kitchen constructed from large flagstones smelled damp. With colors ranging from a deep brown mushroom color to mossy green, someone strong had gone to a site, collected the rocks and brought them back to build. I had pushed enough stones around to know that was hard labor. When I touched one of them with greenery growing through the ancient grouting, it felt cool. Centuries of stories, the aroma of meals, the windy drafts of history—it felt like it belonged to me.

The pastry-cook owner had decided life in the states with her three children was more desirable than remaining in Arles with her chef husband. She quoted us a high price, which I agreed to pass on to Gaston. She pulled her shawl around her and emphasized a few good points, such as the proximity to the train station.

"Since a mention in the Rick Steves's guide, we have reservations booked for the next six months."

"I'll let my friend know." I thanked her as we continued on our way to Saint-Rémy, the asylum where Vincent van Gogh volunteered himself for a stay after leaving the Arles hospital.

Sandrine pointed out a dour building while we lunched at a terraced restaurant. "See the small square windows with bars? That is where the *artiste* set up a studio next to his cell and painted what he could see—irises, lilacs, ivy, his inspiration. All without bars, of course."

A sense of peace passed over me. Maybe it was the setting, the aroma of flowers, the fact that van Gogh created three hundred paintings in the area. Or perhaps it was being with her.

"So. Do you think your friend will buy the place in Arles?" Sandrine stirred her cappuccino.

"I don't know. I'll send him a message later. What did you think of it?"

"I think it's much work, especially for someone who studies rocks and knows nothing about the hospitality industry."

"Should I discourage him?"

"Only if you want to buy it yourself." She grinned at me. A cooler breeze rustled our hair. I pulled my scarf tighter around my neck. "And it's only a four-hour train ride from Paris, not an international flight."

Chapter Thirty Nine

New Haven, Connecticut
February 8, 1994

After my Provence tour with Sandrine I returned to New Haven for a period of self-examination. Who walked away from a Yale professorship? Especially to be with a Frenchwoman who may or may not have wanted me on her turf? And what did I do with all my knowledge? How was I supposed to generate income to live for the rest of my life? Even with savings and my mother's gift, I had to have a purpose.

I stewed around New Haven past the holidays, drank a little too much, called Sandrine in the middle of the night a few too many times and finally put my belongings in storage after contacting a realtor I knew to rent my condominium. No need to make any irreversible decisions. In a college town it was easy to find a renter with visiting professors, especially since I was in the Elm Street Historic District.

My department head, a crusty old guy with owl eyebrows, seemed relieved I was taking an extended leave of absence. He had some new people coming in and my office was prime property. I didn't know when I'd be back, not mentioning if I'd be back.

He wished me well and said, "Michael, take as much time as you need. I can always make space for you." I wanted out of there before the semester ended. It meant fewer explanations. Everyone knew that I supported a hypothesis that crumbled and the auction of God's Gold had been halted.

With only a few goodbyes to colleagues, I preferred to fade away and not answer too many questions. I wanted to focus on what was next. My mother's words echoed: "Whatever happens, happens for the best." Trite but true.

I couldn't see how this was going to work itself out in my favor. Except for inviting Sandrine to New York, I hadn't taken many risks. Strange that my mother created my situation by making an exit and leaving me some cash to do something adventurous, like that first sojourn to Paris last June.

My mother was an unusual woman, bound by the mores of her time, trapped with decisions that cut her off from family and pushing out a vision for another world through me. I wish I had one more day to ask her questions—why she did what she did, what she was thinking, whether any of it mattered.

I got so involved in my own mental machinations I forgot I was an archaeologist and not a philosopher. What I really needed was financial planning. I had a 401K, some savings and most of my mother's nest egg. With some good advice and low living expenses, possibilities pointed me toward another path.

When I first returned to New Haven I called Thomas Gaston, the professor who mentioned the Arles B&B in the first place. He asked some questions with his slight Virginia drawl and then backed off when I told him the condition of the place.

"It needs a lot of work, some TLC from your wife and cash flow until a new owner catches on."

"Sounds too much like another project. Just added a deck onto our house and it almost did us in."

"There's a basement too, but I didn't see it. With the damp chill and the owner's asking price, I let it slide. Figured I'd seen enough cold, dank basements in my life."

"Whoa. More repairs and money tied up for so long? The twins have their eyes on graduate school. I'd say it's a pass."

I called Gaston back the following week after I mulled over living in the south of France, using my physicality to fix something up without all the cerebral maneuverings I forced myself through before finalizing a decision. It would place me in closer proximity to Sandrine. I knew it wasn't a guarantee, that I might never fit into her life.

"I saw it's still on the market. You care if I take a shot at it?"

"Hey man, as long as we can come and visit, I'd say go for it."

After a tough negotiation for the Arles bed and breakfast, the owners, who must have been getting desperate for a buyer in the winter months, conceded. I was the new proprietor of an ancient, dilapidated home that was at least four centuries old.

I didn't know if Sandrine still wanted me. That remained to be seen. My decision was made. The numbers worked as long as I didn't do anything foolish. I was going to France to sort out my life. Most people in my circumstances wouldn't get a second chance to begin again. Nothing was holding me stateside.

Chapter Forty

Arles, France
May 25, 1994

There's something to be said for living in a place where people don't pry or even care about the chronicle of your life. The French are sophisticated that way. Your business is your business. Well, except for their president and his wife, the L'Oreal heiress and her husband's Nazi connections and all the striking workers. It was a bold move, a new place far away where I could fade into anonymity.

Are there things I missed? Of course. The efficiency, the news, even the politics with the crazy extremist voices. There were some things that were uniquely American.

But for now I was more concerned about whether the linens would dry before the rain, what fresh fish was available, whether my favorite *boulangerie* had chocolate croissants with toasted almonds, that the beekeeper had a stock of Miel de Lavande, an all-natural honey with a floral motif on the lid, and that the ingredients for foie gras were ready.

My week of simplicity shaped around the market on Wednesdays and Saturdays that stretched from the stone gates of Arles around many blocks to the Julius Caesar Hotel, probably the most expensive, elegant place in town to stay. I purchased seasonal vegetables, fruit jams and fresh cheese from the farmers who transported refrigerated cases that hummed with generators. Vernal baguettes, squalling chickens cramped in their coops in the back of trucks, eggs in graduated shades of brown and an array of spices set out in shallow round pans tempted me. Who knew being around food preparation would weave my feminine side to the front of my masculinity?

I couldn't resist the plump woman, strands of grey hair falling from her bun, who stirred yellow saffron rice brimming with fresh shrimp and mussels with a wooden spoon. I purchased a small amount to eat in a paper container with a plastic fork, an anomaly for the French. I stood aside to eat, observing two well-known chefs from the popular restaurants in town chatting, woven shopping baskets over their arms. In Provence they were rock stars competing with their Parisian counterparts.

Some American tourists, early for the season, strolled along the crowded aisles, cameras in hand; nylon fanny packs at their waist, deliberately counting out their francs for each purchase. Many made the day trip from Nîmes, Cavillon, Carpenteras and the pedestrian village of Séguret to shop for bright souvenirs that waved in the breeze, sample herbs and spices to bring home and to buy fresh produce, oblivious of the camaraderie among farmers and housewives, haggling over prices.

I'd assisted a few travelers frustrated with the language, Canadians who were polite and Americans who asked incessant questions when they realized I was one too: Do you live here? How is it? Expensive?

Often, they were flummoxed over their change and the francs, a foreign-looking tender. Some farmers lacked patience when the buyer didn't attempt to speak French. Mine was terrible but I tried. The largest market in Provence was a microcosm of my life.

What I learned was that if something's more than four hundred years old, everything leaked or dripped or had to be cleaned. It seemed out of character for me to purchase the bed and breakfast, an impulse buy, but I sought an anchor to keep me in France. Nothing made me want to stay in the States.

Petite Hôtel du Arles needed constant maintenance. Sometimes I wished I had convinced Thomas Gaston, the professor who told me about it, to purchase it instead of me. Initially the price was expensive, but as the owners' civility deteriorated at an exponential rate, it became more competitive. I cursed the old house as I crawled around behind toilets, maneuvered narrow curved stairs built in the sixteenth century and fed the whining cats I brought home from the rescue service to manage the rodent problem. Sometimes I didn't recognize my bandaged fingers, another distraction for a source of income.

At first I was overwhelmed, but now that I was into the rhythm of being a proprietor of a well-known landmark, I looked forward to the guests checking in Thursday through Sunday with their travel tales. I loaded them up with maps and guides after breakfast. They returned late in the day with mementos of Provence: bags of lavender and traditional tablecloths, napkins, aprons in textile designs that hadn't changed since the seventeenth century. Fleur de Sel de Camargue, round salt containers with a picture of the marshy brine south of here where the Mediterranean and the Rhone meet, was another popular purchase, enhanced if the small grey horses ran on the beach. Spring was a little busy, but by summer and fall I'd be booked every weekend.

The guests were surprised to find an American in charge, especially since my heavily accented French was not that fluent, even with weekly lessons. Fortunately, Marie Louise the manager directed the maids so the linens were changed, the long table for breakfast wiped clean and reset, and classical music played from the tinny stereo.

I purchased the ingredients for the continental breakfast, a task I enjoyed. Fresh croissants, herbed goat cheese, butter, homemade jams, hard- boiled eggs, honey at the market twice a week—a splendid spread of exceptional treats that required only minimal preparation in the kitchen, the largest room in the house.

Other days I worked on a book. I found a wealth of material at the archaeological museum, Musée de l'Arles et de la Provence antiques, with the finest collection of Roman sarcophagi outside Rome itself and only a short walk along the embankment of the Rhône River.

Luc Long, the head diver from a subaquatic archaeological research team, brought up hundreds of artifacts from the river including a marble bust of Julius Caesar dated from 46 BCE. And, as usual, various academic factions disputed the date and whether it was placed there by the citizenry after Caesar's assassination to protect it from marauders, or pushed into the river depths by those who wanted to steal the treasures. The French ministry of culture had not issued a statement.

The museum, the market, the guests—all distractions so I didn't think about what catapulted me here almost a year ago.

Chapter Forty One

Arles, France
April 22, 1996

I have everything I need after two years in Arles—a stone wine cellar with Châteauneuf, Pic Saint Loup and Bandol, fresh ingredients prepared by new friends, Claudine's pungent olive oil, the basis of a skincare line she produces, Isabelle's organic honey with a touch of rosemary from her own bee hives, and cheese fashioned from a goat farm I purchased recently on the outskirts of town.

I ask myself what an academic is doing with goats. They're messy, annoying and affectionate; however, I am at peace in the ancient Roman town built on the banks of the Rhône River. The bed and breakfast, profitable even though the blustery winters don't see many guests, runs with efficiency. The Mistral winds keep the buds on the trees from opening until spring.

Fortunately, Paul Pierre and his lovely wife Helene have agreed to assist with the care of goats and the production of cheese. It's wonderful not to have my head cluttered with academia, although the Musée de l'Arles et de la Provence antiques nearby entices me frequently with its extraordinary exhibits of Roman treasures. I work on my book sporadically. Recently, a travel magazine bought one of my articles.

More importantly, my decisions wind around enhancing the creamery, deciding which cheeses to make, calculating quantities and working closely with two cheese technicians, Aimee and her husband Jacky, both from Toulouse. I had no concept that goats give four *litres* of milk a day. They take our product to various outdoor markets in the area, including ours in Arles.

I've also redesigned a milking parlor. After all, my research skills work well in many situations. Platform heights, a cooling system, pipes, ramps, a milk holding tank and a pasteurizing/curdling vat have challenged me more than any supercilious academic. I've gone out there at 5 a.m. to dose the milk with rennet, an enzyme used in the production of cheese, and whey to get the curdling going, assisting with pouring it into molds, flipping, salting and even making yogurt. The rhythm of this work distracts me, so much so that I haven't been plagued with a headache in months.

Now my greatest decision is what kind of cheese to make: Boucheron, cheddar or brie? My mouth salivates at how fresh it tastes right on the spot without packaging to peel away. Quite a few restaurants, even as far away as Paris, make purchases wrapped in paper and secured with a piece of string. The freshness of our product is an incessant lure. And profitable.

With kidding season almost here, I am voraciously learning about raising goats, how to treat them homeopathically and studying with a local butcher on how to cut down chevron meat. The marketing encompasses a wide arena; however, I have enough customers now to keep me busy.

Fifty goats, a cheese-making operation and a B&B pack my days. I enjoy the travelers who stay with us for short periods of time, sharing their adventures, seeing familiar sites with a renewed enthusiasm. In the evenings I listen to classical music near a raging fire and read. I don't feel compelled to tell neighbors or new acquaintances my strange story, although I think about the past often—the artifacts, my mother's death-bed confession, leaving Yale, even the irony of my owning a goat farm like my grandparents in Wisconsin. The absence of a past to reveal cloaks me in mystery.

It doesn't mean I don't ruminate on it though. From what I can discern from the press, the Chinese diplomat Wen Yee and his delegation wove a nefarious plot in tandem with a goodwill mission. Ruthless, willing to commit murder to accomplish their goal of taking possession of the artifacts, the scheme must have been planned with meticulous precision ages ago, although there's still no proof the trucker who sideswiped Maurice's taxi was bribed. A strange coincidence? I might never know. With the ongoing investigation, details might not be revealed for years. Or ever.

I discovered a bit more when Thomas Gaston, the history professor who led me here, and his attractive wife Bettina, a photographer, showed up for a few days in conjunction with an art festival. I had offered a complimentary room when he emailed they would like to visit Arles. I anticipated their arrival with a wanton homesickness that plagued me prior to their visit.

"Hey, thanks for the hospitality. We had to see what we missed. Cabbie gave us a quick tour to get a glimpse of the ruins. Love the town." Gaston glanced around the communal living space, the long table set with lace and fresh wildflowers, love seats and bookshelves against the walls, the tinny stereo playing Bach. "Charming place."

They hugged me, although it felt unfamiliar.

He elbowed his wife. "Hope we didn't miss the opportunity of a lifetime."

"Unless you have a strong back for bending under sinks and a penchant for plumbing problems, I'd say being a visitor will be much easier on you."

Although they didn't mention anything, I felt self-conscious. My trappings of a well-groomed professor had given way to kitchen-cut hair falling on my forehead, grubby clothes and scuffed work boots.

I showed them to the best room in the house with a grotto tiled shower. I worked on it for weeks with a skilled laborer. The room had a view of the street below, funeral wreaths in the shop across the narrow cobblestone street faded with neglect. They seemed pleased with the size of the space, an ancient table placed in the center for camera equipment and art supplies.

Bettina said, "I can't wait to see the light that drew Van Gogh here."

"Yes, he painted in the area, but the town doesn't have any of his works. It's all gone to museums and wealthy buyers." I winced a little as I thought of the auction.

At dinner in an outdoor café on Place de la République with a view of the obelisk, fountain and the church built between the twelfth and fifteenth centuries, we dined on mussels, chicken Cordon Bleu and a chocolate dessert that made Bettina swoon. I wanted to hear the news from Yale and the aftermath of the scandal, but waited until we had eaten and were relaxing with another glass of wine.

"How can the department function without me?" I goaded.

We laughed. Gaston, I had always used his last name, had more current information than I could gather from the international news and a lack of television.

"So what's the update on the Chinese situation?"

"Since the massacre at Tiananmen, we ascertained how reprehensible the Chinese are."

I nodded in agreement, empathetic to the unarmed students who stood up against assault rifles and tanks for democracy in the spring of 1989. Before they declared martial law.

"It was prior to the auction and I was busy with family matters in Florida."

"Well, apparently the auction provided a distraction from the worldwide outrage over innocents mowed down by their own government. With the privatization of businesses in one of the world's largest countries, the lack of information about any events, especially Tienanmen, was not a surprise."

"Ah, the glamorous auction provided an acceptable diversion."

"And more."

"What do you mean?"

"Wen Yee, the Chinese national sent to draw attention to how cultured they were—never mind that most of us in the free world viewed them as blind killers—disappeared in the aftermath of the auction. Diplomatic immunity saved his ass."

"I read that Interpol, the FBI and the CIA were involved, but I lack details. Not much news here and to tell the truth, I'm preoccupied with my business. I have so much to learn."

"Apparently Wen Yee's intention was to stop the auction, discredit the artifacts and buy them on the cheap. Your buddy Farber interrupted the plan."

"How did you hear this?" I sipped my wine for fortification. I hadn't spoken about this in a long time.

"Common knowledge. Chinese conspiracy. No way he acted alone. It had to involve the highest levels of their new, more open government. Someone knew they were counterfeit from the beginning and still wanted them, without witnesses to dispute their authenticity."

"I still don't understand how they pulled it off."

Bettina interrupted. "Mind if I take a stroll around the square? I think Saint Trophime is open this evening and I'd love to see the Romanesque architecture inside."

"Sure, honey, we'll join you in a few minutes."

Bettina wandered off, backpack slung on her shoulder, toward the entrance of the church, the steps near the entrance crowded with slouching local teens smoking cigarettes.

Tantalized with the information of skullduggery, I couldn't believe I had a part in it.

"So, where was I?"

"The conspiracy."

"Right. So this villainous Wen Yee had to eliminate the scientific proponents who authenticated the trumpets, candelabrum and Table of the Divine Presence. No one knows who the Chinese had representing them on their behalf, but a deal was made. Any idea how they did it?"

I hesitated. I had thought about all this for endless hours with no one to bounce off any of my theories of how the Chinese put it together. "It couldn't have been that hard to bribe lab rats." A vision of poor souls in white coats hunched over microscopes for hours, working for a pittance, raced across my mind.

"There are clandestine research facilities in a variety of foreign cities."

"Like where? I never knew the locations Dubois went to authenticate them."

"Apparently no one else did either. They tracked the artifacts from place to place. Complicated trail. Even had some realistic copies turn up, maybe decoys, in Turkey and Italy."

More data I missed while eating croissants and worrying about goats.

"So, what's the latest?" I didn't want to appear too anxious, but my foot started to rattle. This was bringing up my humiliation at the expense of wanting to know the truth.

"Apparently the Chinese were new to the art game and a bit clumsy in their execution. Greed convulses some people." Gaston sipped more wine, glancing around the square at the streetlights that turned on in the hazy twilight.

I wanted more. I raised my eyebrows in expectation while he finished his wine.

"So. People like Wen Yee, drunk with money after years of insulation with endless available manpower took advantage by building huge factories. An ultraimperialism took hold. It was a time of peaceful capitalism where men could accumulate great wealth driven with a sinister fervor, especially since the workers earned little. At least until the Galaxy incident."

"What was that?"

He slapped his hands against the table.

"Hey, Bettina's waiting for me. We'll talk more later."

"Know how to get back?"

"Sure. We follow that street off the square."

"Great. I have to get breakfast ready for the morning."

I strolled off, hands in pocket, mulling over everything Gaston shared. It was more convoluted than I could have imagined.

Chapter Forty Two

Arles, France
April 23, 1996

The next morning, after Bettina and Gaston enjoyed their sumptuous breakfast, we spoke briefly before they took off for a day of sightseeing. Bettina, who spoke a little French, studied maps as the navigator of their last-minute rented Renault.

"Everything satisfactory so far?" I asked Gaston while he relaxed with a second cup of fresh-brewed coffee, the aroma of Carte Noir, my favorite brand, pungent in the room.

"Wonderful. Bed was comfy too. Really appreciate your hospitality. I'll be sure to spread the word back home."

"Listen, I didn't sleep well last night after our conversation about the auction. My computer access is sketchy so I didn't try to find out more about the boat incident. I hadn't paid much attention when the Galaxy hit the twenty-four-hour news cycle three years ago, but I'm interested now. What else do you know?" It made sense to me that a political incident could give Wen Yee a platform.

"Good thing I'm a history prof, although my memory is getting a little vague at this stage of life."

He rearranged his long limbs for comfort.

"At the beginning of September 1993, before the auction, the Chinese ship Yinhe, which means Milky Way, was stopped in Saudi Arabian waters. The US government claimed they were carrying chemical weapons and an episode ensued whereby we boarded their tanker. Among the myriad of containers on the ship that we searched, ironically, only poker cards for exportation to Pakistan were found."

He chuckled. "An embarrassment on a few levels."

"Then what?"

"The U.S. faced accusations of international bullying with our adamant refusal to apologize, fueling Chinese nationalism. Then it died down. We were anxious to do business with them. It's probably why we welcomed Wen Yee and his entourage."

He glanced at his watch, leaning over to pat Bettina's knee.

"Ready, navigator?"

She stood, folding a map, smiling. "See you around dinnertime."

They left a few days later after side trips to Aix and Nîmes. The topic of the auction didn't come up again. I missed their familiarity until a pipe broke and some goats got sick, an awakening in my world.

As I brought the breakfast dishes into the kitchen, I thought about the Yinhe episode. It must have been on people's minds. Wen Yee saw an opportunity to catapult himself and his enterprises onto the world stage, although the convoluted plan must have been in place a long time.

My theory is the Chinese entrepreneur, who was building an empire with low-priced furniture and clothes, thought the artifacts would enhance China's image. The Chinese viewed themselves as superior to other Asian people, often referring to Koreans or Vietnamese as barbarians. I think his plan was to discredit authenticity, eliminate opposition to credibility and buy them at a ridiculously low price. After all, even a fraudulent piece of art would bring him the attention he sought. The backdrop of the Galaxy née Milky Way incident enhanced his position of innocence because America looked the fool.

But Wen Yee's arrangements went awry. The Chinese magnate prepared to disrupt the auction of the most valuable artifacts in the world. He masterminded and executed a bomb scare with his companions, probably including the woman I noticed in the yellow cheongsam at the auction. I learned her name from a newspaper report: Bai Ju. It means one hundred chrysanthemums, if it's even her real name.

When she left the room during the bidding, she alerted another Chinese national to call in the bomb scare. Harmless enough. Empty the building, suspend the bidding and intrude on Shropshire's arrangements for success. In other words, they duped us all. They couldn't have been stolen with the amount of security in place. Yossi Farber's outburst transformed anything that had been planned.

Whenever it's unraveled, Wen Yee and his cohorts will be secreted in China. Their government will never give them up, even as their bubbling cauldron of scandals involving the Olympics, Little League World Series, doping and swimming dominate the news.

In my mind Yossi was still the hero.

The church never owned up to anything.

Swirling around a mist of controversy and investigation, the Catholic Church that housed the artifacts for centuries, clammed up, even with the rabbi's eyewitness report. For all I know the real ones are still in their basement. Someone smarter than I am with access to all the puzzle pieces will figure it out.

Shropshire Auction House relinquished all rights to the items, but even they are suing the church, antique dealers, appraisers and more for costs associated with transfers, security, insurance and personnel as well as misrepresentation damages. And there's a long line behind them of people who paid for catalogues and had expectations of bidding, including Luisa White.

A few of the people at the bottom will serve time for fraud when the plot unravels. I'm sure there's a deal so a few go on trial and serve time while others go free. Wen Yee, the mastermind at the top, will evade the international courts. The People's Republic of China, angry at accusations, ignores public opinion. Interpol, the CIA and the FBI have revealed little information other than a few leaks. That's how these scandals are handled—secrecy, deceit and lies.

The fake God's Gold artifacts, taken off the market, were donated as a peace offering from the Catholic Church to the Israelis, likely guardians, who want to erect an underground site with state-of-the-art security not unlike their structure for the Dead Sea Scrolls.

Credible fakes earn a home. But who made them, when and why?

What if when scientific advancements happen they turn out to be real? That's what the Israelis are hoping. If not, they're still a connection to the biblical era of Moses.

Seymour Sommerstein, who was the darling of the press, his chubby face appearing in numerous print and online stories, was chastised too. I wonder if spunky Heather, his assistant, has remained in her position. I sometimes think of her when I'm supervising the milking of goats. I have no idea why.

Yossi Farber disagreed with me on the verification of the items, interrupting the auction. He would have been better off releasing cockroaches, which actually happened at a contentious board meeting at the Metropolitan Museum of Art years ago. I'm glad we settled our score. The egos of academics don't surprise me, but an apology is rare.

This brings me to Brooks and his mother, Luisa Phillips White, a woman of extreme wealth and snobbery.

He has retained his position at Yale, waiting for a department head to retire so he can move into that slot someday. We don't communicate, but I've heard through the grapevine that his mother has moved forward with her plans to have a building named after her and her late husband at Sommerstein's college. Poor Brooksie. He'll only have millions to spend when she passes, unless she's put a stranglehold on the trust, doling it out to future generations after the age of fifty-five.

I've never followed any religion, skeptic that I am, but I admit to a fascination with a bloodline to the "stiff-necked" people of my forbearers, who endured every plan to wipe them from the face of the earth. It's hard to wrap myself around it, but I'm willing to explore. I'm grateful to have found solace in a new life.

I think back to those conversations with my mother who made the decision not to identify with her people and the pain it caused her. I haven't integrated it yet because the focus was on the auction, but I've done some research on what she shared.

After Jews had been the focus during World War II, a denial settled over them when it ended in 1945, an uncomfortable silence as facts about the camps were revealed. Antisemitism was pervasive in the fifties. I guess my mother wanted to protect me from that. How different would my life been had I known my heritage?

In some respects it might have been the same in that I like learning. On the other hand, I would have moved in a different arena. No country clubs, no Ivy League, no Yale. So how much was my environment and how much did I bring with my gene pool that heralded survival? I'll never know. The urge to explore catapults me to discover more. I want to visit Israel, not as an archaeologist, but as someone who wants to explore his personal history.

What a shame I didn't get to know my mother's parents. I'm interested in the field of genetic memory. How much do our cells remember? Besides physical characteristics, certain diseases, parts of our personality, does DNA store our ancestors' memories? In this case, it might be one to flee in the face of danger or a certain level of paranoia after being persecuted for centuries.

As an aside, I have not been able to locate any relatives from my mother's side, but I connected with some of my father's family in Wisconsin. They are as I remember them from childhood—good, hard-working rural people. We don't have much in common, but I can still smell the aroma of my grandmother baking kringles with remonce, that fragrant buttery pastry, and the smell of goats in the barn.

I'm not much for admonitions of faith, but I have enough respect to examine traditions. French friends invited me to a Passover Seder last year, which was Jesus's last supper. I found the plea for freedom from slavery one that has resonated through time. With their high opinion of scholarly pursuits, Jews really are the People of the Book. They even read one at dinner called a Haggadah. Right up my alley.

The fire thaws my feet. The aroma of *cassoulet*, a meaty stew, wafts by me. Lips brush across mine. I blink my eyes open.

"*Mon ami*, our supper is ready. We have to be up early for the goats. Paul Pierre and Helene are coming with us to the Actilait tomorrow. We are going to learn how to make *pâtes pressées* and *pâtes molles*."

Sandrine has been coming to visit me on weekends and holidays for a long time. Sometimes I take the train to Paris, her family welcoming me with warmth. I pull her toward me, smelling her hair. She tumbles into my lap. "I love you."

"*Je t'aime*. Now you say it in French."

I repeat it after her.

"I went to the doctor yesterday before I left. It is as I thought. I am going to have a baby."

Matter-of-fact as the French are wont to be, she waits for my reaction.

I confess my heart leaps a bit but I am not surprised. I saw her shape rounding more than a few weeks ago, but I thought maybe it was the quality and amount of food we had been consuming. I've gained a few pounds from the fresh cheese and daily croissants myself. If I've learned one thing in all my years of dating, it's never to comment on a woman's shape unless it's positive.

"I do not want to pressure you. I keep it no matter what."

"How do you know I don't want it?"

"Because you say you do not want children."

"But that was before you told me this. Why did you say you'll keep it no matter what?"

"I am thirty-four with no babies and brought up Catholic. My mother will be happy." She looks straight into my eyes.

No room for maneuvers. Not that I want to. I used protection every time.

"And for sure it is mine?"

She pulls back and mock slaps me. "I have not seen Roland for almost two years except as a friend. This is your baby and I want it. It will be smart and good-looking like you." She folds her arms across her chest in defiance as though we argued. "It's mine."

"Did I say I was going to take it away?" I tease her. "And what do you bring to this project?"

"Style and my food preparation."

She has me there.

Then a cloud crosses her face. "Maybe you don't like me with a round shape." She wraps her arms around my neck.

"I don't think that's an issue. And when does our visitor arrive?"

The baby is due in the late fall, a magnificent time in France with the harvest, colors and a nip in the air. I can almost smell the aromas of cappuccinos and burning leaves.

"How do you feel?" I ask her.

"I am happy it is a boy."

I think for a moment. Probably my only child. Yes, a boy.

"Not a girl?"

"Non, non. Trés bien. A boy. I have a name picked out. Maybe we will have a *circoncision* ceremony?"

"A circumcision? You would go along with that?"

"The story of your mother stays with me. Yes. What did you tell me about it?"

"It's the oldest covenant known between man and God. My mother called it a *bris*."

She pulls me closer and kisses me square on the lips. I feel content, ready to be a father.

"My French is weak so I'll ask in English. Will you marry me?"

"Ask in French."

"*Veux-tu m'épouser*?"

"*Oui, oui*!" she shrieks as I look into her coffee brown eyes.

Paris Lamb
Author's Notes

Writing any novel is a journey fraught with many obstacles. I write what interests me and what I would like to read myself. I love the process of research, inhabiting the character's minds and crafting a story with lucid language. This one prompted me to visit Israel with a focus on archaeology. Sometimes stories percolate in me for decades. *Paris Lamb* is one of those.

I want to acknowledge Sean Kingsley, author of *God's Gold: A Quest for the Lost Temple Treasures of Jerusalem*, for inspiration. His book made me ask questions and want to know more. Also, an article published in *Biblical Archaeology Review*, "Tracking Down Shebnayahu, Servant of the King" by Robert Deutsch inspired my passion for the secrets scholars uncover and interpret in their quest for historical accuracy. I have enormous respect for their scholarship and dedication.

As an only child I was privy to my parents' relationship. They had long conversations about books, ideas and people. One afternoon, as I was squirreled away in the back seat of our car with a good book, I overheard my mother sharing what a friend had confessed to her that afternoon. It has stayed with me all these years.

I want to give a special thank you to Beth Lieberman for her expert editorial suggestions and encouragement. Editor Rosa Cays tackled language with good humor. I am also indebted to authors Deborah Hilcove, Judy Starbuck, Deborah Ledford and Virginia Nosky who watched the evolution of the story from the beginning. I am grateful to readers Marsha Reingen and Anne Brown. As always, none of this would have happened without Skip, my love.

Reader's Guide: Paris Lamb

1. Biblical archaeology involves the recovery and scientific investigation of the material remains of past cultures that can illuminate the Bible. It is a major part of this novel. Why is it important to an Israeli like Yossi Farber?

2. Michael says he is not religious. What is his belief system?

3. Sara hides her background and family from Michael. Does it serve her well? What are the pros and cons of her decision? Is she religious?

4. Why does Michael refer to Sandrine as his "Paris lamb"? How does she influence his life?

5. During the 1950s the role of the father was prescribed. Is Byron typical? How has it evolved? What does Michael think about his father?

6. Antisemitism is a theme in *Paris Lamb*. How do the current events of the last half-century support that? How does Sara react? Has it influenced you?

7. How do Sara and Sandrine view their roles as women? Would they have liked each other as Michael surmises?

8. What is the irony in Sara having the BRCA gene? What measures do women take today?

9. Michael, humiliated, suffers a career setback. How does he manage his crisis? Does he make careful decisions or is he impulsive?

10. Is Michael Jewish according to religious law? Does he consider himself a Jew?

11. The attack in the garage of the World Trade Center and the Yinhe incident in 1993 are long forgotten. How are they the harbingers of what is to come?

12. The theme of identity is a strong one. Is it influenced by genetic memory or environment? How does it affect Michael when he learns new information about himself? Is family history important?

INTERVIEW with Marcia Fine about Paris Lamb

Renee Rivers: Michael Saunders, your protagonist, is a biblical archaeologist. What is that and why did you choose that profession for him?

Marcia Fine: A biblical archaeologist studies the historical aspects of the Jewish and Christian bibles as well as the cultures that functioned during the time it was written and beyond. Some believe the Bible is truth and others see only the historical significance. Michael is a conflicted soul so it seemed fitting he would be in a profession with different perspectives. Plus, I find the topic fascinating! There are definitely sites mentioned in the Bible that can be identified now. It doesn't mean all the stories are true, but it does give relevance to the document.

RR: You identify Sandrine Agneau, the female protagonist, as a quintessential Parisian. What does that mean?

MF: French women, especially Parisians, have a *joie de vivre* about them. They exude a confidence that becomes every part of their being. It's the way they walk, their eye contact, the way they express themselves. They're fashionable without trying too hard. They're not all beautiful; however, the way they carry themselves leads you to believe they are.

RR: The novel takes place in 1993. What drew you to this period?

MF: In 1993 the Yinhe cargo ship was stopped in international waters for three weeks by the United States. They were accused of carrying chemical weapons to Iran. Later, proved innocent, our government never apologized. At the time, this was a major incident that most of us have forgotten. It seems to echo current events in the 21st century.

I enjoy placing characters in a time where the world is shifting around them. The year 1993 doesn't seem so long ago, but cell phones were scarcely in use, computers remained clunky and instant messaging didn't exist.

RR: Speaking of cell phones, are Brooks White and his despicable mother based on anyone we know?

MF: I hope not! And if they were, I'd never tell. Despite the lightheartedness, people today still carry prejudices with them. I did not want to write a stereotype of a wealthy, country club lady, but sometimes all that old money just smells the same.

RR: Despite Michael's intention of keeping his life simple, he complicates it by making an impulsive choice. Why did he bring Sandrine to New York with him?

MF: The trauma of losing a parent affects one deeply, especially an only child when there are no siblings to commiserate with in the aftermath. Michael's vulnerability of being bereaved and shocked compromises his usual thoughtful decision-making process.

RR: Sara, Michael's mother, reveals a secret at the end of her life. It seemed to be common in the 1950s. Is it based on someone you know?

MF: Yes, my mother had a friend who confessed her hidden story a few years into the friendship. Her secret and the lengths she went to hide it remained with me.

RR: How do you conduct your research?

MF: I start out reading about my topic of interest. In this case, biblical archaeology and art auctions became my focus. I attended lectures, subscribed to magazines, researched articles. I visited sites in Israel and asked questions of experts. I even talked my way into a tour of the basement in a major New York auction house! I love complexity in a multilayered plot. I want the reader to think and be entertained.

RR: What about Paris?

MF: Ah, my favorite city in the world. It required firsthand knowledge. It is a city of museums, history and extraordinary people watching, especially in one of their beautiful parks. What better place for a romantic liaison to take place? Michael and Sandrine have chemistry and it begins in Paris.

RR: You have written some unforgettable characters—the irascible Yossi Farber in *Paris Lamb*, courageous Paulina in *Paper Children*, feisty Grazia in *The Blind Eye* and the satirical Jean Rubin in your series about Scottsdale. Where do you find inspiration?

MF: In the case of Yossi, I have met many Israelis as well as academics. If they hold an opinion, it's a strong one. They don't cave easily. Plus, academia remains a very competitive place. Paulina is based on my grandmother and letters she received from her family during WWII. Her story echoes through generations of my family. Grazia was pure imagination as I inhabited the decisions people made to survive during a dangerous time. Finally, Jean Rubin is my alter ego who gets to poke fun as we maneuver through our crazy lives. Observing people, their behaviors, how they cope with stress, how they tell their stories fascinates me.

Renee Rivers has extensive background in the literary arts and currently teaches at ASU West, School of Humanities, and Phoenix College. She is the former associate editor of Hayden's Ferry Review Literary Magazine.

My mother and her friend with secrets.